THE VALIANT

THE VALIANT

Michael Jan Friedman

POCKET BOOKS

New York   London   Toronto   Sydney   Singapore

POCKET BOOKS, a division of Simon & Schuster Inc.
1230 Avenue of the Americas, New York, NY 10020

This book is published by Pocket Books, a division of
Simon & Schuster Inc., under exclusive license from
Paramount Pictures.

ISBN: 0-671-77522-7

First Pocket Books hardcover printing April 2000

10 9 8 7 6 5 4 3 2 1

POCKET and colophon are registered trademarks of
Simon & Schuster Inc.

Printed in the U.S.A.

For Cliff

Acknowledgments

I know you didn't buy this book to read the acknowledgments page . . . but since you're here, I need half a minute to thank some people without whose contributions there wouldn't *be* a book.

First, my editors, John Ordover and Carol Greenburg, whose patience and skill helped bring this rather unusual project to fruition. Second, Paula Block, of Viacom, who again gave me the leeway to do something different. And third, but not in any way last, my wife and sons, who did without me for weeks while I banged away furiously at my keyboard.

You see? Half a minute. Now you can go on to the good stuff.

Book One

Valiant

CHAPTER 1

Carlos Tarasco of the *S.S. Valiant* stood in front of his captain's chair and eyed the phenomenon pictured on his viewscreen.

It was immense, he thought. No—it was *beyond* immense. It stretched across space without boundaries or limits, a blazing vermillion abyss without beginning or end.

"Amazing," said Gardenhire, his redheaded ops officer.

Tarasco grunted. "You can say that again."

Sommers, the curly-haired brunette who was sitting next to Gardenhire at the helm controls, cast a glance back at the captain. "You still want to go through it, sir?"

"Do we have a choice?" Tarasco asked her.

The helm officer recognized it as a rhetorical question and returned her attention to her monitors. With her slender fingers crawling across her control dials like an exotic variety of insect, she deployed additional power to the propulsion system.

"Ready when you are, sir."

Was he ready? The captain drew a deep breath.

The phenomenon had puzzled him ever since it came up on the viewscreen earlier that day. Their optical scanners registered what looked like the universe's biggest light show, but there was nothing there as far as their other instruments were concerned.

Unfortunately, it wasn't merely a matter of scientific curiosity. Tarasco and his crew of eighty-eight had set out from Earth years earlier, aiming to chart a stretch of space from their home system to the farthest reaches of the Milky Way galaxy—part of a sector that Terran astronomers had labeled the Alpha Quadrant.

They had almost completed their assignment when they encountered an unexpectedly powerful magnetic storm. At first, it seemed that they might be able to outrun the thing. Then they found out otherwise.

The storm caught them up and flung them light-years off course, well past what Tarasco's cartography team reckoned was the outer edge of the galaxy. If not for the readings their scanners took along the way, they wouldn't even have known which way was home.

But knowing the way was only half the battle. The storm had wrecked both their warp and nuclear impulse engines, forcing them to drift on emergency power until the crew could get them up and running.

Finally, after weeks of languishing under the glare of alien stars, Tarasco and his people got underway again. They knew that their trip back to Earth had been lengthened by nearly eleven months, but no one griped. They were just glad to be heading home.

And all had gone well from that point, the captain reflected. *Until now, that is.*

He couldn't be sure if the phenomenon had been there when the storm threw them so precipitously in the other direction, or if it had sprung up since that time. Certainly, their computer hadn't made any record of it.

One thing was for sure—they weren't going to get back to Earth without passing through the thing.

Tarasco glanced at Sommers. "Let's do it."

He could feel a subtle hum in the deck below his feet as the *Valiant* accelerated to the speed of light. The phenomenon loomed in front of them, a gargantuan, red maw opened wide to swallow them up.

"Still no sign of it on sensors," said Hollandsworth, his tall, dark-skinned science officer.

"Deflectors are registering something," reported Gardenhire. He turned to the captain. "A kind of pressure."

"So we're not just seeing things," Tarasco concluded. "I guess we can take some comfort in that."

"Maintain heading?" asked Sommers.

"Affirmative," said the captain.

The closer they got, the more tumultuous the phenomenon appeared. The ruby light within it began to writhe and shimmer, giving birth to monstrous caverns and towering eruptions.

It was beautiful in the way a stormy, windblown sea was beautiful. And like a stormy sea, it was frightening at the same time.

"All available power to the shields," Tarasco ordered.

"Aye, sir," said Gardenhire.

Suddenly, the ship jerked hard to starboard. Caught by surprise, the captain had to grab hold of his chair back for support. He turned to his operations officer, a question on his face.

"We're all right," Gardenhire reported dutifully. "Shields are holding fine, sir."

Tarasco turned back to the viewscreen. They seemed to be entering a deep, red-veined chasm, pulsating with forces that baffled him as much as they did his scanning devices. Before he knew it, the phenomenon wasn't just in front of them, it was all around.

He felt another jerk, even harder than the first. But a glance at Gardenhire told him that everything was still under control.

Behind the captain, the lift doors whispered open. He looked back and saw that his first officer had joined them. Commander Rashad was a wiry man with a neatly trimmed beard and a sarcastic wit.

"I hope I'm not too late," Rashad said darkly.

"Not at all," Tarasco told him. "The show's just starting."

"Good," said his exec. "I hate to miss anything."

The words had barely left his mouth when the lights on the bridge began to flicker. Everyone looked around, the captain included.

"What's happening?" he asked his ops officer.

"I'm not sure, sir," said Gardenhire, searching his control panel for a clue. "Something's interfering with our electroplasma flow."

Abruptly, the deck lurched beneath them, as if they were riding the crest of a gigantic wave. Hollandsworth's console exploded in a shower of sparks, sending him flying backward out of his seat.

Tarasco began to move to the science officer's side. However, Rashad beat him to it.

"Shields down forty-five percent!" Gardenhire announced.

Another console exploded—this time, an empty one. It contributed to the miasma of smoke collecting above them. And again, the ship bucked like an angry horse.

"The helm's not responding!" Sommers cried out.

Rashad depressed the comm pad at the corner of Hollandsworth's console. "Sickbay, this is Rashad. We need someone up here on the double. Lieutenant Hollandsworth has been—"

Before he could finish his sentence, the first officer seemed to light up from within, his body suffused with a smoldering, red glow. Then he fell to his knees beside the unconscious Hollandsworth.

"Amir!" Tarasco bellowed.

For a gut-wrenching moment, he thought Rashad had been seriously hurt. Then the man turned in response to the captain's cry and signaled with his hand that he was all right.

"Shields down eighty-six percent!" Gardenhire hollered. He turned to the captain, his eyes red from the smoke and full of dread. "Sir, we can't take much more of this!"

As if to prove his point, the *Valiant* staggered sharply to port, throwing Tarasco into the side of his center seat. He glared at the viewscreen, hating the idea that his choices had narrowed to one.

"All right!" he thundered over the din of hissing consoles and shuddering deckplates. "Get us out of here!"

There was only one way the helm officer could accomplish that: retreat. Wrestling the ship hard to starboard, she aimed for a patch of open space.

Under Sommers's expert hand, the *Valiant* climbed out of the scarlet abyss. At the last moment, the forces inside the phenomenon seemed to add to their momentum, spitting them out like a watermelon seed.

Tarasco had never been so glad to see the stars in his life. Trying not to breathe in the black fumes from Hollandsworth's console, he made his way to the science officer and dropped down beside him.

Hollandsworth's face and hands had been badly burned. He was making sounds of agony deep in his throat.

"Is he going to make it?" asked Rashad, who was sitting back on his haunches. He looked a little pale for his experience.

"I don't know," the captain told him.

Before he could try to help, the lift doors parted and a couple of medics emerged. One was a petite woman named Coquillette, the other a muscular man named Rudolph.

"We'll take it from here, sir," said Coquillette.

Tarasco backed off and let the medical personnel do their jobs. Then he did his. "Damage report!" he demanded of his ops officer.

"Shields down, sir," Gardenhire told him ruefully. "Scanners, communications, lasers . . . all off-line."

Beside him, Sommers pounded her fist on her console. "The main engines are shot. That last thrust burned out every last circuit."

"Switch life support to emergency backup," said the captain.

Without waiting for a response, he peered over Coquillette's shoulder to see how Hollandsworth was doing. The science officer's eyes were open, but he was trembling with pain.

"Easy now," Coquillette told Hollandsworth, and injected him with an anesthetic through the sleeve of his uniform.

Tarasco heaved a sigh. Then he turned back to Rashad. "Poor guy," he said, referring to the science officer.

But Rashad wasn't looking at the captain any longer. He was stretched out on his back, eyes staring at the ceiling, and Rudolph was trying to breathe air into his lungs.

Rashad wasn't responding. He just lay there, limp, like a machine drained of all its power.

Tarasco shook his head. "No . . ."

Just moments earlier, his first officer had assured him he was all right. He had even asked the captain about Hollandsworth. How could something have happened to him so quickly?

Then Tarasco remembered the way Rashad had lit up in the grip of the phenomenon, like a wax candle with a fierce, orange flame raging inside it. Clearly, they were dealing with matters beyond their understanding.

Tarasco watched helplessly as Rudolph labored to bring Rashad back to life, blowing into his mouth and pounding Rashad's chest with the heel of his hand. At the same time, Coquillette injected the first officer with a stimulant of some kind.

None of it helped.

"Let's get them to sickbay," a red-faced Rudolph said at last.

Numbly, the captain took hold of Rashad under his arms, though he knew his chief medical officer wouldn't be able to help the man either. On the other hand, Hollandsworth still had a chance to pull through.

He and Coquillette picked up the first officer, while Rudolph and Gardenhire hefted the lanky Hollandsworth. Then they squeezed into the still-open lift compartment and entered sickbay as their destination.

The air in the lift was close and foul with the stench of burned flesh. Fortunately, their destination was just a couple of decks up.

As the doors slid apart, Tarasco and the others piled out with their burdens and made their way down the corridor.

In less than a minute, they reached sickbay. Its doors were wide open, giving them an unobstructed view of the facility's eight intensive care beds, which were arranged like the spokes of a wheel. Three of the beds were occupied, though metallic silver blankets had been pulled up ominously over the patients' faces.

Damn, thought the captain, his heart sinking in his chest. He had assumed the only casualties were those suffered on the bridge.

Gorvoy, the *Valiant*'s florid-faced chief medical officer, looked grim as he approached them and took a look. "Put them down here and here," he told Rudolph and Coquillette, pointing to a couple of empty beds, "and get up to deck seven. McMillan's got two more in engineering."

The medics did as they were told and took off, leaving Tarasco and Gardenhire to stand there as Gorvoy examined Hollandsworth with a handheld bioscanner. The physician consulted the device's tiny readout, crossed the octagonally shaped room and removed something from an open drawer. Then he came back to the semiconscious science officer.

"Hollandsworth will heal," he told the captain. "I wish I could say that for the others. Do me a favor and cover Rashad, will you?"

Tarasco gazed at his first officer, who was lying inert on his bed, his features slack and his eyes locked on eternity. Moving to the foot of the bed, the captain took the blanket there and unfolded it. Then he draped it over Rashad.

"Amir," he sighed, mourning his friend and colleague.

Gorvoy glanced at him as he applied a salve to Hollandsworth's burns. "He lit up like a lightning bug, right?"

Tarasco returned the glance. "The others, too?" he guessed.

"Uh huh. Kolodny, Rivers, Yoshii . . . all of them."

The captain considered the man-sized shapes beneath the metallic blankets. "But why them and not anyone else?"

9

"That's the question," the medical officer agreed. "Was Rashad near an open conduit or something?"

Tarasco thought about it. "No. He was near Hollandsworth's console, though. And it was shooting sparks."

It was possible the console had had something to do with it. However, the captain's gut told him otherwise. And judging by the expression on Gorvoy's face, the doctor didn't believe it was the console either.

Gardenhire was grimacing as he watched Gorvoy spread the salve. Tarasco put his hand on the ops officer's shoulder.

"Go on," he told Gardenhire. "Get back to the bridge. See if Sommers needs any help."

The redhead nodded. "Aye, sir," he said. With a last, sympathetic look at Hollandsworth, he left sickbay.

But Gardenhire wasn't gone long before Tarasco heard the sound of heavy footsteps coming from the corridor. Suddenly, another medical team burst into the room, carrying a young woman between them.

It was Zosky, the stellar physicist who had signed onto the mission at the last minute. She was a dead weight in the medics' arms as they followed Gorvoy's gesture and laid her on another bed.

My God, the captain thought . . . how many more? And what could have killed them, while so many others had been spared?

He watched as they laid Zosky down, as Gorvoy took a moment to examine her with his bioscanner . . . and as they pulled the blanket over her face. *Not the console,* part of him insisted.

The doctor eyed Tarasco. "Maybe you ought to get back to the bridge, too," he suggested.

The captain nodded. "Maybe."

He had started to leave sickbay when Coquillette and Rudolph came huffing in from the corridor. They were carrying yet another victim—a baby-faced engineer named Davidoff.

"McMillan said there were *two* of them," Gorvoy told them. "Where's the other one?"

As if in answer to his question, Chief Engineer McMillan came shuffling in with one of his men leaning on him for support. Tarasco recognized the injured man as Agnarsson, McMillan's first assistant.

Agnarsson was a big man, tall and broad-shouldered, with a strong jaw and a fierce blond mustache. But at the moment, he was weak as a kitten, fighting hard just to stay conscious. The captain helped McMillan get him to a bed and hoist him onto it.

"What's the matter with him?" Tarasco asked.

The chief engineer cursed beneath his breath. "He started to glow—he and Davidoff both. It was the damnedest thing."

The captain looked at him, his pulse starting to pound in his temples. "He was glowing? And he's still alive?"

"I'm fine," Agnarsson muttered, hanging his head and rubbing the back of his neck. "Just a little light-headed is all."

Then the big man picked up his head . . . and Tarasco's jaw fell. Agnarsson's eyes, normally a very ordinary shade of blue, were glowing with a luxuriant silver light.

CHAPTER 2

Captain's log, December 30th, 2069. Tomorrow will be New Year's Eve. We should be preparing our usual celebration, festooning the lounge and watching Sommers mix her killer punch. Unfortunately, with six of our comrades dead, no one feels much like celebrating. So instead of toasting 2070, we're delving under control consoles and wriggling through access tubes, trying to expedite the process of bringing basic systems back online. The problem is every time we think we've fixed something, a new trouble spot rears its ugly head. And even if we can solve all the little snags, we'll still be left with a great big one—the warp drive. Chief McMillan says it may be beyond repair this time. And if we're restricted to impulse power, none of us will live long enough to see Earth again.

Tarasco paused in his log entry, put down his microphone and looked around at his quarters. They were small, cramped—and yet palatial in comparison to those of the average crewman.

They hadn't seemed so bad when the captain first saw them. But back then, he was contemplating spending six or seven years in the place, at most. Now he was looking at living out his life there.

He recalled the story of Moses, the biblical patriarch who led his people through a wilderness for forty years and brought up a new generation in the process. But in the end, Moses was prohibited from entering the Promised Land with his charges.

Is that how it's going to be with me? Tarasco asked himself. After all we've been through, am I going to be Moses? Have I already seen Earth for the last time?

It was a depressing thought, to say the least. Putting it aside, the captain saved his entry, got up and left his quarters. After all, he was needed on the bridge.

Siregar stared at her fellow security officer as if he had sprouted another pair of ears. "You're kidding, right?"

Offenburger, a tall, blond man, pulled his head out from under a fire-damaged control panel. "Not at all. I'm telling you, his eyes were silver. And they were glowing."

"You *saw* him?" asked Siregar, her skepticism echoing through the *Valiant*'s auxiliary control center.

"No," her colleague had to admit. "Not personally, I mean. But O'Shaugnessy and Maciello were in engineering when Agnarsson lit up, and they both told me the same thing. Silver and glowing."

Siregar grunted, then returned her attention to the exposed power coupling she had been working on. Normally, an engineer would have taken care of such repairs. However, with all the damage done by Big Red, the engineering staff couldn't handle everything.

Especially when they were missing two of their best men.

"At least Agnarsson's *alive*," she said.

"For now," Offenburger added cryptically.

Siregar looked at him. "What's *that* supposed to mean? Do they think he's going to die?"

"They don't know what to think," he told her. "They've never seen anyone with glowing eyes before."

"But is he going downhill?"

Offenburger shook his head. "I don't know . . . but I sure hope not. It'd be nice to see at least one of those guys pull through."

Siregar nodded. She hadn't been especially close to any of the victims, but she mourned their loss nonetheless. After she had spent years working alongside them, it would have been impossible not to.

"Yes," she agreed, "it would be nice."

Jack Gorvoy completed the last of his autopsy reports, sat back in his chair and heaved a sigh.

Six casualties, the doctor reflected, and each one showed the same characteristics. Severe damage to the victims' nervous systems, synapses ravaged up and down the line, cerebral cortices burned out as if someone had plunged live wires into them.

Yet none of the victims had suffered external injuries. There were no burns, no surface wounds—nothing to indicate that their bodies had been subjected to electromagnetic shocks.

With that in mind, the open-console theory didn't seem applicable. Besides, only Rashad and Davidoff had been in the vicinity of sparking control panels when they collapsed. Yoshii, Kolodny, Rivers, and Zosky had been in more secure sections of the ship.

It seemed the phenomenon had found a way to affect the victims' brains without intruding on any cells along the way. A scientific impossibility, as far as Gorvoy could tell. And yet, he couldn't think of another explanation for what had happened.

Which led to another question, perhaps bigger than the first. How was it that these six people had died when the majority of the crew had survived unscathed? What was different about them? the doctor asked himself. What was the common denominator?

He glanced in the direction of the intensive care unit, only a small slice of which was visible from his office. He could see Agnarsson, the only patient left to him now that Hollandsworth was well enough to return to his quarters. The engineer was sitting up in his bed, glancing at a printout of his DNA analysis.

Unlike the others who had burned with that strange light, Agnarsson didn't appear to have suffered any ill effects. Though his eyes had changed color, his vision was still perfect. In fact, the man claimed he felt better than ever before.

Under normal circumstances, Gorvoy would probably have discharged him and pronounced him fit for duty. But he couldn't—not when the engineer was their best shot at obtaining an understanding of their comrades' deaths, and by extension, the forces that comprised the space phenomenon.

Abruptly, the medical officer realized that Agnarsson was returning his scrutiny. Like a voyeur caught in the act, Gorvoy pretended to be busy with something else for a moment. When he looked up, his patient was gazing at the analysis again.

No doubt, he told himself, Agnarsson would prefer a novel to an analytical printout. Swiveling his chair around, he examined the lowest shelf of his bookcase, where he kept some of his favorites.

Picking a mystery, the doctor slipped it out of its place and walked it over to the intensive care unit. The engineer didn't look up from his printout as Gorvoy approached him.

"Here," said the doctor, offering his patient the book. "You might find this a bit more interesting."

Agnarsson continued to study the analysis. "Can I see some other printouts?" he asked.

Gorvoy shrugged. "I don't see why not. But if I may ask, what do you want them for?"

The engineer finally looked up at him, his eyes gleaming with silver light. "Just get them," he said softly but insistently, "and I'll show you."

*   *   *

As Captain Tarasco entered Gorvoy's office, he could see the doctor peering at his monitor screen. "You called?" he said.

The medical officer didn't look up. "I did indeed," he replied absently. "Have a seat."

"I'm a busy man," Tarasco ventured.

Gorvoy nodded. "I heard. McMillan says we'll be lucky to get the warp drive up and running this century."

"That estimate may be a little pessimistic," said the captain. *But not by much,* he added inwardly.

At last, the doctor looked up. "Take a look at this," he advised, swiveling his monitor around.

Tarasco examined the screen. It showed him a collection of bright green circles, some empty and some filled in, perhaps a hundred and twenty of them in all.

"I give up," he said. "What is it?"

"It's a DNA analysis," Gorvoy explained. "Those circles are traits. Sexual orientation, height, eye color, and so on."

The captain looked at him, still at a loss. "Is this supposed to mean something to me?"

"Agnarsson created it," said the doctor. "From memory."

Tarasco looked at the screen again, then at Gorvoy. "This is a joke, right?"

"It's not," said the doctor.

"But how could he have done this?"

"I wish I knew," Gorvoy told him. "About an hour ago, he said he was bored with lying in bed while I ran tests on him, so I gave him something to look at—his DNA analysis. He decided to play a game with himself, to see how much of it he could memorize."

"And he memorized *all* of it?" asked Tarasco, finding the doctor's claim difficult to believe.

Gorvoy smiled a thin smile. "All of *them.*"

With a touch of his pad, he brought up a different analysis on the monitor screen. Then another, and another still.

"Seven in all," Gorvoy said. "My analyses of the seven individuals who were afflicted with the glow effect."

The captain absorbed the information. "Obviously, this has something to do with his eyes."

"Obviously," the medical officer confirmed, "but only in that they appear to be symptoms of the same disease—if you even want to call it that. According to Agnarsson he's never felt better in his life, and my instruments back him up in that regard."

Tarasco frowned. "I'd like to see him . . . speak with him."

"Be my guest," Gorvoy told him.

The captain left the doctor's office and followed the radiating corridor that led to the center of sickbay, where the intensive care unit was located. Only one of the eight beds was occupied.

Tarasco could see that Agnarsson's eyes were closed. For a moment, he considered whether he should wake the engineer or wait to speak with him at a later time.

"There's no time like the present," Agnarsson said, speaking like a man still wrapped in sleep.

Then he turned to the captain and opened his eyes, fixing Tarasco with his strange, silver stare. He smiled as he propped himself up on an elbow. "My grandfather was the one who told me that."

The captain felt a chill climb the rungs of his spine. "What made you decide to say it now?"

Agnarsson shrugged. "I'm not certain, exactly. It just seemed to make sense at the moment."

Tarasco tried to accept that, but he had a feeling there was more to it than the engineer was saying. "The doctor tells me you've developed a knack for memorizing things."

"You mean the DNA analyses?" Agnarsson seemed to be staring at something a million kilometers distant. "To tell you the truth, it wasn't that hard. I just gazed at them for a while, and suddenly they were the most familiar things in the world to me."

"That's pretty amazing," the captain observed.

The engineer shrugged again. "I suppose you could say that. But do you know what's *really* amazing?"

Tarasco shook his head. "What?"

Agnarsson pointed past him. "That."

The captain felt a whisper of air on the back of his neck. Whirling in response, he saw something silvery sweeping toward him and put his arms up to protect himself from it.

Too late, he realized what it was—a metallic blanket from one of the other beds. As it sank to the floor like a puppet whose strings had been cut, the engineer laughed.

Tarasco turned to him, uncertain that he could wrap his mind around what Agnarsson had done—and even less certain of how the man had done it. "That wasn't funny," he said, not knowing what else to say.

The engineer bit his lip to keep from laughing some more. "Sorry, sir. I just thought . . . I don't know."

"That it might be interesting to float a blanket over and surprise me with it?" The captain couldn't believe he had said that.

Agnarsson met his scrutiny with his eerie, silver stare. "As I said before," he replied, "it seemed to make sense at the time."

"I see," said Tarasco, not seeing at all.

He was trying to effect a facade of confidence and calm, but he didn't feel those qualities on the inside. He had been prepared to find a lot of things in the vastness of space . . . people as strange as the dispassionate, pointed-eared Vulcans and even stranger.

But this . . . this was the stuff of fantasy.

"I'm not sure you *do* see," said Agnarsson. He laid down on his bed again, gazed at the ceiling and smiled an unearthly smile. "But that's all right, I suppose . . . for now."

The captain wanted to know what the engineer meant by that—and then again, maybe he didn't. Mumbling a few words of goodbye, he left Agnarsson lying there and left the intensive care unit.

He felt an urgent need to talk with Gorvoy.

* * *

Mary Anne Sommers was learning what it felt like to be sitting in the eye of a storm.

An even dozen of her fellow crewmen were laboring around her, punctuating their efforts with grunts, sighs, and colorful language. Some of them were trying to repair the control panels that had blown up. Others were removing and replacing burned-out sensor circuits with new ones.

The helm officer wished they could have replaced the warp drive that easily. Unfortunately, she mused, they didn't carry that spare part.

Sommers would have chipped in some elbow grease, except someone had to keep an eye on the *Valiant*'s progress. At impulse speed, it wasn't all that difficult, of course. But with their shields in such ragged condition, they didn't want to run into any surprises.

"Boy," said Gardenhire as he walked by with a circuit board, "some people have all the luck."

The helm officer begrudged him a smile. "Yes, I feel very lucky. I love being stranded a gazillion light-years from home."

"Hey," said the redhead, looking past her in the direction of the viewscreen, "watch where you're going."

Sommers turned and studied the starfield, with which she'd had ample opportunity to become familiar. To her surprise, Gardenhire was right. They were a half dozen degrees off course.

As she made the correction, she thought she saw something flicker on her monitor. But when she looked down, she didn't see anything—only the black of a system whose sensors were off-line.

"Uh, Mary Anne?" said the navigator.

The helm officer shot another glance at him. "What?"

Gardenhire pointed to the viewscreen with a freckled finger. "I think you may have overcompensated a bit. You're seven or eight degrees too far to starboard now."

Sommers examined the screen again. And to her surprise, her

colleague was on the money. The *Valiant* had deviated from her course in the other direction.

Sommers didn't get it. Nonetheless, she made the necessary correction. "How's that?" she asked Gardenhire.

He leaned closer to her. "You celebrating New Year's a little early this year, Mary Anne?"

She looked back at the navigator, indignant. "No, I am *not* celebrating a little early this year. For your information, I think there's something wrong with the helm. Maybe you can look into it after you finish rebuilding the sensor system."

He chuckled drily. "No problem." Then he went back to his work.

Sommers harumphed. Of all the nerve, she thought. She checked the viewscreen again to make sure everything was all right—which it was. Then, purely out of force of habit, she glanced at her monitor.

And gasped.

"Something wrong?" inquired Gardenhire, who had stopped halfway to his assigned task.

The helm officer stared at her monitor, her blood pumping hard in her temples. There was nothing there, she assured herself. It's blank—completely and utterly blank.

"No," she said. "Everything's fine."

But she wasn't at all certain of that. A moment earlier, she thought she had seen a face on the monitor screen. A man's face, with curly blond hair and a thick mustache.

Agnarsson's face.

Captain Tarasco regarded the handful of staff officers he had summoned to the *Valiant*'s observation lounge. "I think you all know why we're here," he told them.

"We've heard the rumors," said Tactical Chief Womack, a sturdy looking woman with short, straw-colored hair.

"But rumors are all they've been," said Pelletier, the perpetually grim-faced head of security. "I'd like to hear some facts."

"A reasonable request," the captain noted. "Here's what we know. During our attempt to get through the phenomenon—Big Red, as some of us have taken to calling it—Agnarsson lit up and collapsed. But unlike the six who shared his experience, he survived."

"He *more* than survived," said Gorvoy, picking up the thread. "He became a superman. Without even trying, Agnarsson can absorb information at astounding rates of speed, pluck thoughts out of people's minds . . . even move objects through the air without touching them."

"According to Lieutenant Sommers," Tarasco remarked, "Agnarsson manipulated her helm controls from his bed in sickbay. And to add insult to injury, he projected his face onto her monitor."

Womack smiled an incredulous smile. "You're kidding."

"I'm not," the captain told her.

There was silence in the room for a moment. Then Pelletier spoke up. "You want a recommendation?"

"That's why I called this meeting," Tarasco replied.

"In that case," said the security chief, "I recommend you place Agnarsson in the brig and put a twenty-four hour watch on him. And if he tries anything like tugging on the helm again, you have him sedated."

"That sounds pretty harsh," McMillan observed, his eyes narrowing beneath his bushy, dark brows.

"We're out here by ourselves," Pelletier reminded them, "in the middle of nowhere, with no one to help us. We don't have the luxury of waiting until Agnarsson becomes a problem. We have to act now."

"I think you're forgetting something," said the engineer. "Geirrod Agnarsson is a person, just like the rest of us. He came out here of his own free will. He has *rights.*"

"Believe me, Bill," the security chief responded soberly, "I'm not forgetting any of that. I'm just thinking about the welfare of the other eighty-one people on this ship."

"So it's a numbers game," McMillan deduced.

"It *has* to be," Pelletier insisted.

"If I can say something?" Hollandsworth cut in.

Tarasco nodded. "Go ahead."

The science officer looked around at his colleagues. "We're all assuming that Agnarsson is going to use his abilities to hurt us—to work against us. I'm here to suggest that he may decide to help us. In fact," he added, "I think he already has."

"What do you mean?" asked Womack.

"When I was lying in intensive care," said Hollandsworth, "recovering from my burns, I felt as if there were someone there with me—encouraging me, helping me to heal. At the time, I didn't know who it was, or even if the feeling was real. But now, I think it was Agnarsson."

The captain looked to Gorvoy. "Is that possible?"

The doctor regarded Hollandsworth. "He did recuperate a little faster than I had expected. But then, everyone's different."

"Then it *is* possible," Tarasco concluded.

Gorvoy shrugged. "Who knows? The man can read minds and move objects around. Maybe he can help people heal as well."

"Talk about your godlike beings," Womack breathed.

"He's no god," said the chief engineer, dismissing the idea with a wave of his hand. "He's just like you and me."

The security chief chuckled bitterly. "Except he can steer the ship just by thinking about it."

McMillan shot him a dirty look. "Imagine if it was you who had been altered. Would you want to be caged up like an animal? Especially when you hadn't done anything wrong?"

"This isn't about justice," Pelletier maintained. "It's not about right and wrong. It's about survival."

"And what's the point of surviving," McMillan asked him, "if we're to throw right and wrong away in the process?"

"Hundreds of years ago," said Hollandsworth, "people in Salem accused their neighbors of being monsters and murdered them, because they feared what they didn't understand." He looked around the room. "Is that what *we're* doing? Lashing out at our neighbor out of ignorance? And if I do that, who's the *real* monster here—him or me?"

"We're not lashing out at Agnarsson," Pelletier argued doggedly. "We're just talking about restraining him."

"For now," McMillan told him. "But what happens if your restraints don't work? Once you've taken that first step, it's a lot easier to take the next one, and the one after that."

"As someone once said," Hollandsworth added, "we've established the principle . . . now we're just haggling over the price."

Pelletier didn't answer them. Instead, he turned to Tarasco, his eyes as hard as stone. "What are you going to do, sir?"

The captain frowned as he thought about it. Coming into this meeting, his inclination had been in line with his security chief's—he had considered the idea of having Agnarsson watched closely and, if necessary, confined to his quarters. However, McMillan and Hollandsworth had made some good points in the man's behalf.

Agnarsson had been one of them, right from the get-go. He had risked as much as anyone to carry out the *Valiant*'s mission to the stars. And even if he hadn't, he was a human being. As McMillan had stated so eloquently, the man had rights.

"For the time being," Tarasco decided, "I'm just going to talk to Agnarsson—let him know he's treading on thin ice."

Pelletier didn't look happy. "And if he starts throwing people around instead of blankets?"

The captain looked him in the eye. "We'll cross that bridge when we come to it."

CHAPTER 3

Captain's log, supplemental. I have had another conversation with Geirrod Agnarsson. This time, I made it clear to him that I wouldn't tolerate his tampering with any of my ship's systems, or for that matter, frightening any of my crew. I also told him that he was to cooperate fully with Dr. Gorvoy in his efforts to explore Agnarsson's condition. Agnarsson seemed to understand the consequences of diverging from my orders and promised to follow them. For the time being, I'm willing to believe him.

Chantal Coquillette had heard the stories about Agnarsson's manipulation of the helm controls.

But when she entered the intensive care unit, he didn't look like a superman. He just looked like a normal human being, engrossed in one of Dr. Gorvoy's beloved mystery novels.

"How are you doing today?" the medic asked, her voice echoing from bulkhead to bulkhead, emphasizing the loneliness of the place.

Agnarsson looked up from his book. "Just fine."

The eyes, thought Coquillette. She had forgotten about his weird, silver eyes. But truthfully, even those weren't enough to make him seem like some alien entity, ready to tear the ship apart on a whim.

He still looked human. He still looked like the man who had helped bring their engines back when they were stranded.

"Can I get you anything?" she asked.

Agnarsson appeared to think about it for a moment. "I don't think so," he decided. "But thanks for asking."

The medic shrugged. "Don't mention it."

"I guess you're here for another scan," said the engineer, still intent on his mystery novel.

"You don't sound happy," Coquillette replied, removing her bioscanner from its loop on her belt. "I thought you *liked* me."

Agnarsson looked up again. This time, he smiled a little beneath his wild mustache. "I do. I just wish Doctor Gorvoy would let me out of here. I'm going a little stir crazy."

"Hang in there," the medic told him.

She wished she could tell him he would be released soon. However, it didn't look like that was going to take place—not until Gorvoy and his staff understood what had happened to him.

An hour earlier, the doctor had injected a drug into Agnarsson's bloodstream which would make his neural pathways easier to scan. Coquillette's was the second of three scheduled examinations. By the time they were completed, Gorvoy hoped to be able to come up with a hypothesis.

And if he couldn't do that? If the neural scan didn't shed any light on the mystery? The medical team would simply have to come up with another approach to the problem.

Coquillette played her bioscanner over Agnarsson from his feet to the crown of his head. She was almost finished when she noticed something. Agnarsson's hair . . . it had flecks of white in it.

She was sure they weren't there the last time she saw him . . . and that was just the day before. Besides, the engineer was a young man—thirty at the outside. How could his hair be losing its pigment already?

Unless whatever had altered him . . . was *still* altering him. It was a chilling thought—because if Agnarsson was changing on the outside, he might be changing on the inside as well. He might be getting *stronger*.

Fighting to remain calm, Coquillette checked her readout to make certain the requisite data had been recorded. Satisfied, she replaced the device on her belt.

"See you later," she told Agnarsson, hoping her anxiety didn't show, and started for the exit.

"You know," the engineer called after her unexpectedly, "you don't have to go. Not right away, I mean."

His voice sounded funny . . . louder, more expansive somehow. As if it were filling the entire intensive care unit . . . or maybe filling her head, Coquillette couldn't tell which.

He looked at her with those bizarre, silver orbs, not quite eyes anymore, and she felt panic. After all, if he could manipulate the *Valiant*'s helm controls, what might he not be able to do to a human being?

"Actually," she blurted, "I do."

And she left him there.

Jack Gorvoy was studying his monitor screen when Coquillette showed up at his door.

The woman looked pale, frightened. It got his attention immediately. After all, Coquillette was the steadiest officer he had.

"What is it?" he asked.

"It's *him*," Coquillette whispered, sneaking a glance back over her shoulder. "Agnarsson."

Gorvoy looked past the medic. From what he could see of his patient, the man was reading the book the doctor had given him—nothing more. Still, he didn't want to dismiss his officer's feelings out of hand.

"Close the door and sit down," Gorvoy said.

Coquillette did as she was told. Then she described the change she had seen in Agnarsson's hair color.

The doctor frowned. He had examined the engineer less than an hour ago, and he hadn't noticed any graying.

"I'm not imagining it," his officer insisted.

"I didn't say you were," he told her. "Can I see your bioscanner?"

Removing it from her belt, she handed it over to him. Gorvoy called up the scan Coquillette had just done on the device's readout. Then he called up the earlier scan on his computer screen.

"Well?" she asked.

I'll be damned, he thought. "You're right. Agnarsson's changed. And I'm not talking about his hair color."

Coquillette got up and circumnavigated his desk to get a look. "What else?" she demanded.

Gorvoy pointed to the screen. "The neural pathways in his cerebellum have reshaped themselves. They're getting bigger."

She looked at him, her face as drawn and grim as he had ever seen it. "And his powers?"

"May be increasing," he said, completing her thought. He sat back in his chair and rubbed the bridge of his nose. "Congratulations. Your discovery puts mine to shame."

"Your discovery . . . ?" Coquillette wondered out loud.

Gorvoy nodded. "I figured out why Agnarsson and the others were affected by the phenomenon when no one else was . . . why Agnarsson, of all of them, survived and mutated."

Don't keep me in suspense, said a voice—a huge, throbbing presence that seemed to fill the doctor's skull.

Obviously, Coquillette had heard it too, because she whirled and looked back at their patient. Beyond the far end of the corridor, Agnarsson had tossed his blanket aside and was getting up out of his bed.

Gorvoy's mouth went dry. *I'll be glad to fill you in,* he thought quickly, knowing the engineer could "hear" him in the confines of his mind. *You don't have to leave intensive care.*

I've had enough of intensive care, Agnarsson replied, not bothering to conceal an undercurrent of resentment, *and I've had enough of people talking behind my back.*

The doctor glanced at Coquillette. "Leave," he said.

She shook her head. "Not if you're staying."

"Someone's got to tell Tarasco what's going on," he insisted.

Coquillette hesitated a moment longer. Then she opened the door, left Gorvoy's office and darted to her left down the hallway, heading for the exit from sickbay and the nearest turbolift.

In the meantime, Agnarsson had gotten out of bed and was headed toward Gorvoy's office. The medical officer rose from behind his desk and went to meet his patient halfway, thinking that would be the best way to make him forget about Coquillette.

It didn't take long for him to find out how wrong he was.

"Where is she?" Agnarsson demanded impatiently.

"She's got nothing to do with this," Gorvoy argued as they got closer to one another. "This is between you and me."

"That's what you'd *like* it to be," said the engineer. "But I'm tired of listening to you calling the shots—you and your friend, the captain. Now where *is* she?"

The doctor stopped in the middle of the corridor. "Why is Coquillette so important to you?"

Agnarsson's silver eyes narrowed. "She pretended to be nice to me, but I heard her talking to you. She's just like everyone else. She's scared of me." He laughed an ugly, bitter laugh. "And who can blame her?"

Only then did Gorvoy realize the extent of the transformation that had taken place. It wasn't just the engineer's hair and nervous system that were changing. It was his personality as well.

Quite literally, Agnarsson wasn't himself anymore. He was something else—something dark and dangerous, despite what McMillan and Hollandsworth had said about him. And the doctor would be damned if he would let such a thing walk the *Valiant* unchecked.

"Out of my way," Agnarsson snarled.

"We can help you," Gorvoy told him. "We can help you cope with what's happening to you. You just have to go back to intensive care."

The engineer lifted his chin in indignation. "You like it there so much? Why don't *you* go there?"

Before the doctor could do anything to stop him, Agnarsson grabbed him by the front of his uniform and sent him hurtling headlong toward intensive care. The last thing Gorvoy saw was the engineer's blanket-draped bed as it rushed up to meet him.

Then, mercifully, he lost consciousness.

Dan Pelletier hefted the laser in his hand as he made his way toward engineering . . . and hoped that he had guessed correctly.

As soon as he heard from the captain that Agnarsson might be getting belligerent, the security chief had led a team down to sickbay—and discovered Dr. Gorvoy slumped at the base of a biobed, bleeding freely from his nose and mouth. Pelletier wasn't a physician, but he knew a concussion and a set of broken ribs when he saw them.

At that point, Agnarsson had gone from being a misguided fellow crewman to a dangerous and potentially deadly fugitive. And when that fugitive could manipulate objects with the power of his mind, where was he most likely to go . . . other than a place where the slightest manipulation could place the ship in mortal jeopardy?

Especially when that place was where he had spent most of his waking hours over the last few years.

With that theory in his head, Pelletier had used the intercom to get Gorvoy some help and left a man there to look after him. Then he had taken Peavey and Marciulonis and headed for the engine room.

"Remember," he told his men, "fire only on my command. We don't want to blow the warp core with a stray shot."

"Acknowledged," said Peavey.

"Aye, sir," Marciulonis chimed in.

The doors to the engine room were open. Signaling for his officers to fan out on either side of him, Pelletier darted straight ahead, laser pistol at the ready.

When he got inside, he looked around quickly, hoping to find Agnarsson and take him down before the man realized he was there. But all the security chief saw were the surprised faces of McMillan and his engineers.

Agnarsson, it seemed, wasn't there.

Carlos Tarasco paced behind his center seat, wondering if Pelletier and his people had caught up with Agnarsson yet.

He saw now that the security chief had been right. Agnarsson was too dangerous to remain in a medical bed. He had to be incarcerated, for the good of everyone on the ship.

And even that might not be enough, the captain reflected. If the man's powers kept growing, if he became too big a threat, they might have to consider even stronger measures.

Is that how you treat a man who followed you out into space? someone asked, his voice echoing wildly in Tarasco's head.

The captain whirled and saw a strapping, blond figure standing at the threshold of the open lift compartment. Somehow, its doors had slid open without Tarasco's hearing them.

"Don't look so surprised," said Agnarsson, stepping out onto the bridge. "Pelletier's security teams were looking for me everywhere else. This was the only place I could go."

Knowing that the engineer could read his mind, Tarasco tried not to think about the weapons he had secured for himself and his bridge officers. He tried not to think of how those officers would be slipping the pistols from their belts to use them against the man who had been their comrade.

But he couldn't help it.

Agnarsson must have caught the captain's thought, because he whirled in Gardenhire's direction. The navigator had already drawn his laser and was aiming it at Agnarsson.

With a sweep of his arm, the engineer sent the weapon flying out of Gardenhire's grasp. But by then, Womack had drawn her laser as well—and while Agnarsson was disarming the navigator, Womack was pressing the trigger.

A bolt of blue laser energy speared the engineer in the shoulder, spinning him into the bulkhead beside the lift doors. Agnarsson lifted his hand to strike back at Womack, but a second beam caught him in the chest, knocking the wind out of him.

A beam from the barrel of Tarasco's pistol.

Fighting to stay conscious, Agnarsson glared at the captain with his gleaming silver eyes. *I won't forget this,* he thought, each word a reverberating torment in the confines of Tarasco's head.

Then Womack fired a second time and Agnarsson slumped to the deck, looking woozy and deflated.

Tarasco stayed alert, just in case his adversary wasn't as disabled as he looked. But before he could even think about squeezing off another shot, he saw something happen to the engineer's eyes.

Miraculously, the silver glow in them faded. They became the blue of summer skies, the very human blue that Agnarsson had probably been born with.

For a fraction of a second, Tarasco wondered if they might have cured the engineer of his affliction—if all it had taken to drive the phenomenon's energies out of him was a good laser barrage.

Then the light in Agnarsson's eyes returned—and with it came a restoration of his incredible strength. He planted his hand against the bulkhead and tried to stagger to his feet, shrugging off the punishment his body had absorbed.

But Womack wouldn't have any of it—and neither would Gardenhire. They fired their laser pistols at the same time, knocking Agnarsson senseless. And when he crumpled this time, Tarasco was ready.

"Take him to the brig," he ordered.

Instantly, his officers moved to comply.

CHAPTER 4

Captain Tarasco was standing in the corridor outside the brig, watching Pelletier activate the force field that would keep the temporarily sedated Agnarsson under wraps, when Coquillette arrived.

"How's Gorvoy?" the captain asked.

"Sleeping," the medic told him, unable to keep from stealing a glance at Agnarsson. "But he'll be all right. He just needs a little rest."

Tarasco nodded. "I'm glad to hear it."

"Me too," said Coquillette. "I just hope he doesn't sleep too long. I don't think I could stand the suspense."

For a moment, the captain didn't know what she was talking about. After all, he had had plenty to think about in the last few minutes. Then he remembered. "That's right . . . Gorvoy's theory."

"It was more than a theory," the medic insisted. "He told me he had figured out why Agnarsson and the others were affected by the phenomenon . . . and also why Agnarsson was the only one who survived it."

"Did he give you any details?"

She shook her head ruefully. "He couldn't. Agnarsson overheard us at that point and interrupted."

Tarasco sighed. "I'd love to know what Gorvoy came up with."

"He might have made some notes," Coquillette suggested.

"Or crunched some numbers," the captain agreed. "Either way, there would be a record of it in the database."

He tapped a bulkhead pad to activate the intercom. "Tarasco to Gardenhire," he said into the grid below the pad.

"Gardenhire here. How's everything going down there, sir?"

"Agnarsson's under control," the captain assured him. "I've got a job for you, Lieutenant. I'd like you to see if you can find a file the doctor was working on when he was attacked. It had something to do with the victims of the phenomenon."

"Will do, sir," came Gardenhire's response. "I'll let you know as soon as I find something."

"Thanks," said Tarasco. "Captain out." He turned to Coquillette. "It shouldn't be long before we know something."

Coquillette glanced at Agnarsson again. The man hadn't stirred yet from his drug-induced stupor.

"Great," she said. "The sooner we know something about our friend there, the sooner we can help him."

Tarasco wished he could be as optimistic as the medic was.

Jack Gorvoy had treated any number of crew members in his sickbay since the day the *Valiant* left Earth.

However, he himself hadn't previously spent any time in one of his beds. And now that he *had* spent some time there, he didn't like it—especially after he heard what Tarasco had to tell him.

"The file was lost?" the doctor echoed, his voice still a little weak.

"It looks that way," said the captain. "And under the circumstances, I have to entertain the possibility that it wasn't a mechanical failure."

Gorvoy looked at him. "Agnarsson."

"Why not? If he can take over the helm, it's child's play to wipe out a little computer data."

"But why?" asked the medical officer. "He knew I'd be able to tell you about it as soon as I regained consciousness."

Tarasco smiled a sickly smile. "Maybe he didn't believe you were going to do that."

It wasn't a comforting thought. "Maybe," said Gorvoy.

"Or maybe he was just acting out of anger," the captain suggested, "throwing some kind of tantrum. Fortunately, it doesn't matter one way or the other. You *have* regained consciousness."

The doctor could still feel a dull ache where he had hit his head. "If you can call it that."

"So what did you come up with?" the other man asked.

Gorvoy frowned. "Extrasensory perception."

Tarasco looked at him. "That's it?"

"That's it. Mind you, not all of our seven casualties were tested for it, but three were—Agnarsson, Davidoff, and Kolodny. Davidoff and Kolodny scored pretty high . . . but Agnarsson? He was off the charts."

The captain shook his head. "You know what? It makes sense."

"That someone with a predisposition toward mental abilities would develop Agnarsson's brand of powers? I'd have to agree," said the doctor. "I just wish I had thought of the connection sooner."

"What about the rest of the crew?" asked Tarasco. "Are we going to have any delayed cases?"

"I don't think so," Gorvoy told him. "Of the thirty-eight whose records show they were tested, none showed any particular talent for ESP."

"Thank heavens for that, at least."

"You can say that again," said the medical officer. He searched the captain's eyes. "So what happens now?"

"That depends," Tarasco replied.

"On what?"

"Now that we know about Agnarsson's ESP, is there a chance that we can use that knowledge to change him back?"

"Honestly?" said Gorvoy. "I don't think so."

"Then you don't want to know what happens now."

Gorvoy was a physician. He had taken an oath not to hurt anyone. And yet, he couldn't argue with the captain's position.

"Hollandsworth was wrong," he found himself saying. "We weren't just lashing out at Agnarsson. He really *is* a monster."

Tarasco didn't say anything in response. Obviously, he wasn't especially comfortable with the task ahead of him. But who could be?

"Get some rest," he told the doctor.

"I'll try," said Gorvoy. But with what he had to think about, he didn't believe he would be very successful at it.

Security Chief Pelletier saw the engineer stir on the other side of the barrier. Glancing at his watch, he made note of the elapsed time.

An hour and eighteen minutes.

According to Rudolph, the drug he administered would have kept a normal man unconscious for seven or eight hours. Of course, Pelletier reflected bleakly, Agnarsson was anything *but* a normal man.

He glanced over his shoulder at Marciulonis. "Contact the captain," he said. "Let him know that Agnarsson's coming to."

"Aye, sir," Marciulonis replied, and tapped the bulkhead pad that activated the intercom system.

Pelletier turned back to the prisoner and saw that his eyes were open. What's more, they were staring in the security chief's direction.

"You're a fool if you think you can hold me," said Agnarsson.

"Then I'm a fool," Pelletier answered. "But if you were in my place, you'd be doing the same thing."

That made the engineer smile. "No," he said, his voice echoing, "that's not true at all. If I were in your place, I would have killed me some time ago . . . while I still had the chance."

The security chief didn't say that that was still the plan. He didn't even dare to think it.

"You're keeping something from me," Agnarsson observed. "Something you don't think I'll like."

There was no point in denying it—not when he was dealing with a telepath. So Pelletier remained silent.

"You can plot all you want," said the man with the silver eyes. "It won't do you any good. I'm getting stronger all the time."

Suddenly, Agnarsson took a step forward, as if to attack the security chief. As Pelletier jumped backward, fumbling at his hip for his pistol, the engineer laughed.

"Soon I'll be strong enough to grab you for real," he said.

And as if to prove his point, he extended his hand into the vertical plane of the electromagnetic field.

Sparks sputtered around Agnarsson's wrist, making him grimace with pain. But he didn't pull his hand back right away. He left it there, enduring what no mere human could have endured.

Finally, the prisoner staggered backward and cradled his hand. He looked weakened by the experience, even a little humbled. But then, Pelletier told himself, Agnarsson had been weakened before, and he had come back stronger than ever.

The engineer tilted his head, considering the security chief as if he had never noticed him before. "You know," he noted almost casually, "it's only a matter of time."

It was then that Pelletier noticed the patches of white at Agnarsson's temples. The man's appearance was changing again.

"I've notified the captain," Marciulonis told his superior. "He says he's almost finished."

Pelletier didn't take his eyes off the prisoner as he responded. He didn't put his pistol away either.

"Tell Captain Tarasco to hurry," said the security chief. "We may not have much more time."

* * *

Captain's log, supplemental. I'm sending out this message buoy despite my hope that we of the Valiant *will still make it back to Earth. The buoy contains all our computer data from the past several days, which will explain how we wound up in these unfortunate straits . . . and why I've opted for such a drastic response to them.*

Tarasco tapped a square, orange stud on his armrest, terminating his log entry. Then, glancing at Gardenhire, he nodded to show his ops officer that he had finished.

Gardenhire manipulated the controls on his panel. "Releasing the buoy," he announced gravely.

Tarasco turned back to his bridge's forward viewscreen. After a moment, he saw a small, gray object go spinning off into the void like a child's top. It had a squat, graceless body, three sturdy legs and a domed crown, and it would transmit a signal in the direction of Earth for hundreds of years if nothing happened to it.

The message buoy would tell the *Valiant*'s story. It would speak of the magnetic storm that had hurled them through space. It would describe the phenomenon they encountered at the galaxy's edge. And it would say how their first assistant engineer had mutated into a being capable of destroying the rest of the crew.

The buoy would also carry information about extrasensory perception, and how it related to Geirrod Agnarsson's transformation. It would warn other captains who intended to penetrate the barrier about the horrific consequences they might face.

The kind of consequences Tarasco was facing now.

Suddenly, his intercom grid came alive. "Chief Pelletier to Captain Tarasco," it sang.

"Tarasco here. What's the situation?"

"Not good, sir," said the security chief. "Agnarsson is having another go at the force field. He's been in contact with it for nearly a minute and he doesn't seem to have reached his limit yet."

The captain could hear the urgency in Pelletier's voice. No, he told himself, call it what it is. *The fear.*

For the last twenty minutes, while Tarasco was completing his preparation of the message buoy, Agnarsson had been trying to see how much punishment he could take. Each time he penetrated the barrier, it seemed, he was able to endure it a little longer than the previous time.

Eventually, he would be able to pass through it altogether. The captain didn't doubt that for a minute. In time, he reflected, Agnarsson would be unstoppable.

Tarasco desperately didn't want to destroy the engineer or anyone else. That was why he had taken so long to release the message buoy. It was why he was lingering here on the bridge, watching the buoy spin off into space for as long as possible.

But it was becoming increasingly obvious that he had to act. Agnarsson was a deadly threat to the life of every man and woman on the *Valiant*. The engineer had to be sacrificed, and soon . . . or the buoy would be all that was left of them.

And it wasn't just the crew that was at risk. If Agnarsson took control of the ship, he might be able to repair its crippled propulsion system. Then he would have access to every planet in the galaxy, including the ones that boasted sentient populations.

Including, ultimately, Earth.

Tarasco patted the laser pistol on his hip. He couldn't allow a monster to be unleashed on his homeworld. He had to put his dread aside and do something about it.

"I'm coming," he told Pelletier. "Tarasco out."

Slowly, feeling as if he were laden with weights, the captain turned to his helm officer. "Lieutenant Sommers," he said, "you've got the bridge."

The woman turned and looked at him, knowing full well what Pelletier's summons had been about. "Aye, sir."

Pushing himself up out of his center seat, the captain made his way to the lift at the rear of the bridge and tapped the touch-sensitive plate on the bulkhead. The doors slid aside for him and he entered the compartment, then punched in his destination.

It took slightly more than a minute for the lift to convey him to Deck Ten. The doors opened on arrival and he stepped out into the corridor.

The brig was just down the hall. Tarasco followed the bend of the passageway reluctantly. Along the way, it occurred to him that he would have to look Agnarsson in the eyes before he killed him.

It would hurt to do that, no question about it. But it wouldn't stop him. No matter what, he would press the trigger.

Of course, he could have ordered one of his crewmen to destroy the prisoner for him. But Tarasco wasn't the type to put that kind of burden on one of his people. If anyone was going to wake up screaming in the middle of the night, it was going to be him.

He was less than twenty meters from the brig when he realized that something was wrong. It was too quiet, the captain told himself. He couldn't even hear the buzz of Agnarsson's force field.

Drawing his laser pistol from its place in his belt, Tarasco held it before him and advanced more warily. After a few seconds, Pelletier's muscular body came into view. The security chief was sprawled across the floor, his neck bent at an impossible angle, a trickle of dark blood running from the corner of his open mouth.

The captain swore under his breath.

His teeth grinding with grief and anger, he paused to kneel at Pelletier's side and feel his neck for a pulse. There wasn't any. And the man's weapon was fully charged, meaning he hadn't even gotten a chance to fire it before Agnarsson got to him.

Tarasco got up and went on, sweat streaming down both sides of his face, his heart banging against his ribs so hard he thought they would break. At any moment, he thought, Agnarsson might reach out with his mind and strangle him to death.

But it didn't happen. The captain reached the brig unscathed.

It didn't take an expert to see that its force field had been deactivated or disabled. The room itself was empty. And the two security officers who had been helping to guard Agnarsson were laid out on the deck, their necks broken as badly as Pelletier's had been.

Tarasco cursed angrily under his breath and scanned the corridor in both directions. The monster was loose. He could be anywhere, preying on anyone at all. There was no time to waste.

Pressing the intercom pad next to the brig, the captain gained access to every member of his crew in every section of the ship. "Agnarsson has escaped the brig," he said, doing his best to keep his panic in check. "He's already killed three security officers. He is extremely dangerous and to be avoided at all costs. Repeat—"

You're next, Tarasco. The words echoed ominously in his brain, obliterating the possibility of any other thought. Tarasco scanned the corridor in either direction, but there was no one there. *After all, what do I need with a captain? Or a crew, for that matter?*

Tarasco swallowed back his fear. *Where are you?* he asked the engineer in the confines of his mind.

Not so far away, came the coy, almost childlike answer. *And getting closer all the time.*

CHAPTER 5

At the sound of his adversary's thought, the captain could feel a wetness between his shoulder blades. Following his instincts, he whirled—but the corridor was still empty behind him.

Then he spun the other way . . .

And there was Agnarsson, his eyes ablaze with silver light, a cruel smile on his otherwise expressionless face. He had always been a big man, but he seemed even bigger now, more imposing.

You can't kill me, the engineer insisted, his voice expanding to fill the hallway. *Much as you want to, you can't. But I can kill you.*

And he lifted his hand to carry out his threat.

However, Tarasco struck first. His pale blue laser beam slammed squarely into Agnarsson's chest, forcing him back a couple of steps. The engineer's smile became a grimace as he pitted his mysterious power against the laser's electromagnetic fury.

At first, he merely stood his ground. Then little by little, with the beam's brilliance spattering against him, he did even better than that. He began to make his way forward again.

You can't stop me, Agnarsson told him, his voice echoing like thunder. *Nothing can stop me.* And he hurled a crackling bolt of livid pink energy at the captain.

Tarasco didn't have time to duck the discharge or get out of the way. All he could do was try to go limp as the engineer's power hammered him into the bulkhead behind him.

The next thing the captain knew, he was sitting with his back against the bulkhead, feeling as if he had broken every bone in his body. There was blood in his mouth and a wetness in the back of his head that could only have been more blood.

And it hurt like the devil to draw a breath. More than likely, he had cracked a couple of ribs.

Through tears of pain, he looked up at Agnarsson. The man was gazing at his victim triumphantly, in no apparent hurry to finish him off. Almost reluctantly, he lifted his hand.

But before he could accomplish anything with it, the corridor erupted with a blinding, blue light. It caught the engineer by surprise and sent him staggering into the bulkhead.

The captain squinted and was able to make out two high-intensity shafts. Lasers, he thought. On their highest settings. They seemed to be coming from the opposite end of the corridor.

Forcing his eyes to focus, Tarasco saw that two more of his security officers had arrived. Their laser barrage was pummeling Agnarsson without respite, forcing him to expend more and more of his newfound energy just to remain conscious.

The captain knew that this might be his last chance. Looking around for his laser pistol, he found it lying on the deck less than a meter away. Putting aside the pain that squeezed his midsection like a vise, he dragged himself over to the weapon and took hold of it.

When he looked up again, he saw Agnarsson fighting the security officers' lasers to a draw. It was difficult to predict which would give out first—the engineer's stamina or the pistols' batteries.

Tarasco made the question moot by adding his own beam to the equation. Skewered in the back with it, Agnarsson groaned and crumpled to his knees. Then he fell forward, momentarily unconscious.

The captain turned his beam off. So did his security officers, whom he recognized as Siregar and Offenburger. In the aftermath of the battle, they couldn't help glancing at the corpses of Pelletier and the others.

"Are you all right, sir?" asked Offenburger, a tall man with blond hair and light eyes.

Tarasco nodded, despite the punishment he had taken. "Fine, Marc." He managed to get to his feet, though it cost him a good deal of pain. "I need your help, both of you."

"What is it, sir?" asked Siregar, an attractive Asian woman.

"We need to get Agnarsson to the weapons room," the captain told them. "And I mean *now.*"

Their expressions told Tarasco that they didn't follow his thinking. But then, Pelletier had been the only security officer to whom the captain had revealed his intentions regarding the engineer.

Strictly speaking, he didn't owe either Offenburger or Siregar an explanation—but he gave them one anyway. "Agnarsson's become too dangerous. We have to get rid of him while we still can."

The security officers didn't seem pleased by the prospect of killing a fellow human being—a man with whom they had eaten and shared stories and braved the dangers of the void. However, they had seen the engineer's power, not to mention the bodies of their friends on the floor. They would do whatever Tarasco asked of them.

Kneeling at Agnarsson's side, the captain felt the man's neck for a pulse. It was faint, but the engineer was clearly still alive. And that wasn't the only thing Tarasco noticed.

Agnarsson's eyes, or what the captain could see of them through the engineer's half-closed lids, weren't glowing anymore. They had returned to normal again.

As before, Tarasco was tempted to believe that the crisis was over—that their laser barrage had somehow reversed whatever had gotten hold of the engineer, stripping him of his incredible powers. Then he considered the bodies of those Agnarsson had murdered with a gesture and knew he couldn't take any chances.

"Pick him up," the captain told Offenburger and Siregar. "I'll keep my laser trained on him in case he wakes."

Tucking their weapons into their belts, the officers did as they were asked. Offenburger inserted his hands under the engineer's arms and Siregar grabbed his legs. Then they began moving in the direction of the *Valiant*'s weapons room.

There were hatches that were closer to their location. Unfortunately, Tarasco mused, shoving Agnarsson out into space might not be enough. If the engineer was able to survive in the vacuum—and he might be—it was also possible that he could work his way back inside.

The weapons room was a deck above them, which meant they had to use a lift to get to it. It seemed to take forever for the compartment to reach them, and even longer for it to take them to their destination.

After that, they had to negotiate a long, curving corridor. It wasn't long before Offenburger and Siregar began showing the strain of their efforts. Agnarsson was no lightweight, after all. But eventually, Tarasco was able to guide them through the weapons room doors.

The place was dominated by a pair of missile launchers—dark, bulky titanium devices with long, cylindrical slots meant to shoot atomic projectiles through the void. They were empty at the moment, their payloads safely stowed in a series of obverse bulkhead compartments.

But at least one of them wouldn't be empty for long.

The captain pointed to it with his free hand. "Put him in," he told the security officers.

Siregar looked down at Agnarsson and winced at the idea. Offenburger hesitated as well.

"Sir," the security officer began in a plaintive voice, "there must be a better way to—"

"Do it," snapped Tarasco, his stomach clenching.

Offenburger bit back the rest of his protest. With obvious reluctance, he and Siregar placed the unconscious engineer in the open launch slot. Then they started to slide the missile door into place.

That was when Agnarsson woke up.

With a cry of rage, he sat up and slammed the missile door open again, filling the room with metallic echoes. Then he vaulted out of the slot and rounded on Offenburger and Siregar.

The captain wasn't about to let them get hurt—not when he had promised to protect them. Pressing the trigger on his laser pistol, he sent a blue beam slamming into the engineer's back.

It barely slowed Agnarrson down. He released a bolt of raw pink lightning at Offenburger, sending the blond man flying across the room. Then he did the same thing to Siregar.

Finally, he turned to Tarasco. *I told you,* he said in that strangely expansive voice of his, *you can't stop me, Captain— not any more than an amoeba can stop an elephant.*

And with that, he extended his hand toward Tarasco—not casually, as he had before, but with a certain resolve. The meaning of the gesture was clear. He intended to finish the captain off this time.

Tarasco fired at Agnarsson again, producing another stream of electromagnetic force. But the engineer wasn't daunted by it. He simply raised his chin and withstood the barrage, and retaliated with a spidery lightning flash of his own.

Fortunately, the captain was ready for it. Ignoring the crushing pain in his ribs, he ducked Agnarsson's attack and rolled to his right. Then he came up on one knee and fired again.

The engineer actually smiled. *I'm getting stronger with every passing second,* he observed. *You should have done something about me a long time ago. Now it's too late.*

Tarasco saw the wisdom in the remark. He *should* have done something a long time ago. He should have done the hard thing, the heartless thing, and destroyed Agnarsson as soon as he tampered with the ship.

But that didn't help him now. He had to find a way to slow the monster down, to give himself and his crew a fighting chance . . .

Suddenly, it came to him.

As the engineer raised his hand again, the captain fired his laser pistol—but not at Agnarsson, against whom it wouldn't have done any good. Instead, he trained his beam on the deck below Agnarsson's feet.

After all, this was the weapons room—and the *Valiant* boasted two kinds of weapons. One was atomic. The other was a laser cannon system supplied with power by heavy-duty conduits.

And as luck would have it, one of those conduits ran directly under the spot where Agnarsson was standing.

It took a moment for Tarasco's beam to punch through the deck plating. The tactic caught the engineer by surprise, causing him to stumble. But he didn't understand what his adversary was up to, or he would have removed himself from the room immediately.

As it was, he simply levitated himself above the ruined spot in the deck. *You're grasping at straws,* said Agnarsson, looking regal and supremely confident, his technical training obviously forgotten. *What'll you do next, Captain? Try to bring the ceiling down on my head?*

He had barely gotten the words out when Tarasco's beam found its unlikely target. Without warning, a gout of blue-white electroplasma rose up and engulfed the engineer.

Agnarsson writhed horribly in the clutches of the energy geyser. Finally, with a prolonged snarl, he hurled himself out of harm's way and landed on the deck with a thud.

However, the engineer's exposure to the deadly electroplasma had taken its toll. He was curled up in a fetal position, his clothes burned off, his skin and hair blackened and oozing with blood.

But his eyes still glowed with that eerie, silver light. And as Tarasco looked on, Agnarsson's flesh began to repair itself. Despite everything, he and his power had survived.

The captain bit his lip. It wouldn't be wise to try to launch the engineer into space a second time—not at the rate his strength was coming back. And he could think of only one other option.

Cradling his damaged ribs, he raced across the room to the intercom grid. Then he pressed the pad that activated it.

"This is Tarasco," he gasped. "All hands abandon ship immediately. Repeat, all hands abandon ship."

There was no time to elaborate, no time to explain. There was only enough time to issue the order and hope his people would follow it, because Agnarsson was already healed enough to focus his thoughts.

That was clever, the monster reflected through the haze of his pain. *But how many conduits can you open without destroying your ship?*

The captain didn't allow himself to think of the answer. Instead, he aimed his weapon at the deck below Agnarsson and fired again. This time it took a little longer for him to pierce the surface and reach the conduit, but the result was just as spectacular.

As the engineer was enveloped in the seething, blue-white flame, he screamed a high, thin scream. Then he lurched out of the plasma's embrace and fell to the deck, thin plumes of black smoke rising from him.

Tarasco's heart went out to the man. After all, Agnarsson hadn't asked for what had happened to him. He hadn't done anything to deserve it. In a sense, he was a victim as much as those security officers he had killed.

But as Pelletier had pointed out, this wasn't about right and wrong. This was about evolution. This was about survival.

And the captain would be damned if he was going to let his engineer shape the future of the human race.

As Agnarsson whimpered and clutched at himself with black-

ened, clawlike hands, Tarasco tried to rouse Siregar and Offenburger. Both of them were still alive, it turned out, though badly
battered.

"Get out of here," he told them. "That's an order. Grab the
nearest escape pod and get off the ship."

Offenburger glanced at the engineer, too dazed to fully grasp
what was happening. "What about you, sir?" he asked the captain, his words slurred and difficult to understand.

"I'll follow when I'm certain Agnarsson can't come after us,"
Tarasco assured him. It was a lie, of course. He had no intention
of following the security officers.

Siregar's eyes narrowed. Unlike Offenburger, she seemed to
divine his intentions. "Let me stay and help," she suggested.

"No," the captain told her. "Now get going."

Siregar hesitated for a moment longer, loathe to leave him
there alone with Agnarsson. Then she put her arm around Offenburger and helped him stagger out of the weapons room.

Tarasco turned back to the engineer. To his amazement, the
man was almost healed again, his skin raw but no longer charred.
Agnarsson glowered at him with eyes that had known unbelievable pain.

You can't keep this up forever, the engineer told him. *Sooner
or later, I'll destroy you.*

The captain's only response was to walk over to the launch
console and punch in some commands. The first one armed the
ship's atomic missiles, overriding the protocol that would have
kept them from exploding inside the *Valiant*. The second command accessed the missiles' timers.

What are you doing? Agnarsson demanded.

"That's simple," Tarasco told him with an inner calm that surprised him. "I'm blowing up the ship."

You won't do that.

"Won't I?" asked the captain.

He estimated that it had been two minutes since he had given the order to abandon ship. By then, all surviving members of his crew should have cast off, with the possible exception of Offenburger and Siregar. And even they should have reached a pod.

With that in mind, he tapped in a detonation time. Then he took a moment to reassess Agnarsson's condition.

With an effort, the engineer had propped himself up on his elbow. Slowly, laboriously, he was reaching out in Tarasco's direction, no doubt intent on blasting him with another energy surge.

The captain didn't wait to see if Agnarsson had recovered enough to generate a charge. He simply fired at the deck below the man. As before, it took a few seconds to penetrate the plating and open the conduit.

A third time, the engineer was bathed in electrocharged fire. And a third time, he escaped its clutches to collapse on the deck, a crisped and bloody thing that barely resembled a man.

Tarasco almost allowed himself to believe that Agnarsson was dead—that he could deactivate the missiles and save his ship. Then the husk that had been the *Valiant*'s engineer began to stir again—began to roll over so it could see its tormentor.

Its eyes had the same startling silver cast to them. And they pulsated with hatred for the captain.

Damn you, Agnarsson rasped in Tarasco's brain, *you don't know what you're doing. I'm your future, your destiny . . .*

If the captain had needed a sign, he had gotten one. He didn't dare think about turning back.

So instead, he stood there and waited, counting down the seconds. He watched the engineer recuperate as he had before, but it didn't seem that Agnarsson was going to mend quickly enough to be a problem.

Tarasco's last thought was for his crew. Like Moses, he was going to be denied the Promised Land—but after all his people had been through, he hoped they, at least, would make it back to Earth alive.

Book Two

Stargazer

CHAPTER 1

Jean-Luc Picard regarded his opponent through the fine steel mesh of his fencing mask.

Daithan Ruhalter was tall, barrel-chested, and powerfully built . . . and for all of that, quick as a cat. Like Picard, he was clad entirely in white—the accepted garb for fencers for the last several hundred years.

At first, Ruhalter just stood there on the metallic strip in a half-crouch, only his head moving as he took stock of Picard's posture. Then he edged forward with a skip step, lunged full length and extended his point in the direction of his adversary's chest.

It wasn't his best move—Picard knew that from experience. It was just an opening salvo, Ruhalter's effort to feel his opponent out—and Picard, who had been trained by some of the best fencing masters in twenty-fourth-century Europe, didn't overreact. He merely retreated a couple of steps and flicked his opponent's point aside.

Undaunted, Ruhalter advanced and lunged again—though this

time, he took a lower line. Picard had no more trouble with this attack than the first. In fact, he launched a counterattack just to keep his adversary honest.

Ruhalter chuckled in his mask, his voice deep and resonant. "Let's begin in earnest now, eh?"

"If you say so," Picard rejoined.

Suddenly, the other man's point was everywhere—high, low, sliding in from the left, zagging in from the right. Picard wove an intricate web of protective steel around himself, defending against each incursion as soon as he recognized it.

Ruhalter used his fencing blade the way he commanded his crew. He was aggressive, improvisational, inclined to go with his instincts first and last. Also, he was a devout believer in the philosophy that the best defense is a good offense.

It was an approach that had garnered the man his share of prestigious medals and left more than one hostile species cursing his name. Years earlier, before the landmark Treaty of Algeron, Ruhalter had even gotten the best of the crafty Romulans.

However, Picard was no pushover either. Though his style was to rely on skill, discipline, and a carefully considered game plan, he was so surgically precise that few opponents could prevail against him.

Ruhalter continued to advance against the younger man, relentless in his onslaught. His sword darted like a living thing, a steel predator hungry for a taste of its prey.

Picard had no chance to go on the offensive, no opportunity to drive his opponent back in the other direction. It was all he could do to keep Ruhalter's point away from himself—but he did that admirably well.

And he knew his adversary couldn't keep up his intensity forever. Eventually, Ruhalter would have to falter. If I bide my time, Picard told himself, I'll find the opening I need.

Then, suddenly, there it was . . . *the opening.*

In an attempt to lunge in under Picard's guard, Ruhalter had failed to extend his lead leg quite far enough. As a result, he had dropped his upper body. Off-balance, he was eminently vulnerable.

Picard moved his opponent's point out of the way, encountering little resistance. With practiced efficiency, he leaned forward into a forceful but economical counterthrust.

Too late, he saw his error. Ruhalter hadn't made a mistake after all. His overextension had been an act, a ruse designed to draw Picard into a subtle trap . . . and it had worked.

Thwarting the younger man's attack with the polished dome of his guard, Ruhalter came at Picard with a roundhouse right. Before Picard could retreat and erect a new defense, Ruhalter's point was pushing against the ribs beneath his left arm.

"Alas!" the older man barked, making no effort to mask his exuberance.

The best fencing masters in Europe would have been ashamed of him, Picard thought. On the other hand, it was devilishly difficult to deal with someone who was so unpredictable.

"Your point," Picard conceded drily.

Careful not to forget his manners, he swung his blade up to his mask in a gesture of respect. Then he settled back into an en garde position. Ruhalter, who was smiling behind his mask, did the same.

"You know," he remarked good-naturedly, "you look a little sluggish this morning, Jean-Luc."

"Only in comparison to my opponent," Picard told him. *Though that will change,* he added, resolving to win the next point.

He succeeded in that objective. However, Ruhalter came back and won the next two in succession. In the end, Picard's determination notwithstanding, he lost the match 5-3.

Ruhalter removed his mask, revealing his rugged features and thick, gray hair. "Thanks for the workout," he said.

Picard removed his mask as well. "Thank *you,* sir," he responded, ever the good sport.

"You know," Ruhalter told him in a paternal way, "you need to trust your instincts more, Commander. A man who ignores his instincts is defeated before he starts."

Tucking his mask under his sword arm, Picard managed a smile. "I'll try to keep that in mind, sir."

He would, too. After all, Ruhalter was more than his captain. He was also the twenty-eight-year-old Picard's mentor—a man the second officer greatly admired, despite the differences in their personalities.

"Perhaps you would care for a rematch," Picard suggested.

Before the captain could answer, a voice echoed throughout the gym: "Leach to Captain Ruhalter."

The captain looked up at the ceiling, as if he could see the intercom grid inside it. "Yes, Mr. Leach?"

Stephen Leach was Ruhalter's first officer. He had been left in charge of the ship's bridge while the captain and his second officer took their exercise in the gymnasium.

"You have an eyes only message from Admiral Mehdi at Starfleet Command, sir," Leach reported. As usual, he projected an air of cool efficiency.

Ruhalter looked at Picard. "Eyes only, eh? I guess I'll have to ask for a rain check on that rematch."

Picard nodded. "I understand, sir."

The captain glanced at the ceiling again. "I'll take it in my quarters, Mr. Leach. Ruhalter out." Replacing his mask and sword on a wall rack, he nodded in Picard's direction and left the gym.

As the younger man watched his captain depart, he wondered what the message from Starfleet Command might be about. After all, it was rare for headquarters to send an eyes only missive to *any* vessel, much less a deep-space exploration ship like the *Stargazer.*

The second officer ran his fingers through his sweat-soaked, auburn hair. Few eyes only messages remained that way for long, he mused. He hoped this one wouldn't be an exception.

* * *

Idun Asmund was running a diagnostic routine at her helm console when the turbolift doors opened and her twin came out onto the bridge.

Gerda Asmund was Idun's mirror image—tall, blond, and eminently well proportioned. Men invariably found the two of them attractive, though the reverse wasn't true nearly often enough for Idun's taste.

One of the drawbacks of having been raised among Klingons, she reflected. Unless a man smoldered with a warrior's passions, she wasn't likely to give him a second look.

Negotiating a path around the captain's chair, which was occupied at the moment by the tall, rail-thin Commander Leach, Gerda relieved Lieutenant Kochman at the navigation console. Then, as she sat down and surveyed her control settings, Gerda shot her sister a look.

Idun had no trouble divining the intent behind it. Clearly, Gerda was bored. For that matter, so was Idun.

They had joined the *Stargazer*'s crew with adventure in mind. After all, the *Stargazer* was a deep-space exploration vessel, its mandate to push out the boundaries of known space. However, in more than seven months of service, they had seen nothing but routine planetary surveys and the occasional space anomaly—hardly the kind of excitement they had hoped for. Gerda had even broached the subject of transferring to another ship.

Idun was a bit more optimistic than her sister. And less than fifteen minutes ago, she had been given reason to believe her patience might finally be rewarded.

"Commander Leach?" came a voice over the ship's intercom system. It was the captain, Idun realized.

The first officer looked up, his dark eyes alert in their oversized orbits. "Yes, sir?"

"Set a course for Starbase two-oh-nine," the captain said. "And don't spare the horses."

Idun saw Leach frown. He was a man who liked to deal in hard facts, not colorful colloquialisms.

"Warp eight?" the first officer ventured.

"Warp eight," the captain confirmed. "Ruhalter out."

Leach turned to Gerda. "You heard Captain Ruhalter, Lieutenant. That survey of Beta Aurelia will have to wait."

"Aye, sir," said Gerda, bringing up the appropriate cartography on her monitor and charting a course. A few moments later, she sent the results to her sister's console.

A comment went with it: *Warp eight. Sounds serious.*

Idun sent a return communication: *Preceded by an eyes only message not fifteen minutes ago.*

Surprised, Gerda looked up from her monitor and glanced at her sister. For the first time in months, a smile spread across her face.

Gilaad Ben Zoma, the *Stargazer*'s chief of security, heard a beep and looked up. "Come in," he said.

A moment later, the doors to his small, economically furnished office slid apart, revealing a compact, baby-faced young man with short, sandy hair in a uniform that seemed a tad too big for him. He looked uncomfortable as he stepped into the room.

But then, Ben Zoma mused, Lieutenant Peter "Pug" Joseph probably had an idea as to why he had been summoned. The security chief smiled to put the man at ease and gestured to a chair on the other side of his desk.

"Have a seat, Mr. Joseph."

"Yes, sir," said the younger man. He sat down, but he didn't look any more comfortable than before.

Ben Zoma leaned forward. "As you may have guessed, I called you here to talk about what happened last night."

Joseph looked contrite. "Yes, sir."

"You know," said the security chief, "it's good to be alert, especially when we're dealing with something as tricky as the inlet manifold. But sometimes, it's possible to be a little *too* alert."

"Sir," Joseph replied, "I thought there was a real danger—"

Ben Zoma held his hand up, silencing the man. "I know exactly what you thought, Lieutenant. And I must say, I admire the quickness with which you responded. But for heaven's sake, you've got to be a little more certain before you sound a ship-wide alarm."

"But, sir," Joseph argued respectfully, "if there *had* been a problem with the inlet manifold—"

"Then it would have been picked up by our engineers," the security chief assured him. He reached for his computer monitor and swiveled it around so the other man could see its screen. "Just as they would have picked up that field coil overload you were certain you saw a couple of days ago . . . and that apparent injector malfunction over which you shut down the warp drive."

The other man sighed and slumped back into his chair.

"Then," Ben Zoma went on as gently as he could, "there was the time you called an intruder alert without verifying your sensor data. And the time before that, when you thought an unidentified ship was approaching and it turned out to be a neutrino shadow."

Joseph hung his head.

The security chief was sympathetic. Not too many years earlier, he himself had been a fresh-faced, junior-grade officer.

"I don't bring up these incidents to make you feel bad," Ben Zoma explained. "I just want you to see that you're overreacting a bit. Granted, a threat to life and limb occasionally rears its head on a starship . . . but it can't be lurking *everywhere.*"

Joseph nodded. "I see what you mean, sir."

"Good," said the security chief. "Then we've accomplished something."

The younger man looked up, his eyes hard and determined. "I'll do better," he vowed. "I promise you that."

"I'm sure you will," said Ben Zoma.

But in reality, he wasn't sure at all.

* * *

Chief Medical Officer Carter Greyhorse hadn't intended to walk into the ship's gym. Distracted as he was, he had believed he was entering the neighboring biology lab, where he meant to review the work of a Betazoid biochemist who claimed to have synthesized the neurotransmitter psilosynine.

The doctor had expected to be greeted by the sleek, dark forms of a computer workstation, an industrial replicator and an electromagnetic containment field generator, all of them packed into a small, gray-walled enclosure. Instead, he found himself gazing at a tall, blond woman in a formfitting black garment pursuing some exotic and rigorous form of exercise.

The woman's cheeks, he couldn't help noticing, were flushed a striking shade of red. Her full lips had pulled back from her teeth, endowing her with a strangely wolflike appearance, and her ice-blue eyes burned with an almost feral intensity.

And the way she moved . . . it took Greyhorse's breath away. She punched and kicked and spun her way through one complex maneuver after another, her skin glistening with perspiration, her long, lean muscles rippling in savage harmony.

Harsh, guttural sounds escaped her throat, occasionally devolving into a simple gasp or grunt. But they didn't signal any pause in her routine. Despite whatever fatigue she might have felt, she went on.

In the presence of such passion, such vigor, Greyhorse felt oddly like an intruder. He experienced an impulse to go back the way he had come, to retreat to his safe and familiar world of scientific certainties.

But he didn't go. He couldn't.

He was mesmerized.

The woman, on the other hand, didn't even seem aware of the physician's presence in the room. Or if she *was* aware of it, it didn't appear to faze her. She pursued her regimen with uninhibited energy and determination, pushing her finely tuned body to levels of speed and precision that few other humans could even contemplate.

Then she did what Carter Greyhorse would have thought impossible. She turned it up a notch.

As the doctor watched, spellbound, the woman attacked the air around her as if it were rife with invisible enemies. She whirled, struck, gyrated, and struck again, faster and faster, until it seemed her heart would have to burst under the burden.

Then, suddenly, she stopped . . . and in a spasm of triumph and ecstasy, tossed her head back and howled at the top of her lungs. The sound she made was more animal than human, Greyhorse thought, more the product of the woman's blood than her brain.

Finally, her chest still heaving, sweat streaming down both sides of her face, she fell silent. Only then did she turn and take notice of the doctor standing by the door. Their eyes met and he could see the raw emotion still roiling inside them.

He felt he should say something, but speech escaped him. All he could do was stare back at her like an idiot.

The woman drew a long, ragged breath. Then she went to the wall, pulled a towel off the rack there, and stalked past him. A moment later, Greyhorse heard the hiss of the sliding doors as they opened for her. Another hiss told him they had closed again.

Looking back over his shoulder, he saw that the woman was gone. A wave of disappointment and relief swept over him.

The doctor was new on the ship, so he didn't know many people outside of Ruhalter and his command staff. Certainly, he didn't know the woman he had just seen . . . not even her name.

But he would make it his business to find out.

Lieutenant Vigo was sitting in the *Stargazer*'s mess hall, staring at his plate of *sturrd,* when his friend Charlie Kochman sat down next to him and lowered a tray of food onto the table.

"Now that," said Kochman, who was the ship's secondary navigator, "is what I call a replicator program."

Vigo glanced at Kochman's tray, which featured a large wooden bowl full of hard, gray mollusk shells with dark, rubbery tails emerging from them. "Steamers?" he asked.

"Steamers," his colleague confirmed with a grin. "It took a while, but the replicator finally got them right." He glanced at Vigo's plate. "You've got some more of that Pandrilite stuff, I see."

"*Sturrd.* It *is* the signature dish of my homeworld," Vigo noted.

Kochman held up a hand. "Don't get me wrong, buddy . . . the last thing I want to do is keep a big blue guy like you from eating what he really likes. I just figured you might want to try something else sometime."

Vigo glanced at his friend's mollusks, which he didn't find the least bit tempting. "Sometime," he echoed.

Kochman chuckled. "To each his own, I guess." And with unconcealed gusto, he used his fork to crack open one of the clams.

Vigo considered his own food again. One of the other humans on the ship had described *sturrd* as a mound of sand and ground glass smothered in maple syrup. But to a Pandrilite, it was as appetizing as any dish in the universe.

Usually, he amended. At the moment, Vigo didn't have much of an appetite.

Kochman noticed. "What's wrong?" he asked between mollusks.

Vigo shook his head. "Nothing."

His friend looked sympathetic. "It's Werber again, isn't it?"

Wincing, the Pandrilite looked around the mess hall. Fortunately, Hans Werber was nowhere to be seen. "I told you," he reminded Kochman. "There's nothing wrong. Nothing at all."

"Right," said his friend. "Just like there was nothing wrong a couple of days ago, and a couple of days before that. Admit it— Werber's on your back and he won't get off."

Vigo didn't say anything in response. He was a Pandrilite, after all, and Pandrilites were taught from an early age not to complain. They shouldered their burdens without objection or protest.

However, Kochman was right. Lieutenant Werber, the *Star-*

gazer's chief weapons officer and therefore Vigo's immediate superior, was a supremely difficult man to work for.

He routinely held Vigo and the ship's other weapons officers to unrealistic standards. And when they didn't meet those standards, Werber would make them feel unworthy of serving on a starship.

Kochman shook his head sadly. "Somebody's got to stand up to the guy. Otherwise, he'll just keep on making people feel like dirt."

Perhaps my colleague is right, Vigo reflected. Perhaps the only way to improve the situation in the weapons section is for someone to let Werber know how we feel.

But the Pandrilite knew with absolute certainty that that someone wouldn't be him.

Standing at his captain's left hand, Picard watched Idun Asmund bring the *Stargazer* to a gentle stop. Then he eyed the bridge's main viewscreen and the Federation facility that was pictured there.

Starbase 209 was shaped roughly like an hourglass top, its bulky-looking extremities tapering drastically to a slender midsection. In that regard, it was no different from a dozen other starbases Picard had visited in the course of his brief career.

What's more, he had seen plenty of ships docked at those facilities. But none of them even vaguely resembled the dark, flask-shaped vessel hanging in space alongside Starbase 209—a vessel whose puny-looking warp nacelles projected from its flanks as well as its hindquarters.

Ruhalter leaned forward in his center seat. "Interesting design, isn't it?" he asked, clearly referring to the ship and not the base.

"Interesting, all right," said Leach, who was standing on the captain's right. "And if I may hazard a guess, it's the reason we're here."

The captain didn't respond to the remark. But then, he didn't seem to know much more than the rest of them.

Suddenly, Picard was struck by a feeling that he had seen the flask-shaped vessel somewhere after all . . . or something very much like it. But if not at a starbase, where would it have been? The second officer wracked his brain but couldn't come up with an answer.

"Sir," said Paxton at the communications console, "I have Captain Eliopoulos, the base's ranking officer."

Ruhalter sat back. "Put him through, Lieutenant."

A moment later, the image of a fair-haired man with a dark, neatly trimmed beard appeared on the screen. "Welcome to Starbase two-oh-nine," he said. "You must be Captain Ruhalter."

"Pleased to meet you," said Ruhalter. "Your place or mine?"

The casual tone seemed to catch Eliopoulos off guard. It took him a moment to reply, "Yours, I suppose."

"Done," said Ruhalter. He turned to Leach. "See to Captain Eliopoulos's transport, Number One. The command staff and I will be waiting for you in the ship's lounge."

The first officer darted a glance at Picard, no doubt wondering why his subordinate couldn't have taken care of Eliopoulos's arrival. Then he turned and entered the turbolift.

As the doors slid closed with a whisper, the second officer regarded the viewscreen again. The more he studied the strange vessel, the more familiar it seemed to him. He could barely wait to hear what Captain Eliopoulos had to say about it.

CHAPTER **2**

Picard watched the ship's new chief medical officer enter the lounge with some difficulty. Carter Greyhorse was so big and broad-shouldered, he could barely fit through the door.

"Good of you to make it, Doctor," said Ruhalter, from his place at the head of the dark, oval table.

Greyhorse looked at him, then mumbled an apology. Something about some research he was conducting.

"Be thankful I'm inclined to be lenient with ship's surgeons," the captain told him. "I never forget they can relieve me of my command."

The doctor's brow furrowed beneath his crop of dark hair.

"That was a joke," Ruhalter informed him.

Greyhorse chuckled to show that he got it, but his response lacked enthusiasm. Clearly, Picard reflected as the doctor took a seat beside him, humor wasn't Greyhorse's strong suit.

In addition to Ruhalter and Picard himself, five other section heads had arrived before Greyhorse. They included Weapons

Chief Werber, Chief Engineer Phigus Simenon, Communications Chief Martin Paxton, Sciences Chief Angela Cariello and Security Chief Gilaad Ben Zoma.

Simenon was a Gnalish—a compact, lizardlike being with ruby-red eyes and a long tail. Everyone else at the table was human.

The assembled officers sat in silence for more than a minute. Then, just as some of them were beginning to shift in their seats, Leach arrived with Eliopoulos in tow.

"Commander Eliopoulos," said Ruhalter, "may I present my command staff." He reeled off their names. "Naturally, they're all most eager to learn why we've made this trip."

"I'm not surprised," the bearded man responded.

Leach indicated a chair and Eliopoulos sat down. Then the first officer took a seat next to him and said, "Go ahead, sir."

Eliopoulos looked around the table. "No doubt," he said, "you noticed a strange-looking ship as you approached the base. It arrived here seven days ago. There were only two people aboard—a man named Guard Daniels and a woman named Serenity Santana."

"Humans?" asked Werber, a stocky, balding man with piercing blue eyes and a dense walrus mustache.

"From all appearances," Eliopoulos confirmed. "But from what they told us, they weren't just any humans. They were descendants of the crew of the *S.S. Valiant* . . . the ship that went through the galactic barrier nearly three hundred years ago."

The remark hung in the air for a moment as its significance sank in around the room. Picard, who was more excited by history than most, felt his pulse begin to race.

Three hundred years . . .

It was then that he realized where he had seen the strange-looking ship before. Or rather, not the ship itself, but elements of it.

Back at the Academy, one of his professors had showed him a picture of the *S.S. Valiant.* He recalled its wide, dark body and its abundance of small, curiously placed nacelles. The vessel hanging in space alongside the starbase could easily have evolved from that primitive design.

Then something occurred to Picard—something that seemed to preclude the claim made by Eliopoulos's visitors. "Wasn't the *Valiant* destroyed by order of her captain?"

Ruhalter nodded. "That was my understanding as well."

The second officer knew the story. For that matter, everyone did. James Kirk, the last captain of the original *Starship Enterprise,* had embarked for the galactic barrier on a research mission in 2265. Just shy of his destination, he encountered an antique message buoy—a warning sent out by the captain of the *Valiant* two centuries earlier, chronicling his experiences after penetrating the barrier.

Though the details provided by the buoy were sketchy, it seemed one of the *Valiant*'s crewmen had become a threat to his colleagues . . . and to Earth as well, if he lived to return to her. To eliminate that possibility, the *Valiant*'s captain was forced to blow up his ship.

That seemed like a good reason to turn back. And as far as most people in Kirk's time knew, that was exactly what he had done.

But he hadn't turned back. He had braved the barrier despite the warning. And in doing so, he had shed some light on the fate of the *Valiant* . . . albeit at a terrible price.

The man who paid it was Kirk's navigator, Gary Mitchell, in whom exposure to the barrier had touched off a gradual but startling transformation. Mitchell became a superman, a being capable of increasingly improbable feats of mental and physical prowess . . . telepathy and telekinesis among them.

Unfortunately, Mitchell's perspective began to change as well. He came to see his crewmates as insects, hardly worthy of his notice . . . much less his compassion. In the end, Kirk was compelled to kill him.

Had he hesitated, he might have found himself in the same predicament as the captain of the *Valiant,* who had likely been confronted with a superman of his own—or so Mitchell's transformation seemed to indicate. Then Kirk too might have been forced to destroy his vessel as a last resort.

"But Daniels and Santana," Ruhalter continued, "are saying the *Valiant* wasn't destroyed after all?"

"They agree that it was destroyed," Eliopoulos replied. "However, they maintain that a portion of the *Valiant*'s crew survived her destruction . . . then found an M-Class planet and settled there."

"Hard to believe," said Simenon, his speech harsh and sibilant. "Hundreds of years ago, escape pods didn't have any real range. And M-Class planets weren't any easier to find then than they are today."

Ruhalter regarded Eliopoulos beneath bushy, gray brows. "Assuming for the moment that your guests were telling the truth, what made them decide to return to our side of the barrier?"

Eliopoulos smiled a tired smile. No doubt, he had grown weary of disseminating the information.

"They say they're here to warn the Federation about an impending threat—an immensely powerful species called the Nuyyad, which has been conquering the scattered solar systems on the other side of the barrier and sending native populations running for their lives."

Ruhalter stared at Eliopoulos for a moment. They all did. Then the captain said, "I see."

"Quite a revelation," Picard remarked.

"Stunning, actually," said Leach. He cast the second officer a sideways look. "Assuming it has some basis in fact."

"You sound skeptical," Ruhalter observed.

"I'm more than skeptical," the first officer told him. "I'm afraid—and not of the Nuyyad."

"Of what, then?" asked Picard.

"Of Daniels and Santana," said Leach. "Think about it, Commander. If these people's ancestors went through the galactic barrier more than two hundred years ago, they might eventually have developed some of the same powers Gary Mitchell displayed. And in Mitchell's case, those powers came with a need to dominate others."

The second officer smiled patiently. "But that doesn't mean—"

"I know what you're going to say," Eliopoulos interrupted. "The need to subjugate might have been a quirk of Mitchell's personality. But I have to confess, I had the same concerns as Commander Leach. I had to be careful—I had a starbase to think about."

Ruhalter cocked his head. "Wait a minute . . . didn't Mitchell's transformation have something to do with extrasensory perception?"

"It did," Eliopoulos agreed. "He was a documented ESPer and therefore more sensitive to the barrier effect. So, apparently, was the affected crewman on the *Valiant.*"

"And so was that other crewman on the *Enterprise,*" Cariello added. "The woman who became Mitchell's ally . . ."

"And later turned against him," said Eliopoulos. "That would be Dehner. And yes, she was an ESPer as well. However, the *Enterprise* had better shielding with which to filter the barrier's effects. The *Valiant* was all but naked, by today's standards."

Picard tried to imagine it. The chaos . . . the destruction . . . the blinding flash of powerful, unknown energies . . .

"For all we know," Eliopoulos told them, "even a hint of ESP might have been enough to trigger an eventual transformation—and how many humans aren't blessed at least a little in that regard?"

There was silence around the table. Werber was the one who finally took the air out of it.

"So what did you do with them?" the weapons chief asked. "Daniels and Santana, I mean?"

Eliopoulos scowled. "I did what I had to do. I had the two of them placed in detention cells, pending orders from Starfleet Command."

He paused, looking just the least bit uncomfortable with his actions. And Picard knew why. The pair was human . . . and as far as he could tell, they hadn't done anything to merit imprisonment.

"They seemed disappointed, of course," said Eliopoulos. "And more than a little displeased, I might add. But not surprised."

"Why's that?" asked Ruhalter.

Eliopoulos scowled again. "They said their colleagues had warned them that they would be taking a chance. As they were escorted to the brig, they quoted a twentieth-century Earthman . . . a fellow named Thomas. Apparently, he's the one who said, 'No good deed ever goes unpunished.' "

Picard smiled a grim smile. "It sounds like the type of remark one might make if his ancestors were Earthmen."

"Or if it served one to create that impression," Leach added cynically.

"Go on," Ruhalter instructed the bearded man.

"Naturally," said Eliopoulos, "I didn't like the idea that I might be detaining innocent people. But when I contacted Command, Admiral Gardner-Vincent applauded my judgment . . . and ordered me to run a battery of tests on Daniels and Santana."

"Tests?" Picard echoed.

"Brain scans, for the most part," the starbase commander elaborated. "Also, some blood workups."

"And what did you find?" asked Ruhalter.

Eliopoulos looked at him gravely. "While both Daniels and Santana looked perfectly normal—perfectly *human*—on the outside, their brains were different from those of normal *Homo sapiens*. Their cerebellums, for instance, were a good deal more developed, and the blood supply to their cerebral cortices was greater by almost twenty-two percent."

"Which suggested what?" Ruhalter wondered. "That they had been born with the mind-powers that Mitchell acquired?"

"That was the inescapable conclusion," Eliopoulos told him. "With the cooperation of our guests, we performed additional tests designed to gauge the extent of their telepathic and telekinetic abilities."

Picard leaned forward in his chair, eager to hear the results. Ruhalter leaned forward as well, he noticed.

"Mind you," said Eliopoulos, "Daniels and Santana could have been holding back and we would have been hard-pressed to detect it. However, what we *did* see was remarkable enough. They could tell me what I was thinking at any given moment, as long as I didn't make any effort to conceal it. And they could maneuver an object weighing up to a kilogram with reasonable precision for an indefinite period of time."

Remarkable indeed, thought Picard.

"In addition," Eliopoulos went on, "Daniels and Santana underwent psychological tests. If we're to believe the results, they're a good deal more independent and desirous of privacy than the average human being. Whoever said that no man is an island never met these two."

"Did you ask them why that might be?" Picard inquired.

Eliopoulos turned to him. "We did. They told us that in a society where people can read each other's thoughts, privacy necessarily becomes an issue of paramount importance."

"I'll bet it does," said Werber.

"So you were right about them," Leach observed. "Both of them had powers like Lieutenant Commander Mitchell's."

"*Like* them, yes," Eliopoulos noted. "But we didn't find any evidence that their abilities are as devastating as Mitchell's were. For what it's worth, both Daniels and Santana claim that they demonstrated the full extent of what they could do."

Leach grunted. "And if you believe that, I've got some prime land to show you in an asteroid belt."

Werber laughed at the remark.

"This is all very interesting," Ruhalter said, his tone putting a lid on his officers' banter, "but what's the *Stargazer*'s role in it?"

Eliopoulos looked at him. "Despite our suspicions about Daniels and Santana, we've yet to prove they're telling anything but the truth. As a result, Command wants a vessel to go through the barrier and investigate their story about the Nuyyad invasion force."

Leach rolled his eyes, making clear his incredulity. At the same time, Werber muttered something under his breath.

Ruhalter eyed them, the muscles in his jaw bunching. "Let's maintain an air of decorum here, shall we, gentlemen?"

"Of course, sir," the first officer responded crisply.

Werber frowned and said, "Sorry, Captain."

But to Picard's mind, neither of them looked very apologetic.

"I don't blame your officers for being wary of Santana and Daniels," said Eliopoulos. "As I said, I was wary too . . . until I received verification that the Nuyyad exist."

Leach's brow creased, just one indication of his discomfort with the announcement. "Verification? From whom?"

"I'd like to know that myself," said Ruhalter.

"From Nalogen Four," replied the starbase commander.

Picard knew the place. "There's a colony there," he said. "A *Kelvan* colony, if I'm not mistaken."

Eliopoulos nodded. "Since it was established more than a century ago by refugees, they've been accepting other Kelvans from the far side of the galactic barrier."

"And they've encountered the Nuyyad?" Cariello asked.

"One of them has," Eliopoulos told her. "One of the colony's more recent arrivals—an individual named Jomar. He told a Starfleet investigator that he had witnessed Nuyyad aggression and atrocities with his own eyes just a few years back."

"Was he told of the claims made by Daniels and Santana?" asked Ruhalter. "That the Nuyyad were gearing up to cross the barrier?"

"He was," Eliopoulos reported soberly. "And according to Jomar, those claims could well be true."

Ruhalter leaned back in his seat and regarded his officers. "All right," he declared. "I think we understand the situation. When does Command want us to leave for the barrier?"

"Immediately," said Eliopoulos. "But on the way, you're to

make a stop at Nalogen Four. Apparently, Jomar is an engineer by training. He feels certain that he can adapt Starfleet tactical systems to make them more effective against the Nuyyad."

That got Werber's attention. Simenon's, too.

"What's wrong with the systems we have now?" asked Leach.

"I don't have the details," Eliopoulos told him. "You'll have to ask Jomar that question."

"I intend to," the first officer said.

"One other thing," Eliopoulos remarked. "For the sake of convenience, Jomar will assume a human appearance. However, he'll be more comfortable in his natural form and at times may wish to revert to it."

"His . . . natural form?" asked Paxton. "And what might that be?"

"Something with a hundred tentacles," Eliopoulos told him. "That's all I know, I'm afraid."

"That's enough," said Cariello.

"We'll accommodate our friend Jomar as best we can," Ruhalter declared. "Just as we would any guest on the *Stargazer*."

Picard changed the subject. "Naturally," he said, "we'll need the coordinates of the Nuyyad positions if we're to investigate them."

Leach scowled at the notion. "Assuming, of course, that there *are* any Nuyyad positions." Clearly, he wasn't convinced yet.

"You'll have the coordinates," Eliopoulos promised them. "But Command doesn't want you searching for the Nuyyad on your own, given our lack of experience beyond the barrier. That's why they've provided you with a guide."

Simenon looked at him askance. "Meaning?"

Eliopoulos glanced at the engineer. "Meaning Jomar won't be your only guest. Either Daniels or Santana will accompany you as well."

Werber cursed beneath his breath. Simenon didn't look very happy either.

"Captain," said Leach, turning to Ruhalter, "someone didn't

think this through very well. As soon as these people arrived, they were thrown into the brig . . . that's how little we trusted them. And now we're ready to give them the run of the *Stargazer?*"

"Not the run of her," Ruhalter assured his exec.

The captain seemed a good deal less perturbed about the prospect than Leach was. At least, that was how it appeared to Picard.

"In fact," Ruhalter added flatly, "whoever comes with us will be watched day and night. Isn't that right, Mr. Ben Zoma?"

The security chief nodded. "It is, sir," he said crisply.

"Nonetheless, sir . . ." Leach began.

"Thank you for your input," the captain told him pointedly.

Then he turned to Eliopoulos again. "Tell me," he said, "did Starfleet Command determine which of your guests I'm to take along?"

The bearded man shook his head. "They left that up to us."

"In that case," Ruhalter told him, "I'd like to meet Daniels and Santana. Now, if possible. And unless you've got some objections, I'd like to bring a couple of my officers with me."

Eliopoulos shrugged. "Suit yourself, Captain."

"I usually do," said Ruhalter, quirking a smile. He turned to his second officer. "Commander Picard, Lieutenant Ben Zoma . . . you're with me." He glanced at Leach. "You've got the conn, Number One."

His first officer didn't look very happy about the decision. Clearly, he would rather have beamed over to the starbase with the captain. However, he couldn't object to Ruhalter's choice . . . not in front of Eliopoulos and the entire senior staff.

"Aye, sir," was all he said.

On that note, the captain dismissed his officers and sent them back to their respective assignments. Then he led Eliopoulos, Picard, and Ben Zoma out of the lounge.

As he followed Ruhalter down the hall, the second officer

caught sight of Leach out of the corner of his eye. The first officer was standing with Simenon and Werber and scowling at him.

Ben Zoma leaned closer to him and spoke sotto voce. "Looks
like you're developing quite a fan club, Commander."

Picard glanced at the security chief. Gilaad Ben Zoma was a
handsome, darkly complected man with a ready smile. He was
also the second officer's closest friend and colleague on the ship.

Like Picard's father, Ben Zoma's had disapproved of his join-
ing Starfleet. From the day they met, the coincidence had given
the two men a common ground, something about which to com-
miserate—and had created a warm rapport between them.

"Fan club indeed," the second officer responded in the same
soft voice.

Up ahead, Ruhalter was too engrossed in conversation with
Eliopoulos to pay much attention to what his officers were saying. Still, Picard didn't want to utter anything even vaguely in-
subordinate.

"That's all you have to say?" Ben Zoma wondered. "You
know, if you're not careful, our pal Number One is going to stab
you in your sleep."

Picard chuckled drily. "He's welcome to try."

CHAPTER 3

Picard stood outside a pair of gray sliding doors, alongside Ruhalter, Ben Zoma, and Eliopoulos, and watched an armed Starfleet security officer punch a code into a wall pad.

A moment later, the doors parted, revealing a fairly large, well-lit chamber. A translucent force field bisected the place, denying access to two separate cells. One was empty. The other contained two very human-looking figures—a man and a woman in dark green jumpsuits.

The man was of average build, with curly, red hair and a robust mustache. The woman was dark and petite, her thick, black tresses drawn back into a long, unruly ponytail.

Daniels, Picard thought. And Santana.

They eyed Eliopoulos and the others as they entered. There wasn't any anger in their expressions, despite their captivity. There wasn't any apparent resentment. But there *was* an almost palpable sense of impatience.

"Commander Eliopoulos," said the redhaired man. "I hope these gentlemen are from the ship you told us about."

"They are," Eliopoulos confirmed. He introduced Ruhalter, Picard, and Ben Zoma one by one.

"Pleased to meet you," the woman replied.

Up close, Serenity Santana was strikingly beautiful, with big, dark eyes and full, cherry-colored lips. So beautiful, in fact, that Picard had difficulty taking his eyes off her.

It seemed to him that her gaze lingered on him for a moment as well. But then, the second officer was quick to concede, that might well have been a product of his imagination.

"And your mission?" Daniels asked, his eyes narrowing. "To investigate what we've been telling you about the Nuyyad? That's still on, I hope."

"It is," Eliopoulos confirmed for him. "In fact, that's what we're here about. Captain Ruhalter wants to decide for himself which of you he'll take along as a guide."

Santana frowned. *"Which* of us?"

"Starfleet Command has decided it would be better for one of you to remain here," Eliopoulos explained. "For security reasons."

Picard saw Santana and Daniels exchange glances. Judging from the looks on their faces, this was yet another indignity in what they perceived as a long list of indignities.

"Fine," said the red-haired man.

Santana looked at Ruhalter. "Who are you going to take?"

The captain returned her gaze for a moment. Then, in a voice that betrayed nothing, he said, "I'll take you."

The woman seemed unprepared for such a quick decision. "Just out of curiosity," she asked, "why me?"

Ruhalter smiled an easy smile. "As my second officer will tell you, I like to go with my instincts."

Santana glanced at Picard. Again, it seemed to him that her

scrutiny lasted a little longer than necessary. Then she looked at Daniels, and finally at the captain again.

"I'm ready when you are," the woman told him.

Idun Asmund had been waiting at her helm console for what seemed like forever before she heard her captain's voice flood the bridge: "We're aboard, Number One. Take us out of here."

Commander Leach, who had been sitting in Ruhalter's center seat, responded to the order. "Aye, sir." He turned to Asmund. "You heard the captain, Lieutenant. Half impulse."

"Half impulse," the helm officer confirmed.

She had laid in a course already, based on the coordinates transmitted to her minutes earlier by Commander Eliopoulos. Applying starboard thrusters, she gently brought the *Stargazer* about. Then she engaged the impulse engines and left Starbase 209 behind.

As usual, Gerda was bent over the navigation station. Idun glanced at her sister—and saw that she was typing something on her comm pad. The helm officer was able to guess the sense of the message before she saw it appear on one of her monitors.

Where now? Gerda wanted to know.

Idun smiled to herself. Where indeed? Clearly, they were headed for the other side of the galactic barrier—her sister knew that much already. But what did they expect to find there? What did they hope to accomplish? That was what Gerda was really asking.

Eventually, both Idun and her sister would be briefed by Commander Leach or Commander Picard and given the answer to Gerda's question. But for now, Idun was more than content to savor the question itself.

And judging by the expression on her sister's face, Gerda felt the same way.

Pug Joseph had taken a turbolift down to the brig just as soon as Lieutenant Ben Zoma contacted him.

After all, he'd had to make certain that everything was in running order. The last thing he wanted was to have his superiors arrive with their prisoner and find that the force field was on the blink.

Of course, the security officer reflected, as he leaned on the wall beside the field controls, Ben Zoma hadn't actually *called* the woman a prisoner. But if she was anything else, she would have been given a suite of guest quarters instead of a small, spartan cell with a guard outside.

Abruptly, Joseph heard the clatter of boot heels from around a bend in the corridor. Straightening, he listened to the sounds grow closer, louder. Finally, Lieutenant Ben Zoma turned the corner.

He wasn't alone. Fox and Sekowsky were with him, carrying phasers. And a woman was walking between them—a small, slender woman with a black ponytail and dark, exotic eyes.

"Mr. Joseph," said Ben Zoma, acknowledging him. "This is our guest, Serenity Santana. Please see that she's not any more inconvenienced than she needs to be."

"I will, sir," Joseph answered.

Santana, he repeated inwardly. The name suggested energy and exhuberance, spice and spirit. In his mind, at least, it seemed to fit her.

The woman didn't wait to be escorted into her cell. She walked in of her own volition. Then she sat down on the bench seat within and watched as Fox manipulated the force field controls.

A moment later, a not-quite-transparent barrier sprang into existence across the cell mouth. It was powerful enough to cause any human who came into contact with it to lose consciousness.

But Joseph, along with every other security officer on the ship, had been warned—Santana wasn't just any human. It was possible, if only remotely, that the electromagnetic field wouldn't hold her. Hence, the need for live, armed guards, who would monitor her every minute of the day.

And if she was as adept a telepath as they suspected, even armed guards might not be enough to keep her from escaping. So Joseph and whoever else was watching Santana would have to check in with a superior every five minutes . . . just in case.

Not so long ago, Ben Zoma had lectured him about his overzealousness. But surely, this was one case where he *couldn't* be overzealous. No amount of caution would be too great, Joseph told himself.

Even if the woman *did* look pretty harmless.

Ben Zoma put his hand on Joseph's shoulder. "You'll only be here a couple of hours. Then I'll get you some relief."

The security officer nodded. "Acknowledged."

Ben Zoma smiled at the terseness of Joseph's response. Then he left, and Fox and Sekowsky followed in his wake.

Joseph turned to Santana. For a moment, their eyes met and locked. Then, made uncomfortable by the contact, the security officer turned away.

"I don't bite," she told him.

He looked back at her, but he decided not to reply. He didn't want to be distracted by conversation.

Santana smiled a wan smile. "You know," she said in a friendly, almost playful tone, "the guards on the starbase talked to me. Are the rules that different here?"

It seemed rude not to speak to her at all. No, Joseph reflected, more than rude. Cruel, really. After all, the woman was going to be in that cell for a long time.

"If you need anything," he responded finally, "let me know."

"Ah," said Santana, her smile blossoming into something lovely. "So you *can* talk. That's good to know."

With an effort, he kept from smiling back. "Is there?" he asked. "Anything you need, I mean?"

She thought about it for a moment. "Not right now," she told him. "But if I think of anything, you'll be the first to know."

Then he *did* smile.

"We're making progress," Santana observed. "First a conversation. Then a smile. Next thing you know, I'll have you in my power."

Joseph felt his heart jump up his throat. Instinctively, his hand went to the phaser on his hip.

She took note of it. "Actually," she said, her voice a good deal more measured, "I was joking with you."

As quickly as he could, he took his hand off his weapon. "So was I," he answered, trying to salvage some of his dignity.

Santana smiled again. "Listen," she said, "I should probably let you believe you fooled me just now, but . . . well, I'm a telepath. I can tell when you're joking and when you're not. And just now . . ." She shrugged.

Joseph blushed.

"So," she said, "now that we've shared an incredibly awkward moment . . . what's your name?"

There didn't seem to be any harm in telling her. "Joseph. Peter Joseph. But everyone calls me 'Pug.' "

"Pug," Santana echoed, tilting her head to the side as if to get a better look at him. "Yes . . . I can see why."

The scrutiny made Joseph feel self-conscious. But in a way, it was also flattering. It wasn't often he had beautiful women staring at him.

"Tell me something, Pug."

"What's that?" he asked.

"I don't mean something in particular," she explained. "I mean tell me anything. Anything at all. It'll make it easier to pass the time."

The security officer tried to think of something, but he couldn't. He had never been much of a conversationalist.

"All right, then," said Santana. "I'll tell you something. I'll tell you about the place I come from."

And she did.

* * *

Picard reported to the ship's lounge as soon as he received the captain's summons. But by the time he arrived, Ruhalter and Leach were already seated around the sleek, black table.

"Have a seat, Jean-Luc," said the captain.

Picard pulled out a chair across from Leach and sat down. Then he gave Ruhalter his attention.

"I think one of us should get to know Santana better," the captain declared. "I'm not saying Eliopoulos's conclusions aren't valid, but I'd prefer to have a second opinion."

"Makes sense," Leach agreed.

Ruhalter regarded the second officer. "I noticed some . . ." He smiled. "Let's call it magnetism . . . between you and Santana."

Picard felt his cheeks heat up. "Magnetism?"

"That's what I said," came Ruhalter's reply. "I didn't get where I am by being oblivious to that kind of thing. She's attracted to you, Jean-Luc, no question about it."

Suddenly, the second officer's uniform seemed a size too tight for him. He lifted his chin. "If you say so, sir."

"I'd like you to spend some time with her," the captain told him. "Take her out of her cell, if you like. See what you can learn."

Picard didn't entirely like the idea of weaseling his way into someone's confidence. On the other hand, he knew there might be a lot at stake.

"As you wish," he responded.

"I object, sir," said Leach.

Ruhalter turned to his first officer, making no effort to conceal his surprise. "On what grounds, Commander?"

Leach didn't even glance at Picard as he spoke. "On the grounds that I've got a degree in xenopsychology and a higher rank . . . all of which makes me better qualified to do the job."

There was a rather obvious note of bitterness in the first officer's voice, but the captain seemed willing to ignore it. "You know I'm a man who listens to his gut," he told Leach. "And right now, my gut is telling me this assignment should go to Mr. Picard."

Leach seemed to wrestle with the decision. Finally, he conceded the point with a nod. "I understand," he said.

But he *didn't* understand. Picard could tell. And so could Ruhalter, the second officer imagined.

Nonetheless, the captain thanked them for their help and dismissed them, and remained in the lounge for a scheduled meeting with Simenon and Werber. Picard and Leach left the room together, the silence between them thick and full of hostility.

Finally, as they made their way toward the nearest turbolift, the first officer spoke. "I know what you're doing," he said.

Picard glanced at him. "What do you mean?"

Leach's mouth twisted with unconcealed resentment. "Don't play innocent with me, Commander. You're worming your way into the captain's good graces more and more each day, hoping to squeeze me out and land yourself a fat promotion. But I've worked too long and hard to let someone like you undermine my authority."

"Undermine your . . . ?" Picard smiled incredulously and shook his head. "I had no such thing in mind, I assure you."

"The hell you didn't." Leach's eyes had become as sharp as chips of obsidian. "Don't push me, Commander. I'm liable to push back."

Picard didn't know what to say to that. And before he could think of anything, two crewmen turned the corner ahead of them. The second officer recognized them as Pernell and Zaffino—a couple of Simenon's engineers.

"Just the men I wanted to see," said Leach.

The engineers looked surprised. "Us, sir?" asked Zaffino.

Picard doubted that Leach had any real business with Pernell and Zaffino. More likely, he was simply looking for an excuse not to share a turbolift with the second officer.

That was fine with Picard, who hadn't been looking forward to the company either. Leaving his colleague with the two engineers, he made his way down the corridor on his own.

The second officer wasn't thrilled that he had made an enemy—especially of the ship's first officer, who happened to be his immediate superior. However, he wouldn't let it stop him from discharging his duty. Turning left at the first intersection, he came to the turbolift and summoned it.

When the compartment arrived, Picard stepped inside and uttered a single word: "Brig." Then, his command filed and noted, he let the lift carry him to the vicinity of Santana's cell.

CHAPTER 4

Picard gazed at Serenity Santana across a table in the *Stargazer*'s mess hall. She, in turn, was gazing into her drinking glass, her raven hair liberated from its ponytail.

The woman had been happy to leave the brig, no question about it. It couldn't have been a picnic sitting in the same small enclosure hour after hour, denied access even to the ship's library computer lest she stumble across something of some small tactical value.

The second officer glanced at the open doorway, through which he could see a watchful Pug Joseph. A necessary precaution, he conceded, but one that made having a casual conversation a bit awkward.

"You're right," Santana observed. "It *is* a little awkward."

Picard turned to her. "You read my mind," he said, hearing a mixture of surprise and delight in his voice.

"Of course," she returned.

"You know," he said candidly, "I haven't had much experience with telepathy. Few Federation species are capable of it. And none of them are capable of telekinesis."

"Unfortunately," Santana replied, "neither talent is very highly developed in our case. Captain Eliopoulos must have mentioned that."

The commander nodded. "He did. Still . . ."

The woman's dark eyes narrowed with mock suspicion. "Are you angling for a demonstration, Commander?"

He chuckled. "Can't you tell?"

Santana looked at him askance. "If you've spoken to our friend Eliopoulos, you know I'm only privy to active thoughts."

"I do know that," he admitted. "And for the sake of expediency, I'll make no bones about it . . . I *would* like to see a demonstration."

She seemed charmed by his manners. "All right. One feat of mental dexterity coming up."

Gradually, her eyes took on a harder cast. Then the skin around them began to crinkle. It was clear that she was focusing on something, concentrating as hard as she could, though the second officer didn't know what kind of task she had set for herself.

Then he heard a tinkling sound and he looked down. Santana's drink was moving, levitating off the table, the ice in it clinking merrily against the sides of the glass.

As Picard watched, the drink gradually rose to a height of perhaps twenty centimeters. Then, just as slowly, it descended, eventually coming to rest on the table again.

He looked up at Santana. "Impressive." He meant it.

She shrugged. "Eliopoulos didn't think so. He kept waiting for me to send his station spinning through space like a top."

"You have tops where you come from?" Picard asked.

"We *are* human," she reminded him. "If you saw my world, I'm sure you'd see a lot that's familiar about it."

He found himself smiling. "And a lot that's *not,* no doubt. To be honest, it's the latter that intrigues me."

"You want to know how we're different?"

"I do indeed."

Santana thought for a moment. "As Eliopoulos must have told you, we value our privacy."

"He mentioned that," Picard conceded. "But surely, that's not the only quality that sets you apart from us?"

She thought some more. "We're good gardeners, as a rule. And good musicians. Unfortunately, I'm one of the few exceptions to the rule. I couldn't carry a tune if my life depended on it."

"Anything else?"

Santana shook her head. "Nothing. Except for our mental powers, of course. But I think we've already covered that topic."

"Not completely," the second officer said. "You haven't shown me much of your telepathic abilities."

She waved away the suggestion. "They're not very impressive in comparison to my drinking glass trick."

"Nonetheless," Picard insisted.

"Persistent, aren't you?"

"So I'm told."

Santana sighed. "Have it your way, Commander. You'll have to think of something, of course. Something pleasant, I hope."

"I'd be happy to," he told her. And he did as she had asked.

Santana's brow furrowed for a second. Then she said, "Your mother was a lovely woman. And if I'm not mistaken, a wonderful cook."

Picard was intrigued. He had created an image of his mother in his mind's eye, but he hadn't pictured her preparing food.

"Why do you mention her cooking?" he wondered out loud.

"The smell of her," Santana explained. She closed her eyes. "I don't recognize it, but it's some kind of spice. Sharp, pungent . . ."

Abruptly, the second officer realized what she was talking about. "Cinnamon," he said. "She would use it in her apple tarts."

Her eyes still closed, Santana inhaled deeply, as if she were in Picard's mother's kitchen. "And you liked those tarts, didn't you?

In fact, you used to think about them on your way home from somewhere."

"School," he confessed.

She opened her eyes. "Yes. School."

"Extraordinary," said Picard.

Santana shook her head. "No. What would be extraordinary is if I could read your mind like a book, finding any memory at all. They say some of our people could do that in the days when the colony was first founded. But we can't do it anymore."

Perhaps it was the look on her face, a little sad and a little dreamy, as she contemplated something she considered wondrous. Perhaps he had crossed some invisible threshold of familiarity. Perhaps many things.

Picard couldn't explain it. He just knew that he was intensely aware of how beautiful Serenity Santana was, and that that awareness was making his heart beat faster.

Then he saw her blush, and he realized that she had read his thoughts again. He felt embarassed and ungainly, like a youngster whose crush on some girl had inadvertently been exposed.

"I'm sorry," the second officer told her.

Santana looked sympathetic. "Don't be."

"No," he said, shaking his head, "I didn't mean to—"

She held up a hand for silence. "I'm serious, Commander. There's no need to feel awkward." Unexpectedly, her expression turned coquettish. "After all, who knows how embarassing *my* thoughts might be."

For a heartbeat, Picard was lost in the dark, sorcerous pools of Santana's eyes. Then he swallowed and pulled himself back out again.

"An . . . intriguing notion," he replied.

She seemed on the verge of saying something in response. But instead, she picked up her glass and sipped her drink. By the time she put it down again, the second officer had regained his composure.

"I hate to say it," the commander began, but—"

"I know," Santana said, saving him the trouble. "It's time I was returning to the brig."

He nodded soberly. "Yes. After all, I have a shift starting on the bridge. But I enjoyed our conversation. Perhaps we—"

"Could have another one some time? Here in the mess hall?" The woman shrugged. "Why not?"

Picard couldn't help feeling there was more to say. However, he didn't want to make this any more personal than it had to be. When it came to Serenity Santana, he was simply doing his duty. He was following the orders his captain had laid out for him.

He didn't dare consider the possibility of falling in love with the woman.

Without another word, the second officer got up and gestured to the doorway. Santana rose as well and preceded him out into the corridor. Then she allowed Pug Joseph to accompany her back to the brig.

Picard watched them go for a moment. Heaving a sigh, he turned and headed for the bridge.

Carter Greyhorse was sitting behind his desk, studying the results of the examinations he had already conducted, when he spied Gerda Asmund through one of his office's transparent walls.

The last time the doctor had seen the woman, she had been wearing a tight-fitting exercise garment, her lips pulled back from her teeth, her skin tantalizingly moist with perspiration. Now, she was dressed in the cranberry tunic and black trousers of Starfleet, looking like anyone else in the *Stargazer*'s crew.

No, Greyhorse corrected himself quickly and emphatically . . . *not* like anyone else. Not at all. Even in her standard-issue uniform, with her spun-gold hair woven into an austere bun, Gerda Asmund was a most attractive woman.

A most *exciting* woman.

But she was there to see him as a physician, not someone with whom she might share a love interest. He forced himself to remember that. Taking a deep breath, he assumed his most professional demeanor.

Unaware of Greyhorse's inner turmoil, the blond woman came to a stop at the entrance to his office. "Lieutenant Asmund," she said in a husky but eminently feminine voice, "reporting as requested."

The doctor smiled—not an activity at which he had had a lot of practice—and gestured for his patient to take a seat on the other side of his desk. She complied without comment.

Her eyes were so blue it almost hurt to look at them. He tried his best not to notice. "Thank you for coming," he told her. "Do you have any questions about why you're here?"

She shrugged. "You need to test my extrasensory perception quotient before we penetrate the barrier. It's straightforward enough." She frowned. "Though, as you must know, I've been tested before."

Greyhorse tapped his key padd and brought up Gerda's medical file. It took no time at all to locate the results of her last ESP test, which showed she had no talent in that area whatsoever.

"Let's see," he said. "ESPer quotient . . . oh-one-one. Aperception quotient . . . two over twenty-five. As you say, you've been tested before." He looked up from his monitor. "However, things can change, and Starfleet regulations are rather specific in this regard."

The woman nodded. "Of course. Let's just do what we have to."

The doctor pretended to review other parts of her file, though he had come to know them pretty much by heart. "You're the primary navigator," he noted, "and have been since the ship left Utopia Planitia some seven months ago."

"That's correct," she said.

"Prior to that," he observed, "you served on the *da Gama,* and before that you graduated from the Academy with honors."

"Correct again," Gerda told him.

Greyhorse looked up at her. "It also says here that you were raised in a . . . Klingon household?"

"Yes," the navigator said matter-of-factly, as if such things happened all the time. "As children, my sister Idun and I were the only survivors of a Federation colony disaster. After several days had gone by, Klingons intercepted the colony's distress signal and rescued us. Apparently, we impressed them with our resourcefulness."

He grunted thoughtfully, seeing an opportunity to establish some kind of rapport with her. "It must have been quite . . ."

"Yes?" Gerda prodded.

He felt himself wither under her scrutiny. "Nothing," he said at last. "Nothing at all."

It was no use, he reflected. He wasn't good at small talk. Truthfully, he wasn't good at *any* kind of talk.

If someone gave him a disease to cure or an injury to heal, he was as sharp as any physician in the Federation. But when it came to being a person, a social creature capable of interacting with other social creatures, he fell significantly short of the mark.

Greyhorse had come to grips with his shortcomings a long time ago. He had gotten to the point where they didn't bother him. But they bothered him now, he had to admit.

And it was all because of Gerda Asmund.

"Doctor?" she said.

He realized that he had been silent for what must have seemed like a long time. "Yes," he responded clumsily. "Sorry. I was just thinking of something. Er . . . let's begin, shall we?"

Gerda nodded. "Indeed."

"I'll bring a picture up on my screen," Greyhorse explained for the fifteenth time that day. "You try to develop an impression of it in your head, using any means that occurs to you. And while you're at it, the internal sensors in this room will monitor your brainwaves."

She smiled a weary smile. "I know. As we've established, I have undergone this test before."

He smiled back as best he could. "So you said."
And he began the examination.

Picard studied the small, blue-and-green world on the *Stargazer*'s forward viewscreen from his place beside Captain Ruhalter.

"Establish a synchronous orbit," said Ruhalter.

"Aye, sir," replied Idun Asmund from the helm console.

Nalogen IV was an M-Class planet, which meant it was inhabitable by most oxygen-breathing species. Indeed, there was only one sentient form of life on the planet, and it required oxygen to survive. However, it wasn't an indigenous form of life. It had originated in a solar system one hundred thousand light-years away.

Nearly a century earlier, several ships' worth of Kelvans had set out from their home in the Andromeda Galaxy to find a new place for their people to live. One of their vessels was damaged as it penetrated the galactic barrier and its crew was forced to abandon ship.

Since Kelvan technology allowed them to change form, they took on the appearance of humans—a populous species in that part of the Milky Way galaxy—and put out a distress call. Ultimately, they hoped to commandeer a starship and use it to return to their homeworld.

However, their takeover attempt was thwarted by Captain James Kirk—the same near-legendary Starfleet officer who had dealt with the menace of Gary Mitchell a few years earlier. Once the threat to his vessel was defused, Kirk arranged for the Kelvans to settle on a world in Federation space.

That world was Nalogen IV.

"Hail the colony," said Captain Ruhalter from his captain's chair.

"Aye, sir," responded Paxton.

The comm officer's fingers flew over his communications panel. A few moments later, he looked up again.

"I've got the colony administrator," Paxton reported. "His

name is Najak. But he says he'd like to restrict communications to audio only."

Ruhalter frowned as he considered the viewscreen. "Very well, Lieutenant. Tell him I'll comply with his request."

Picard had to admit that he was disappointed, if only to himself. He had hoped to get a glimpse of Kelvan civilization. Now it looked as if he wouldn't get the chance.

Abruptly, a deep and commanding voice filled the bridge. "This is Administrator Najak," it said.

Ruhalter looked up at the intercom grid. "Captain Ruhalter here. It's a pleasure to speak with you, Administrator."

"The pleasure is mine," said Najak. "And thank you for respecting my privacy, Captain. Over the years, we have come to appreciate how monstrous we seem to other Federation species. This fact has occasionally led to . . . let us call them 'misunderstandings.' "

"It's no problem at all," Ruhalter replied. "We don't want to intrude on you any more than we have to."

"Jomar will be ready in a matter of minutes," Najak advised. "If you give us the coordinates of your transporter room, our technicians will be pleased to effect his transport."

"Acknowledged," said the captain. He turned to Paxton. "Send them whatever they need, Lieutenant."

"I'll do that, sir," Paxton responded.

Ruhalter returned his attention to the Kelvan. "With luck, I'll have good news when I bring Jomar back to you."

"With luck," the administrator echoed. "Najak out."

The captain glanced at Leach, who was standing beside Simenon at the engineering console. "You've got the conn, Number One. Commander Picard, you're with me."

With that, he got up and made his way aft to the turbolift. As the second officer followed him, he saw the expression on Leach's face. If looks could have killed, Picard would have been torn atom from atom.

Ruhalter couldn't have failed to notice his exec's displeasure.

However, he didn't comment on it as he and Picard entered the lift and watched the sliding doors close behind them.

Instead, he said, "I was really looking forward to beaming down and seeing that Kelvan colony."

Picard nodded. "So was I, sir."

"I guess we shouldn't complain. We'll no doubt be seeing plenty on the other side of the galactic barrier."

"No doubt," the second officer agreed.

Just then, the turbolift doors opened again. The captain exited ahead of Picard and led the way to the transporter room, where a woman named Vandermeer was working the control console.

"Anything yet?" Ruhalter asked her.

"No, sir," said the transporter operator, consulting her monitor. "Wait . . . I'm getting a message from the surface."

"The colony administrator's office?" asked the captain.

"Yes. They say they're ready to beam someone up."

Ruhalter nodded. "Contact the bridge and tell Mr. Leach I want the shields dropped. Then let the Kelvans know we're ready. But as soon as our visitor arrives, I want the shields back up again."

"Aye, sir," said Vandermeer, carrying out her orders.

Picard too felt uneasy when the *Stargazer*'s deflectors were lowered. After all, it left the ship vulnerable to all manner of mishaps. Unfortunately, they couldn't effect a transport with the shields in place.

"He's on his way," Vandermeer announced.

Picard turned to the raised, oval platform in the back of the room. A shaft of light appeared there, then slowly resolved itself into a humanoid form. A moment later, the light died, leaving a tall, fair-skinned man with unruly red hair and haunting, pale-blue eyes.

"You must be Jomar," Ruhalter observed. He smiled a craggy smile. "Welcome to the Federation *Starship Stargazer*. I'm Captain Ruhalter . . . and this is Commander Picard, my second officer."

The Kelvan stared at Ruhalter for a full second before he answered. "Thank you, Captain." He turned to Picard. "Commander."

Jomar's tone was flat and utterly devoid of enthusiasm. And his expression—or rather, his lack of one—would have been the envy of many a logical Vulcan.

"If you'll follow us," said the captain, "we'll show you to your quarters. I think you'll find them—"

"I have a great deal of work to do," the Kelvan declared, unceremoniously interrupting Ruhalter's invitation. "I would prefer to familiarize myself with your ship's tactical systems and subsystems before I give any thought to sleeping accommodations."

The captain appeared unoffended. "Of course," he told Jomar. "We can start in engineering, if you like."

"That would be satisfactory," said the Kelvan.

Ruhalter tapped the Starfleet insignia on his chest. "Captain to bridge. Break orbit, Mr. Leach. We've got our passenger."

"Acknowledged, sir," said Leach.

The captain turned to Jomar. "Next stop, engineering."

The Kelvan didn't respond. He just waited for Ruhalter and Picard to lead the way, then fell in behind them.

Charming, thought the second officer. But then, they hadn't enlisted Jomar's assistance because of his advanced social skills. If all went well, he would be their secret weapon against the Nuyyad.

CHAPTER 5

Picard sat in his usual place at the black oval table in the *Stargazer*'s lounge and watched Captain Ruhalter bring the meeting to order.

Unlike the last meeting the second officer had attended there, this one didn't call for the presence of the entire senior staff. The topic was a largely technical one, so all of the officers present— with the exceptions of Ruhalter, Commander Leach, and Picard himself—were from the weapons and engineering sections.

And then, of course, there was the Kelvan. He was sitting beside the captain with his bright red hair in disarray, a deadpan expression on his face that betrayed his lack of humanity.

"I called this meeting," said Ruhalter, "so you could all meet Jomar here and hear his plans for the *Stargazer*'s tactical systems." He turned to the Kelvan. "Go ahead."

Jomar inclined his head. "Thank you, Captain." He scanned the other faces at the table without a hint of emotion. "As you may have heard," he went on abruptly, "the Nuyyad are a formidable enemy, with a long list of conquests to their credit."

"So we've been given to understand," said Ruhalter.

"However," the Kelvan went on, "the Nuyyad's vessels are no faster or more maneuverable than this one. Their shields are no stronger than the *Stargazer*'s shields. In fact, they may be a little weaker. Where the Nuyyad far outstrip Federation technology is in a single area . . ."

"Firepower?" Simenon suggested.

"Firepower," Jomar confirmed ominously. "More specifically, a quartet of vidrion particle cannons, any one of which could pierce your shields with a single high-intensity barrage."

It wasn't good news. For a moment, they pondered it from one end of the table to the other.

Then Picard spoke up. "Vidrion particles? I don't believe I've ever heard of them."

"That is because they have not been discovered on this side of the barrier," the Kelvan explained. "My people have known of them for centuries, though we always considered them too unstable to be harnessed as directed energy. The Nuyyad have apparently solved that problem."

Ruhalter leaned forward. "You've got our attention, Jomar. How can we defend ourselves against these vidrion cannons?"

"By fighting fire with fire," said the Kelvan, "as the human expression articulates. We have discovered that lacing a standard, graviton-based deflector shield with a certain percentage of vidrion particles renders it all but impermeable to the Nuyyad's beams."

"And that," observed Ruhalter, "will give us a chance to launch an offensive of our own."

Jomar regarded the captain with his strange, pale-blue eyes. As in the transporter room, he seemed to stare. "Yes," the Kelvan said finally, "that is the intention."

Suddenly, Picard realized something. Jomar wasn't staring after all. It was just that his eyes weren't blinking.

But then, when the second officer thought about it, that made sense. The Kelvan had only assumed this form for the sake of convenience. His "eyes" were ornaments, lacking function, created to make the humanoids on the *Stargazer* feel more comfortable in his presence.

As for his true sensory organs, the ones he used to see and hear and so on . . . where *they* were located was anybody's guess.

"However," Jomar went on in his monotone, "it will not be enough to merely defend ourselves. If we are to hold our own against the Nuyyad, we must increase the power of our own weapons."

"Increase it *how?*" asked Werber.

The Kelvan shrugged. "By routing your warp chamber's plasma flow to your emitter crystals in a more pure and unadulterated form."

The weapons chief's eyes narrowed warily. "Go on."

"As the system is currently configured," said Jomar, "electroplasma must pass through a flow regulator, a distribution manifold, and a prefire chamber before it reaches the crystal. I propose that we delete the flow regulator and distribution manifold in favor of a single device, which would do the work of both of them—and at the same time, facilitate a higher subatomic energy level at the end of the process."

For a moment, every technician in the room was silent. Picard could see them pondering the Kelvan's idea, turning it over in their minds. Then Simenon broke the silence.

"Where did you come up with this?" he asked.

"Actually," Jomar told him, "it is the approach we have taken in Kelvan vessels for the last seventy years."

Vigo, a Pandrilite officer in the weapons section, leaned forward in his chair. "I don't understand," he confessed. "How can you achieve higher energy levels in the crystals without—"

Werber cut Vigo off with a preemptive wave of his hand. "Without compromising the integrity of the conduit network?" he asked, finishing the Pandrilite's question himself.

As Picard watched, Vigo slumped back in his chair again and fell silent. However, he didn't look at all happy about it.

Meanwhile, the Kelvan answered Werber's question. "Starfleet Command has made available to me considerable data concerning the conduit network and its rated tolerances. As far as I can tell, it is somewhat less durable than the energy channels in my people's ships—but nonetheless strong enough to withstand even a substantial increase in subatomic activity."

Simenon shook his lizardlike head from side to side. "Not from where I stand, it's not."

"No question about it," Werber added. "That plasma will never reach the prefire chamber. It'll blow up in the conduits first."

"And send us all to kingdom come," Leach agreed.

For once, Picard found himself on the first officer's side. He turned to Ruhalter. "It would be imprudent to make the kind of changes that are being discussed without considerable study. I advise against it."

"As do *I*," Leach chimed in, obviously reluctant to let Picard receive the credit for anything.

Ruhalter addressed the Kelvan. "To be honest, Jomar, I'm not thrilled with the idea either. It seems too damned dangerous. But your strategy for beefing up the shields . . . that I like." He glanced at Simenon, then Werber. "I want you to get started on that as soon as possible."

"Aye, sir," said the weapons chief.

"As you wish," the engineer added.

If the Kelvan resented the rejection of his phaser idea, he didn't show it. His expression was as neutral as ever.

"What else?" asked the captain.

"*Nothing* else," Jomar told him. "I have discussed all the possibilities I meant to discusss."

Ruhalter nodded. "All right, then. Thank you all for attending. Now let's get to work."

And with that, the meeting ended.

As Pug Joseph approached the *Stargazer*'s brig, he was forced to admit something to himself.

He had guarded his share of prisoners in the course of his brief career. Every security officer had. But he had never actually looked forward to guarding one until now.

Garner, the officer on duty in the brig, acknowledged Joseph with a businesslike nod. "All quiet," she reported.

"Good," he replied.

Not that he had expected Garner to say anything else. After all, it wasn't exactly a Nausicaan slave-runner they were holding. It was just a woman, and a very cooperative woman at that.

He looked past the brig's translucent, yellow barrier and saw Santana sitting upright on the edge of her sleeping pallet, her eyes closed, her hands held out in front of her as if in supplication. She had told Joseph about the technique during his last shift—a form of meditation, it was used widely in her colony as a way of achieving calm . . .

And perspective. She certainly needed that right now.

"Go ahead," he told Garner. "I can take it from here."

His colleague smiled as she passed him on her way out. "I'll see you later," she said.

"Later," he echoed.

But his mind was already focused on Santana, who hadn't fluttered an eyelash since he arrived. He considered saying something to let her know he was there, but he didn't want to disturb her.

"Mr. Joseph," she said abruptly. "Nice of you to drop by."

The security officer chuckled. "As if I had a choice."

Santana opened her eyes, disappointment etched in her face. "You mean you only come to see me because you *have* to?"

For a moment, he felt the need to apologize. Then he realized that she was just joking with him . . . again.

"Funny," he said.

"I'm glad you think so," Santana replied. "After all, you *are* my only audience."

"You didn't get along so well with Garner?"

She rolled her eyes. "She's not the friendliest person around. So, tell me . . . have you met the Kelvan yet?"

Joseph shook his head. "I haven't even caught a glimpse of him."

The woman's expression turned sour. "Figures. He's the one you *really* ought to be watching."

"Why do you say that?" he asked.

Santana looked as if she were about to say something critical—then stopped herself. "Never mind. I don't want to start any controversies. This mission is too important to all of us."

But it was too late. She had roused the old Pug Joseph—the one who couldn't help seeing danger at every turn.

"Are you saying he poses some kind of threat?" Joseph asked.

"Not necessarily," Santana said. "My people have had some unpleasant experiences with Kelvans, that's all. It doesn't mean this particular one is going to be a problem."

He searched her eyes. "Do you really believe that?"

She smiled disarmingly. "Why would I lie?"

Why indeed? Joseph asked himself. He couldn't come up with a good answer. When Santana first came aboard, he had been as suspicious of her as anyone else. Now he knew better.

"So," he said, switching tacks, "where were we?"

She knew exactly what he meant. "Let's see . . . you were telling me about the place where you were raised. Boston, wasn't it? And there's a river there where your parents took you for picnics . . ."

Joseph was pleased that she remembered. "The Charles."

"Yes," she said, closing her eyes so she could pick the image from his brain. "The Charles." Her brow creased with concentration. "And you had a little brother named Matthew, who lost his sneaker somehow and put his foot in the potato salad . . ."

Suddenly, Santana began to laugh, and before he knew it he was laughing with her, both of them caught up helplessly in the memory of little Matt stepping where he shouldn't have. The brig rang with their hilarity.

Pug Joseph found that he liked Santana very much, no matter what Commander Leach or anyone else said about her. In fact, he wished he could have felt this way about *everyone* he guarded.

Vigo wasn't particularly enamored of Jefferies tubes. His Pandrilite musculature made crawling through the cylindrical, circuit-laden passageways a cramped and uncomfortable proposition at best.

Fortunately for him, Starfleet weapons officers seldom had to negotiate the tubes the way engineers did. Their maintenance and repair activities were typically restricted to one of the ship's weapons rooms, or on a rare occasion, the bridge.

But there were exceptions to every rule. And at the moment, Vigo was caught up in one.

For some political reason that escaped the Pandrilite, Lieutenant Werber wanted his section to be well represented in the effort to implement the Kelvan's shield strategy. As a result, Vigo and several of his fellow weapons officers had been asked to assist their counterparts from engineering in retrofitting field generators and distortion amplifiers from one end of the ship to the other.

And that meant crawling through one Jefferies tube after another, enduring muscle cramps and skin abrasions in the process.

"Pass the spanner," said Engineer First Class Pernell, a spare, fair-haired man lying just ahead of the Pandrilite in the passageway.

Vigo found the requisite tool and removed it from his equipment bag. "Here it is," he said, and handed it to Pernell.

They were busy installing new graviton relays in one of the *Stargazer*'s field generators. The relays, which had been fabricated only an hour earlier, were designed to expedite the passage of vidrion particles through the deflector system.

The Pandrilite wiped perspiration from his brow with the back of his hand. It was hot in the tube too, so hot that he had begun to wonder if something had gone wrong with the ventilation system.

But that wasn't the worst of it. His shoulders stung where he had rubbed them raw against the walls of the passage, his hip hurt where he was forced to press it against a circuit bundle, and his legs were so contorted he could barely feel his feet.

But Vigo wasn't going to complain. He was a Pandrilite. He had been given an assignment and he would carry it out.

Suddenly, the weapons officer saw something move into the tube from a perpendicular passageway far down the line. At first, he thought it was one of his fellow crewmen, on his way to an assignment much like his own.

Then he realized that it wasn't a crewman. It wasn't even humanoid. It was the kind of life-form one might have seen at the bottom of an alien ocean, slithering out from under a rock to snatch unsuspecting sea creatures with its long, dark tentacles.

As Vigo watched, anxious and fascinated at the same time, the thing pulled itself along the tube with chilling efficiency. His hand darted to his hip instinctively, but he wasn't wearing a phaser.

"What is that?" Pernell asked, his voice thick with consternation.

The Pandrilite shook his head, his eyes glued to the tentacled monstrosity. "I don't know. I—"

Before he could finish his sentence, before he could even think about getting out of the Jefferies tube and calling for security, the thing began to change. Right before his eyes, its tentacles grew shorter and the mass at its core lengthened, until it wasn't nearly as horrific.

In a matter of seconds, it became the kind of figure Vigo had expected all along: a black set of work togs accommodating two arms and two legs and—in this case—a head full of fiery red hair.

"Bloody hell," Pernell whispered, his skin pale and slick with perspiration. "It's the *Kelvan.*"

The Pandrilite nodded. It *was* the Kelvan. And now that he thought about it, he had been warned that Jomar might return to his original shape on occasion. He just hadn't been prepared for what that shape might be.

The Kelvan continued to make his way toward Vigo and Pernell, though he seemed somewhat less adept at maneuvering a human body through the tube. Finally, he got close enough to speak with them.

"Any problems?" Jomar asked.

"None so far," the weapons officer managed.

"Good," said the Kelvan.

Apparently, he was just checking up on them. No doubt, he meant to do that with the other retrofit teams as well.

"Do not let me keep you," Jomar added.

Then he made his way back down the tube. Eventually, he came to another perpendicular passageway and vanished into it. Vigo was glad the Kelvan had opted to retain his human form until he was out of sight.

"What a nasty thing *he* is," Pernell observed.

The weapons officer looked at him. "He's our ally, remember?"

But deep down inside, Vigo had to admit, where his instincts were stronger than his intellect, he thought of Jomar exactly the same way.

As Stephen Leach negotiated the long, subtle curve of the corridor, casting blue shadows in the light of the overheads, he felt as if he were finally making some progress.

For months, ever since the *Stargazer* left Earth's solar system, the first officer had been forced to take a backseat to Commander Picard when it came to the important assignments around the ship—assignments that required knowledge and leadership and experience.

And there was no one but Picard to blame for it. The second

officer had a way of ingratiating himself to Captain Ruhalter that Leach couldn't seem to get the hang of.

Things had been different on the *Merced*. Leach had been the fair-haired boy there, a second officer who could do no wrong. He had had the kind of relationship with Captain Osborne that sons have with their fathers, and only then if they're very lucky.

If not for Picard, he might have had the same kind of relationship with Captain Ruhalter. No . . . not *might* have, Leach assured himself. *Would* have, without question.

But right from the beginning, Picard had upstaged and undermined and sabotaged the first officer, to the point where Ruhalter didn't seem to feel he could trust Leach's instincts—and instincts were more important to the captain than anything else.

It was insulting. It was frustrating. And Leach had decided that he had taken all he was going to take of it. He had promised himself that he was going to confront Ruhalter the next time he gave Picard a job that should have been the exec's.

Then, as if he had read Leach's mind, the captain contacted him in his quarters and put him in charge of the Kelvan's deflector modifications. Finally, Leach had a task he could sink his teeth into—and an opportunity, as well, he was quick to note. If he could see the retrofit schedule completed quickly and efficiently, he would prove to Ruhalter that he was good for something more than meeting visitors at the transporter platform.

Smiling to himself for the first time in a long time, the first officer stopped in front of the lounge doors and tapped the metal padd set into the bulkhead. A moment later, the doors slid aside, revealing the room's long, oval table.

There were three figures seated around it—Simenon, Werber, and Jomar. The Kelvan sat apart from the two officers, his pale blue eyes glazed over as if he were deep in thought.

But he wasn't. Leach knew that. It was simply one of the flaws in Jomar's imitation of a human being.

The first officer pulled out a chair and took his seat. "Thanks for coming," he told the others. "I'm hoping we can keep this short, so we can attend to our respective duties. All I need is an update on how the deflector modifications are going."

"They are going well," the Kelvan answered, before anyone else could be consulted. "We should be done on schedule."

Werber frowned. "As our colleague says, we'll be finished on time . . . barring any unforeseen complications, of course."

"No snags, then?" Leach asked.

"None," Jomar blurted. "Neither with the field generators nor the distortion amplifiers. Everything is proceeding smoothly."

Simenon regarded the Kelvan with disdainfully slitted eyes. "So far, so good," the engineer agreed.

Given the climate of optimism, Leach didn't think anything else really needed to be said. "All right, then. We'll reconvene at this time tomorrow. Until then, you're all—"

"You do not like me," the Kelvan observed abruptly, cutting off the first officer's directive.

It took Leach a full second to recover from the remark—perhaps because it had some truth to it. "I beg your pardon?" he said.

"You do not like me," Jomar repeated.

The first officer shifted uncomfortably in his chair. "Why would you say something like that?"

The Kelvan shrugged his narrow shoulders. "I am different. I do not emote as you do. I lack social graces. Do not bother to tell me that these facts are irrelevant. I know differently."

Leach could feel his opportunity to impress the captain slipping away . . . and quickly. Hiding his anxiety behind a smile, he dismissed Jomar's statement with a wave of his hand.

"Listen," he said, "we're Starfleet officers. We've each had experience with dozens of sentient life-forms—hundreds, in some cases—and believe me, you're not as different as you might believe."

"Nonetheless," Jomar insisted, "you do not like me. You resent my being here. Perhaps you feel that my contributions are unnecessary."

The Kelvan leaned forward in his chair. His face was still devoid of expression, but his posture suggested a purposefulness Leach hadn't seen in Jomar to that point.

"It does not matter to me what you think," the Kelvan told them. "You have not witnessed Nuyyad atrocities. You have not seen my people writhing in agony. You have not seen them die. But I have. That is why I will go to any length to halt the Nuyyad's advance."

The first officer didn't quite know what to say to that. Fortunately, Simenon baled him out.

"We all have the same purpose in mind," the Gnalish assured Jomar. "Let's not waste any time arguing over how to pursue it."

The Kelvan considered Simenon, then nodded. "I will take you at your word." He turned to Leach. "If you have no further need of me, Commander, I will return to my duties."

The first officer was only too happy to accommodate Jomar. "You're dismissed," he said, completing his earlier thought.

The Kelvan got up stiffly and left the room. As the doors slid closed behind him, Leach felt a wave of relief. Grinning, he glanced at his colleagues. "Now, *that* was interesting."

Werber grunted disparagingly. "I'll say."

"Give him credit," Simenon rasped. "He's got the courage of his convictions. We should be glad he's on our side."

The first officer knew that the Gnalish loved sarcasm. For a moment, he thought Simenon was demonstrating that love. Then he realized that his friend was serious.

"You really think so?" asked Werber.

"I do," the engineer told him.

"Maybe Phigus is right," Leach conceded, though in the privacy of his mind he sincerely doubted it.

"Maybe," said Werber. "And maybe not."

"Time will tell," the first officer noted diplomatically. "Come on. Let's get some lunch."

CHAPTER 6

The galactic barrier was like a gaping wound in the fabric of space . . . a raw, red chasm seething with waves of violent energy. At least, that was the way it appeared to Picard, as he stood beside Captain Ruhalter's chair and gazed at the forward viewscreen.

As far as the *Stargazer*'s instruments were concerned, it was a different story entirely.

"The barrier registers on optical scanners," said Gerda Asmund from her navigation console, "but that's it. I can't get anything from any other sensor modality. Wideband electromagnetic, quark resonance, thermal imaging, neutrino spectrometry . . . not so much as a blip on any of them."

"No gravimetric distortions either," Idun observed. "Subspace field stress is zero."

Ruhalter got up from his center seat and approached the viewscreen. "So as far as most of our expensive, state-of-the-art instruments are concerned, this thing doesn't exist."

Gerda glanced at him. "That would be one way of putting it, sir."

It was a remarkable state of affairs indeed—and it came as no surprise to any of them.

In the sixty-eight years since Captain Kirk's vessel plunged through the barrier, the Federation had sent out numerous expeditions to study the phenomenon. They all came back with the same results. In other words, none at all.

The barrier defied conventional analysis. It could be seen, certainly. It could be felt, once one got close enough. But for all other intents and purposes, it was a phantom.

"Helm, take us down to warp one," said Ruhalter. "Navigation, divert all available power to the shields."

"Done, sir," the Asmunds replied at virtually the same time.

Despite the reduction in speed, the barrier loomed closer. Patterns of light began to emerge in it, taking the shape of globules and then flares. Picard felt his jaw clench.

He knew, of course, that there wasn't really any cause for concern. Deflector shield technology had come a long way since Captain Kirk braved the barrier in the original *Starship Enterprise*. The chances of any ESPers being exposed to the phenomenon and metamorphosing into modern-day Gary Mitchells were ridiculously remote.

Nonetheless, the sight of the phenomenon strained the second officer's nerves. If the shields dropped at the wrong moment, or if some part of the barrier proved much fiercer than the others . . .

"Status?" Ruhalter demanded.

"There's some turbulence up ahead," Idun reported evenly, "but nothing we can't handle."

Just then, the turbolift doors opened and Leach emerged. He had been overseeing a last-minute diagnostic on Jomar's shield alterations.

The captain glanced at him. "Any problems, Commander?"

Leach frowned as he took in the spectacle on the viewscreen. "None, sir. Everything's functioning perfectly."

The first officer was still perturbed about the idea of taking Santana back to her side of the barrier. He hadn't made any secret of that. And the bizarre spectacle on the screen couldn't have made it any easier for him.

The captain turned back to Idun. "Steady as she goes," he said.

"Aye, sir," his helm officer responded.

"Five million kilometers and closing," Gerda Asmund announced. "Four million. Three million . . ."

Picard felt a shudder run through the deck beneath his feet. He put his hand on the back of Ruhalter's chair, just in case the shudder was a portent of something worse.

"Two million," the navigator continued.

The barrier loomed in front of them, bigger than anything Picard had ever seen. He could discern vast shadows of light twisting within it, testing the limits of the screen's illumination dampers.

Gerda Asmund looked up at the screen. "One million . . ."

As she spoke the words, the phenomenon engulfed them, closing its jaws on the *Stargazer* as if the ship was a helpless minnow and the barrier was a colossal, writhing serpent.

The deck shuddered again, then slid to the right. Picard tightened his grasp on the captain's chair.

"Report," Ruhalter snapped.

"Shields at eighty-eight percent," the navigator responded.

"Warp drive operating at peak capacity," her sister added.

The viewscreen was a confusion of ruby-red twisters, a maelstrom of heaving, burning lava. The *Stargazer* bucked once, twice, and again, and the second officer had to fight to keep his feet.

But it didn't get any worse than that. Even under immense pressure, the shields held. The control consoles on the bridge managed not to spark or explode. And most importantly, no one was caught in the spasm of light that had signaled the beginning of Gary Mitchell's transformation.

The *Stargazer* endured one last buffet from the barrier's unknown energies, one last surge of hull-shivering fury. Then it burst free of the phenomenon into normal if unfamiliar space.

Picard took a deep breath . . . and smiled.

Without question, their passage through the barrier had been tense and plagued with uncertainties. It had been a study in faith and humility. But in retrospect, it had also been a thing of wonder.

It was for just such experiences that the second officer had joined Starfleet. Looking around, he saw that he wasn't the only one who felt that way. Paxton, the Asmunds, Cariello . . . they all looked pleased.

Even Ruhalter seemed to have relished the experience, if the bright glint in the man's eyes was any indication. Only Commander Leach looked vaguely disapproving. But then, knowing the man as he did, Picard wouldn't have expected anything else.

"Shields at seventy-eight percent," Gerda Asmund observed.

"All systems operational," said Idun.

The captain nodded. "Excellent." Then he turned to his first and second officers. "You're with me, gentlemen."

Without any explanation, he rose and made his way to the turbolift. Picard saw Leach hurry to fall in behind Ruhalter, as if it made a difference who was behind the captain as he entered the lift. Sighing, the second officer followed Leach into the compartment.

The doors whispered closed behind them. "Ship's lounge," said Ruhalter, his voice echoing in the enclosure.

Apparently, the captain meant to conduct a meeting with his two senior officers. However, Picard had no idea what the meeting was about.

The lift's progress through the ship was imperceptible to its occupants, except for a tiny monitor that showed their location. They were halfway to their destination when Ruhalter did something surprising.

"Computer," he said, "stop turbolift."

Picard looked at him. So did Leach.

"It just occurred to me," said the captain, "that we don't have to go to the lounge to have this meeting. After all, there's only the three of us, and this shouldn't take long."

"As you wish, sir," Leach responded.

Ruhalter regarded each of them in turn. "I have one question, gentlemen—and that's whether Serenity Santana can be trusted."

The first officer smiled a lopsided smile. "Since you're asking, sir, I don't think the woman is even remotely trustworthy—and for the record, I've felt that way since we arrived at Starbase Two-oh-nine."

The captain nodded, then turned to Picard. "What about you, Jean-Luc? What do you think?"

The second officer took some time to consider the question. "As you know," he said finally, "I've had a chance to get to know Ms. Santana. However, I would have to know her a lot better before I could vouch for her with any assurance."

"Unfortunately," Ruhalter told him, "we don't have time for you to get to know her better. You'll have to give me your appraisal of her based on what you know *now*."

Picard frowned, hating to be pinned down this way. "Based on that," he said, "I'm inclined to believe she *can* be trusted."

Leach didn't seem surprised. "It's clear," he pointed out, "that Commander Picard is quite taken with Ms. Santana. I don't think he's thinking as clearly as he should be."

"Perhaps not," the captain conceded.

Leach looked pleased with himself.

But the second officer felt betrayed. He was thinking as incisively as ever, he assured himself. If Ruhalter disagreed with his conclusion, that was one thing. But to question his clarity . . .

Suddenly, a mischievous smile broke out on the captain's face. "Then again, Number One, Commander Picard may be right on target."

Leach's mouth fell open. "Sir . . . ?"

"You see," said Ruhalter, "I agree with Picard one hundred

percent. I too think Ms. Santana can be trusted—and like you, Mr. Leach, I formed my opinion the moment I met her."

The second officer understood. "You went with your instincts."

"Yes," said the captain, his eyes twinkling. "As always."

"But, sir," Leach began, "if you had already made your decision—"

"Why did I ask for your opinions? Simple, Commander. I wanted to make sure I hadn't missed something."

The first officer looked as if he had been slapped in the face. "I have to protest, sir. If necessary, through official means."

Ruhalter seemed unperturbed by the remark. "That's your option, Mr. Leach—as always. But I hope you'll refrain from exercising it until after we've completed our mission."

"By then," Leach said coldly, "it may be too late."

"We'll see," the captain rejoined. "In any case, Santana has given us two sets of coordinates. One describes the location of her colony. The other will lead us to a Nuyyad supply depot."

"We're going to head for the depot," Picard guessed.

"Absolutely right," Ruhalter confirmed. "Why waste time? If there's a threat, let's see it."

"And if it's a trap?" Leach suggested.

"Then we'll see that too," said the captain. "Though my instincts tell me that won't happen."

The first officer's nostrils flared, but he didn't say anything more.

"Thank you for your input," Ruhalter told them. "Both of you. Computer, return us to the bridge."

Again, the turbolift began to move.

Pug Joseph closed his eyes and concentrated. "Okay," he said. "See if you can picture this."

Santana answered from the other side of the translucent barrier. "Protruding brow ridge, bony forehead, a preference for facial hair. Strong, by the look of him. And fierce."

Opening his eyes, the security officer smiled at the woman's skill. "He's called a Klingon."

"Friend?" Santana guessed.

"Friend *now*," Joseph told her.

"But not always?"

"Until fifty years ago," he said, "the Klingons were almost constantly at war with us. Then we signed a nonaggression treaty with them."

"Got it," she responded. "Who's next?"

Again, the security officer closed his eyes and conjured an image. "How about this one?"

"Let's see," said Santana. "Aristocratic bearing, pointed ears, painfully precise haircut. If not for the subtle ridges above the eyes, I'd be tempted to say he's Vulcan."

Joseph laughed softly. "Very good. He's called a Romulan. And his people are an offshoot of the Vulcan species."

"Enemy?" she suggested.

"I'll say. We haven't seen them in more than twenty years, but people still worry about them."

"Give me another one," Santana told him.

"All right," he said, picturing someone else. "Here's one."

"Hmmm. Mottled red skin, long jaw tusks like an elephant's, spiny scalp projections instead of hair."

Joseph opened his eyes and shook his head in admiration. "A Vobilite."

"An enemy?"

"A friend. In fact, the Vobilites were one of the first species to support the idea of a United Federation of Planets. I served with one of them on my previous assignment."

Santana nodded. "Now it's my turn."

The security officer felt a chill climb his spine. "I didn't know you could project your thoughts."

She smiled. "I can't. I meant I was going to describe them out loud."

Joseph blushed. "Oh."

The woman thought for a moment. "Here's one. Tall and thin, with jet black fur and silver eyes."

He tried to put the information together. What he came up with seemed pretty elegant. "Sounds easy on the eyes."

"I've always thought so. They're called the Yotaavo."

"Friend?" he ventured, playing the game.

"Friend. We've done quite a bit of trading with them over the years. Want another one?"

Joseph shrugged. "Sure."

Again, Santana took a moment to choose. "Small and muscular, with four arms, short legs, and scaly, yellow skin."

The security officer constructed an image in his head. "I think I've got it. What are they called?"

"The Caddis."

"I'll say . . . friend."

"Actually," said the prisoner, "they've been both. When we first established the colony, they were always making life difficult for us. In the last fifty or sixty years, they've gotten to know us better. As a result, things have improved."

"How about an enemy?" Joseph asked. "A current one, I mean."

She frowned. "We've only got one of those. Big and fleshy, with shiny, black eyes and a fringe of dark hair around their skulls."

"The Nuyyad?" he asked.

Santana nodded. "Not that we've ever had a run-in with them—but we consider them our enemy just the same."

"I can't wait to meet them," Joseph said, injecting a note of sarcasm into his voice.

The woman didn't seem to notice the irony. "Oh yes, you can, Mr. Joseph. *Believe* me, you can."

Picard sat down at the black, oval table in the *Stargazer*'s lounge and faced his captain. "You wanted to see me, sir?"

Ruhalter nodded from the other side of the table. "I do indeed,

Commander." He paused, as if choosing his words more carefully than usual. "According to regulations, we shouldn't be having this conversation. Nonetheless, I feel it's necessary."

The second officer waited patiently. The captain wasn't the sort to need any prodding.

"As you've no doubt noticed," said Ruhalter, "Commander Leach and I don't often see eye to eye. Don't get me wrong—he's an efficient officer, with an impressive background and considerable skill in some areas. But he's not a *first* officer. At least, not in my book."

Picard was surprised. Captains didn't normally make such comments about their execs—especially to subordinate officers.

"It's unfortunate, really," Ruhalter went on. "Captain Osborne expressed every confidence in Leach, and I relied heavily on his recommendation. It was one of the few times since I became a captain that I *didn't* go with my instincts—and look what happened."

The second officer had wondered how Ruhalter could have made such an error in judgment. Now he understood.

"I wound up with a man I can't get along with," said the captain. "A man eminently capable of carrying out a project on his own, yet plainly *in*capable of leading others." He shook his head ruefully. "It's not a good situation, Jean-Luc. And I'd be remiss if I didn't do something about it."

Do something? Picard repeated to himself. Might that mean what he thought it meant?

"As soon as we come back from this mission," Ruhalter told him, "I'm going to arrange for Commander Leach to be transferred to another ship. Or, failing that, to some other Starfleet facility. Of course, that's going to leave me short a first officer . . ." He smiled. "And I can't think of anyone I'd rather have serving in that capacity than you."

The second officer was at a loss for words. Finally, he found a few. "I would be honored, sir," he replied graciously. "That is, when the appropriate time comes."

The captain nodded approvingly. "I'm glad to hear you say that, Commander. It'll give me something to look forward to when I'm wrangling with your predecessor over Serenity Santana."

"Commander Leach still insists it was a mistake to bring her along?"

"Yes," said Ruhalter, "he does. And at every opportunity, I might add. It's making my head spin."

Picard understood. The first officer made *his* head spin sometimes too.

"In the meantime," the captain told him, "we have an important mission on our hands—and frankly, I'm afraid that Leach will do something to muck it up. I want you to keep an eye on him for me. If he gives an order that you think will lead to trouble, you're to let me know immediately. Is that understood?"

"It is," the second officer assured him.

"Good," said Ruhalter. "I—"

Abruptly, the lounge filled with the voice of the very man they were talking about. "Captain," said Leach, his tone taut with concern, "we've got a situation up here."

Ruhalter's brow knit. "Elaborate."

"There's a vessel approaching on an intercept course," Leach reported. "Bearing two-four-four-mark two. I have to tell you, sir, it doesn't look like anything we've encountered before."

The captain frowned and got to his feet. "Go to red alert, Commander. I'm on my way."

Picard was right behind him as he headed for the doors. His stomach muscles clenched as he wondered what they were up against. And then, all of a sudden, it came to him.

The Nuyyad.

CHAPTER **7**

As Picard pelted along the corridor in pursuit of Captain Ruhalter, he turned the idea over in his mind. *The Nuyyad.*

It was just a hunch, of course. He had no proof to back it up, no information on which to build a case. For all he knew, they hadn't been detected by the Nuyyad at all, but rather by some other species—one that only meant to investigate the *Stargazer's* unfamiliar presence here.

But his instincts—the kind his commanding officer always spoke about—were working overtime, and they had come to a conclusion on their own.

Ruhalter might have been thinking along the same lines, but he needed some corroboration. Slightly more than halfway to the turbolift, he tapped his communicator badge. "Jomar," he said, "this is the captain. I need you on the bridge immediately."

The Kelvan replied just as the lift compartment arrived. "Coming," he said over the intercom system, his voice as empty of inflection as ever.

Then Picard and his commanding officer were inside the lift, the doors closed, moving silently toward the *Stargazer*'s bridge. Ruhalter scowled, but he didn't say anything. There was no point in doing so, Picard recognized, until they could see the problem for themselves.

Finally, after what seemed like an eternity, the turbolift doors opened and they emerged onto the bridge. The place was bathed in the crimson light of a red alert. As the captain replaced Leach in the center seat, Picard took in the sight depicted on the viewscreen.

"You see?" Leach asked Ruhalter.

The captain saw, all right. And so did Picard.

He saw an almost flat, silver diamond—one so large that it seemed to dominate the dark spaces around it. The similarly diamond-shaped appendages on either side of it were probably its warp nacelles, or whatever analogous equipment the vessel's occupants used for propulsion.

A cold and efficient-looking ship, Picard reflected. No doubt, it had been built by a cold and efficient people.

Ruhalter turned to Gerda Asmund. "How much time do we have before our paths converge, Lieutenant?"

"At the alien vessel's current rate of speed," said the navigator, "she'll reach us in less than six minutes."

The muscles in the captain's jaw rippled uncomfortably. "Keep me posted," he told Gerda.

Just then, the lift doors hissed open again. Glancing over his shoulder, Picard saw Jomar come out onto the bridge. The Kelvan's pale-blue eyes were immediately drawn to the viewscreen.

He uttered a single, colorless word: "Nuyyad."

Ruhalter grunted. "I had a feeling you were going to say that."

Jomar turned to him. "Captain," he said, "we did not expect to encounter the enemy so quickly. The modifications to the deflector grid have not yet been completed."

Ruhalter swore under his breath. "How far along are we?"

"We have finished perhaps eighty percent of the job," said the Kelvan. "But it would take several hours to do the rest."

"And we don't *have* several hours," Leach reminded them.

Picard looked at the first officer. Leach's expression seemed to say "I told you so." He had predicted that they would run into trouble if they followed Santana's instructions—and now, it seemed, they had.

"Four minutes," Gerda announced.

The second officer moved to the navigator's console, planted the heel of his hand on its edge and leaned in to get a better look. He could see a green blip crawling across the black background of Gerda's monitor.

The blip seemed so abstract, so theoretical. But the ship it represented was making warp eight, if their sensors were correct, with no sign whatsoever of slowing down.

"Activate what we have," Ruhalter said, referring to the shields. "And keep working. Let's see if we can get some more capacity on-line."

"As you wish," Jomar responded dispassionately, and made his way back to the turbolift.

The captain eased himself back in his seat, his expression as grave as Picard had ever seen it. They were at a disadvantage, the second officer told himself, and the captain knew it.

On the other hand, the *Stargazer* was a fast, well-equipped ship, and her crew had been battle-tested on other Starfleet vessels. They could yet prevail, Picard told himself.

"Three minutes," said Gerda.

Ruhalter's eyes narrowed. "Battle stations. Raise shields where we have them. Power phasers and arm photon torpedoes."

"Done, sir," said Lieutenant Werber, working at his weapons console aft of the center seat.

The second officer looked around the bridge. In addition to the captain, Leach, and himself, there were four officers present—the Asmunds, Werber, and Paxton. Every one of them was going about his business cooly and methodically, as if this sort of thing happened all the time.

For a moment, he almost thought he saw Idun Asmund smiling. Then the moment passed and he chalked it up to his imagination.

"Two minutes," Gerda told them.

The captain glanced at his communications officer. "Hail them, Mr. Paxton. Let's see what they do."

"Aye, sir," said Paxton.

Everyone waited for the results of his efforts. Finally, the communications officer looked up from his console.

"Nothing," he told Ruhalter.

The captain nodded. "Can't say I'm surprised."

"One minute," said Gerda, "and closing. Fifty seconds. Forty . . ."

Picard latched onto the back of the navigator's chair with his free hand. It made him feel a trifle more secure.

"Thirty seconds," Gerda announced. "Twenty. Ten . . ."

"Weapons range," said Lieutenant Werber, sounding too eager by half for Picard's taste.

"They're firing!" Gerda announced.

A barrage of green witch-lights streamed from the Nuyyad's weapons ports and exploded to spectacular effect on the viewscreen. The Federation ship bucked under the impact of the vidrion assault, but not so badly that anyone was hurt.

"Shields down twenty-two percent!" Werber called out.

Not good, Picard reflected. But if not for the Kelvan's modifications, they might have been destroyed altogether.

Ruhalter leaned forward in his seat, a look of determination on his face. "Target and fire!"

A moment later, the *Stargazer* released a series of yellow-white photon torpedoes—packets of matter and antimatter bound together by magnetic forces. They found their target in quick succession, returning the enemy's attack blow for ponderous blow.

But the Federation vessel couldn't continue to trade punches with her adversary—not when the Nuyyad possessed a weapon as devastating as a vidrion cannon. She had to make her move—and quickly.

"Evasive maneuvers!" the captain barked. "Pattern Delta!"

Idun Asmund pulled the *Stargazer* into a tight upward turn, taking her out of the enemy's sights for a moment. The Nuyyad obviously hadn't expected such an action, because they sent an emerald-green vidrion volley slicing through empty space.

"Target and fire!" Ruhalter bellowed.

Again, Werber released a flight of photon torpedoes. Again, they found their mark, wreaking havoc with the enemy's shields.

Picard's heart leaped. They were winning. If they could keep it going, the battle would be over in short order.

Unfortunately, the Nuyyad seemed to have another outcome in mind. They pumped out yet another round of vidrion particles, hammering the *Stargazer* even harder than before.

An aft console erupted in flames, prompting the second officer to grab a fire extinguisher and douse the blaze with white spray. Before he was done, he heard Gerda's status report.

"Shields down forty-eight percent, sir! Damage to decks six, seven, eight, and eleven!"

"Dispatch repair crews!" the captain told her.

It was a setback, Picard told himself, but no more than that. If anything, the enemy had only evened the odds.

"Pattern Episilon!" Ruhalter called out.

This time, Idun sent the ship veering to starboard—just as the Nuyyad hurled another barrage at them. For a heartbeat, the second officer thought the maneuver would do the trick.

Then he found out otherwise. The deck slipped out from under him, pitching him forcibly into an aft console.

"Shields down eighty-two percent!" Gerda thundered. "Damage to decks five, nine, and ten!"

She had just gotten the words out when the viewscreen

flooded with bright green fury. Picard barely had time to brace himself before the ship staggered hard to starboard, jerking his fellow officers half out of their seats.

Ruhalter thrust himself to his feet and came forward to glare at the screen, as if he could stop the Nuyyad by force of will alone. "Pattern Omega!" he snarled.

Idun sent them plummeting in a tight spiral, vidrion bundles bursting savagely all around them. Somehow, they emerged unscathed—but the enemy didn't let them go far. The Nuyyad ship banked and dogged their trail, like a predator that had smelled its victim's blood.

"Pattern Omicron!" the captain cried out, trying desperately to give them some breathing room.

Idun coerced the ship into a sudden, excrutiatingly tight loop, causing the hull to groan and shiver under the strain. But the maneuver worked. Unable to stop in time, the Nuyyad vessel shot past them.

"Maximum warp!" Ruhalter commanded.

The *Stargazer* tore through the void at a thousand times the speed of light, putting a hundred million kilometers between herself and the enemy with each passing second. Picard eyed the viewscreen, but he saw no sign of the Nuyyad. All he could see were the stars streaming by.

The tension on the bridge eased a notch. Commander Leach, who had lost all the color in his face, sighed and eased himself into a vacant seat by the forward engineering console.

"Report," breathed the captain.

Gerda consulted her monitor. "Hull breaches on decks twelve, thirteen, and fourteen. Repair teams have been deployed to all damaged areas. Sickbay reports nine injured."

"Dead?" asked Ruhalter.

"No one," the navigator replied.

The captain seemed relieved. "Well," he said, "that's something to be thankful for. What about our shields?"

Gerda glanced at him and shook her head. "There aren't any, sir. That last volley took out the last of them."

No shields, thought Picard. It was a good thing they had escaped when they did. Another barrage like the last one, and—

"Captain!" exclaimed Werber, his face caught in the ruddy glare of his control panel. "They're on our tail again!"

"Give me a visual," said Ruhalter.

Once again, the viewscreen showed them the Nuyyad ship. Picard felt his jaw clench. Though they were pushing the *Stargazer*'s warp drive as hard as they dared, the enemy was slowly catching up to them.

"Weapons range," Werber told them.

"Stand by, helm," the captain told Idun. "If we can't outrun them, we'll have to outfight them."

Picard stared at him, wondering about the wisdom of Ruhalter's strategy. As if he sensed the younger man's scrutiny, Ruhalter looked back.

I know, Jean-Luc, his expression seemed to say. *Without shields, we don't stand much of a chance. But what choice do I have?*

Picard wished he had a good answer. *None,* he conceded silently.

"Target photon torpedoes," said the captain.

"Aye, sir," came Werber's response.

Ruhalter's eyes narrowed with resolve. "Pattern Alpha."

All at once, Idun swung them hard to port. The *Stargazer* wheeled more quickly and gracefully than she had a right to, coming about a full one hundred and eighty degrees. Before the second officer knew it, he found himself face-to-face with the Nuyyad.

And the enemy hadn't cut his speed one iota.

"Fire!" the captain roared.

A swarm of photon torpedoes took flight, illuminating the void between the two combatants. At the same time, the Nuyyad vessel unleashed its most devastating attack yet.

It was a glorious, breathtaking spectacle, emerald green mingling with gold, brilliance weaving its way through brilliance. Unfortunately, it lasted only a fraction of a second.

Then the *Stargazer* reeled under the hull-buckling onslaught, sending Picard crashing into a bulkhead. Pain shot through his ribs and the side of his head and blackness began to overwhelm him.

No, he told himself, fighting to regain his senses. I cannot give in. I need to know what has happened. The taste of blood strong in his mouth, he pulled himself up along a console and took stock of the bridge.

The air was full of smoke and sparks and fire. Unmanned consoles beeped frantically and open conduits hissed deadly plasma. The second officer blinked, trying to see through the haze with badly stinging eyes, and spied someone sprawled on the deck near the captain's chair.

It was Ruhalter—and he wasn't moving.

Darting to the captain's side, Picard saw why. Half the man's face had been burned away in the explosion of a still-sputtering plasma conduit.

The second officer shook his head. No, he thought, denying it as hard as he could. It cannot be. It is not possible.

But it *was*.

Daithan Ruhalter was dead.

Abruptly, he realized that someone was standing next to him. Looking up, he saw that it was Paxton.

"My god," said the communications officer, gaping at the captain's corpse in disbelief.

Picard saw the look on Paxton's face and imagined the same look on his own—and a feeling of shame welled up inside him. He had to accept the situation, he told himself. He had to move on.

After all, the ship was in deadly danger. Their shields were down and they had an enemy taking shots at them with impunity.

As Picard thought that, he felt another jolt run through the ship—but it wasn't nearly as bad as the last one. Obviously, Idun Asmund was still at the helm, doing her job.

They needed a leader, however. And with Ruhalter dead, that left Leach—whether the man was up to the task or not. Starfleet protocol wouldn't tolerate anything less.

"Commander Leach!" Picard hollered into the miasma of fireshot smoke.

There was no answer.

Leaving Ruhalter's side, the second officer made his way forward. He had last seen Leach at the engineering console. With luck, the man would still be there.

But when Picard reached the spot, he couldn't find any sign of the first officer. He looked around, hoping to catch a glimpse of him—and instead saw Gerda Asmund hunched over near her navigation console.

His first thought was that the woman had been hurt. Then, as he got closer, he saw a body stretched out on the deck beyond her. Gerda turned and looked up at the second officer.

"It's Leach," she told him, her concern evident in the knot of flesh at the bridge of her nose.

Picard moved around her and saw the first officer. His eyes were closed, his features slack, and there was blood seeping from a gash in his smoke-blackened temple.

"Dead?" the second officer said numbly.

Gerda shook her head. "No. He still has a pulse."

"Get him to sickbay," Picard told her. "And send some hands up here to see to the captain."

"Aye, sir," said the navigator.

Picking Leach up with athletic ease, she headed for the turbolift. The second officer watched her go for a moment, open plasma conduits and flaming consoles illuminating her passage.

As the lift doors opened, Picard felt another impact. But like the last one, this one had been tolerable.

He looked at the officers still left to him. Idun, who was battling her controls to keep them in one piece. Paxton, who had returned to his post at communications. And Werber, who looked eager to fire again if only someone would give him the order.

With Ruhalter and Leach victims of the Nuyyad, Picard would have to be the one to do that. In fact, he would have to give *all* the orders.

"Mr. Paxton," he barked, "take over at navigation."

"Aye, sir," the communications officer replied, and moved forward to do as he was asked.

Picard turned and gazed at the viewscreen, where a reverse perspective showed the Nuyyad ship clinging to them in pursuit. It only took him a moment to realize that there was something curious about the sight—and another moment to figure out what it was.

The enemy vessel was slightly atilt as it sped through space, slightly off-line relative to the axis of its forward progress. Picard knew enough about propulsion systems to understand the reason for such an aberration.

One of the Nuyyad ship's warp nacelles was misfiring. The one on the port side, it seemed to him. That suggested a weakness of which his helm officer could take advantage.

"Lieutenant Asmund," he said, "the enemy will have difficulty turning to starboard. Reprise Pattern Epsilon on my mark."

"Aye, sir," the helm officer replied.

Next, the second officer turned to Werber. "Target photon torpedoes."

"I've been doing nothing *but* targeting," Werber told him.

Ignoring the man's tone, Picard eyed the screen again. "Lieutenant Asmund—execute your maneuver. Lieutenant Werber—fire when ready."

The words had barely left his mouth when the Nuyyad spewed another wave of green fire at them, trying to finish off the *Stargazer*. But by then, Idun had gone into her turn.

The vidrion assault shot harmlessly by them. And as the Federation vessel continued to perform her maneuver, the enemy shot by as well—much to Werber's delight. Cheering beneath his breath, the weapons officer released a hail of golden photon torpedoes.

The first wave ripped into the Nuyyad's flank, shredding what remained of her shields. The second wave clawed chunks out of the vessel's hull. And the third penetrated to the very heart of the ship, finding and obliterating critical power relays.

A moment later, Picard knew that at least one torpedo had reached the enemy's warp core—because the Nuyyad ship tore itself apart in a ragged spasm of bright yellow fire.

The second officer watched the fragments of the shattered craft pinwheel end over end through space, expanding outward from the point of the explosion. There was a macabre grace to the scene, a feeling of something strangely akin to serenity.

He looked back over his shoulder. Ruhalter's corpse was gone, having been spirited away while Picard was busy with the Nuyyad.

But his work wasn't done yet. They were still in unfamiliar territory, with wounds to lick and the ever-present threat of another attack—not to mention some serious questions to answer.

And his bridge was on fire.

As Werber, Paxton, and Idun Asmund watched him, Picard moved to the rear of the bridge and found the fire extinguisher he had used before. Then he began spraying down the ruined remnants of the nearest console.

Carter Greyhorse ran his sleek, palm-sized regeneration unit over the flesh of Lieutenant Cariello's bare shoulder, creating a few more healthy, new cells to replace the ones she had lost to a white-hot spurt of plasma.

The doctor took a moment to examine his work. Satisfied with it, he checked Cariello's vital signs on her biobed's overhead readouts. The lieutenant's systems were all stable, he observed. In a day or so, after she had gotten some rest, there would be no indication that she had been within minutes of losing her life.

Activating an electromagnetic barrier around Cariello to guard against infection, Greyhorse moved to the next bed in line. Lieutenant Kochman was lying there in a stasis field, outwardly unharmed but inwardly suffering from broken ribs, ruptured organs, and considerable hemorrhaging.

He would require a good deal more work than Cariello, the doctor reflected. But at least the man was alive.

Greyhorse glanced at the corpses laid out under metallic blankets in the corner of his sickbay. There were four of them in all. Barr, Janes, Harras . . . and, of course, Captain Ruhalter.

If the chief medical officer had had more than twelve biobeds at his disposal, he wouldn't have subjected the deceased to the indignity of lying on the floor. But to his chagrin, he didn't have more than twelve beds—and his priority had to be the living.

Greyhorse was on the verge of deactivating Kochman's stasis field when he heard the sickbay doors hiss open. Glancing in that direction, he fully expected to see someone bringing in another casualty.

But this time, it was different. It wasn't just anyone being brought in. It was *her.*

At least, that was the way it looked to the doctor for a split second. Then he realized he was mistaken, and a wave of relief washed over him. It wasn't Gerda Asmund who was being carried into sickbay. It was Gerda who was doing the carrying.

And it was Commander Leach wrapped up in the woman's arms, Greyhorse realized—Commander Leach who was lying as limp and pale as death. Clearly, the first officer's condition would have to take precedence over anyone else's for the time being.

Leaving Kochman's side, the doctor crossed the room to the bed containing Ensign Kotsakos, whose injuries weren't nearly as severe. Deactivating the protective field around the ensign, Greyhorse picked the woman up as gently as he could and deposited her on the floor beside the bed.

He would have preferred to give her the benefit of the field for the next several hours. That would have been the ideal approach.

However, Kotsakos would survive without the field. He couldn't say the same for Leach.

"Put him down here," Greyhorse told Gerda.

She did as he said, easing the first officer onto the biobed.

The doctor looked up to study the bed's readouts. Clearly, Leach was in bad shape—even worse than the ragged gash in his temple suggested. His vital signs were badly depressed.

"What can I do?" asked Gerda.

Greyhorse looked at her with the same longing and admiration he had felt the other day, when he had checked her ESPer capacity. But this time, he wasn't tongue-tied in the least.

"Check the other beds, one at a time, and call out their readings to me." He pointed to Kochman. "Starting with that one."

"And Leach?" the navigator asked.

"I'll take care of him," the doctor assured her.

She hesitated for just a moment, as if there was something else she wanted to say to him. Then she left the first officer in his capable hands and went to see how Kochman was doing.

Greyhorse drew a deep breath and wiped sweat from his brow with the back of his hand. In that moment when he thought Gerda was injured, he had gone through an eternity of hell in a single second.

He didn't like the idea of people getting hurt. He was a physician, after all. But if it came down to the navigator or someone else . . . he was glad it hadn't been Gerda.

As the turbolift doors opened, Ben Zoma emerged from the compartment and made his way down the corridor—phaser in hand.

He had good reason for concern. The moment the battle with the Nuyyad had ended, he had tried to contact the officer on duty in the brig. But there hadn't been any response—not a promising sign by anyone's reckoning.

And with the battering the *Stargazer* had taken, power conduits had been compromised on every deck. There was no guarantee that the brig's electromagnetic force field was still in place.

Which meant Serenity Santana might be free to go wherever she wanted. *Do* whatever she wanted.

That made Ben Zoma nervous, given the fact that the woman's motivations were still in question—maybe more so now than ever, considering they had followed her directions straight into the sights of an enemy battleship.

He hadn't been particularly suspicious of Santana when Captain Ruhalter brought her aboard. He had believed they were doing the right thing by checking out her warning. And even now, he wasn't convinced that she was in on the Nuyyad attack.

But he was the ship's security chief. With hundreds of lives at stake, he had to believe the worst of everyone.

Striding purposefully, Ben Zoma negotiated a bend in the corridor and came in sight of the brig. The first thing he saw was a body laid out on the deck. He recognized it as Pug Joseph, Santana's guard.

Instantly, the security chief broke into a run. When he reached Joseph, he dropped at the man's side and saw the blood running from Joseph's nose and mouth. He also saw the burgeoning bruise over Joseph's right eye.

He felt for a pulse—and found one. Tapping his combadge, he said, "Security, this is Ben Zoma."

"Pfeffer here, sir."

"I'm at the brig," the chief told Pfeffer. "Joseph is down. I'll need help getting him to sickbay."

"Acknowledged," said the security officer. "What about Santana, sir? Is the field still in place?"

Ben Zoma cursed under his breath and glanced in the direction of Santana's enclosure. "Stand by."

He had been so concerned about Joseph, he hadn't taken the time to check on their guest yet. Getting to his feet, he approached the entrance to the brig cautiously, phaser at the ready.

Stopping at the doorway, he craned his neck to get a look inside at Santana's cell.

The force field was still in place, all right. But Santana was crumpled in the corner.

"Ms. Santana?" he called out, his voice echoing.

The woman didn't answer. She just lay there.

The security chief sighed. "Santana looks like she's in a bad way," he told Pfeffer. "I'll need help with her as well."

"On its way, sir," the officer assured him.

CHAPTER 8

Captain's log, supplemental, second Officer Jean-Luc Picard reporting. Now that I have had a few hours to assess our situation, I find that it is even more troubling than I anticipated. Six brave members of our crew perished in the course of the battle with the Nuyyad. One of them was Captain Ruhalter, for whom I had a great deal of personal respect and affection. Fourteen others are recuperating from serious injuries—among them Commander Leach, who has lapsed into a deep coma. The Stargazer did not fare much better. Her ability to travel at faster-than-light velocities has been significantly curtailed, her starboard phaser batteries are nearly useless and her supply of photon torpedoes has been all but depleted. However, it's the ship's deflector grid that sustained the greatest damage. At this point, it can barely protect us from spaceborne particles. Perhaps needless to say, the vidrion-generating enhance-

ments endorsed by Jomar were completely and utterly destroyed in the clash with the Nuyyad. Unless and until we can secure replacement parts for our shield generators, we will remain vulnerable in the extreme. As for Serenity Santana, our mysterious advisor . . . like Commander Leach, she was rendered comatose in the melee. We are thus deprived of an opportunity to determine her role in what appears to have been a carefully calculated trap—if she indeed had any role in it at all.

Picard gazed at Serenity Santana. She lay still and pale on the flat surface of the biobed, her raven hair spread around her head, her chest rising and falling mechanically.

The second officer wished the woman were awake—and not just because he hated to see her lying there like that, limp and helpless, when she had once been so charming and vibrant. Not just because she was, quite possibly, the most beautiful woman he had ever seen.

As Picard had indicated in the log he had filed only a few minutes earlier, there were questions he wished to ask Santana. Mainly, he wanted to know how the Nuyyad had discovered the *Stargazer*—because he didn't believe for a second that the enemy had just stumbled onto them.

Space was a vast place, on this side of the galactic barrier as much as on the other one. The odds of two ships sensing each other even with long-range instruments were so slim as to almost be absurd.

And yet, they had barely penetrated the galactic barrier when the Nuyyad descended on them. If Santana had something to do with that, if she had betrayed them as Leach feared she would—

"You see, Commander?" called a deep voice.

Picard turned and saw Greyhorse coming toward him, his huge frame looking out of place in his lab coat. The doctor had been attending to an injured crewman on the other side of sickbay.

"As I indicated," Greyhorse went on, "Ms. Santana has retreated into a deep coma. But at least she's stable."

The second officer gazed at the colonist again. Even in her debilitated state, she was a compelling sight.

"Will she come out of it?" he asked.

"That's difficult to say," Greyhorse told him.

"Because her brain is different from ours?"

"Among other reasons, yes." The doctor pointed to the bed's readouts. "I want to show you something. Do you see those lines, Commander? The two near the top?"

Picard nodded. "What about them?"

"Those are the patient's brain waves," Greyhorse explained. He pressed a keypad next to the readout and it changed instantly—the top two lines in particular. "And these were her brain waves when she first came aboard. Do you see the difference?"

He did—but he didn't know what conclusion he was supposed to draw from the observation. "I'm sorry. I don't see what—"

The medical officer held up a large, powerful-looking hand. "I didn't expect you to draw any real conclusions. Let me walk you through it."

Picard thought that would be a good idea.

"A woman in Ms. Santana's condition should exhibit precious little brain activity. For example, she should have a very quiet cerebral cortex. However," said Greyhorse, pointing to the topmost line on the readout, "we see that her cerebral cortex is anything *but* quiet. In fact, it's busier now than when she was awake. The same goes for portions of her cerebellum."

Picard mulled over the information. "So . . . you're saying some parts of her brain are actually busier in her comatose condition than they were when she was conscious?"

"Exactly," the doctor confirmed.

"And what do you make of that?"

The doctor shrugged his massive shoulders. "Again, difficult

135

to say. The patient's brain may have gone into some kind of healing mode. Or . . ." His voice trailed off.

"Or?" Picard nudged.

"If her brain works like those of other telepaths, the patient may have purposely emphasized certain functions at the expense of others—which would suggest the possibility that this is not a naturally occurring coma, but one she induced on her own."

On her own? Picard thought. He looked at Greyhorse. "I don't understand. Why would she do such a thing?"

The other man returned his glance. "You are in a better position to know that than I am, Commander."

Picard turned to Santana again, as if he hoped to find the answer written on her lips. Was it possible that she had shut herself down purposely, in order to avoid answering difficult questions?

Somehow, the second officer didn't think so. Or was it just that he didn't *want* to think so?

"Thank you," he told Greyhorse. "You've given me much to think about. If there's any change in her condition, even a small one—"

"I'll be sure to let you know," the doctor assured him.

Picard nodded. Then, with a last glance at Santana, he left sickbay and returned to the bridge.

Pug Joseph touched the itchy spot just above his right cheekbone and recalled Doctor Greyhorse's orders not to scratch it.

In a day or so, his regenerated flesh would complete the healing process. Then no one would ever know he had hit his head against a bulkhead hard enough to knock himself out.

Fortunately, the security officer thought, he had suffered nothing more serious than a concussion. Otherwise, he would still be in sickbay along with Kochman and the other worst cases.

And they were the lucky ones, he reminded himself. The captain and some of the others hadn't made it at all.

Removing his food from the replicator enclosure, Joseph

placed it on his tray. First his meat, then his rice, then his vegetables, and finally his juice. Then he moved across the crowded mess hall in the direction of one of its few empty tables.

His crewmates, who were all working triple shifts on one repair crew or another, had gathered in clusters all around the room. They were obviously seeking comfort in numbers—taking the opportunity to vent their sorrows and air their concerns, of which they had many.

The *Stargazer* had been hobbled pretty badly in the battle with the Nuyyad. With key systems on the blink, people were worried about what they would do if another vessel showed up.

Joseph had thought about that possibility too, of course—and he probably felt the need to talk about it as much as anyone. But there were certain things he wanted very much *not* to talk about just then, so he had decided he would keep to himself.

Arriving at his solitary destination, he put his tray down and deposited himself in a chair. Then he pushed himself into his table and began to eat, mindful of the fact that he had to get back to work soon.

He was halfway finished when some of his crewmates walked in and took a table next to his. He recognized them as Lieutenant Werber, Chief Engineer Simenon, and a couple of the men who worked for him.

They didn't acknowledge Joseph's presence. In fact, they didn't acknowledge anyone. They were too engrossed in their conversation.

Joseph didn't want to eavesdrop. He was the kind of person who respected the rights of others, the right of privacy in particular. However, Werber and his companions were speaking so loudly, it would have been difficult not to hear them.

"—upstart is taking the captain's place," said Simenon. His expression was a distinctly sour one.

"And he was the one who convinced Ruhalter to trust Santana," Werber pointed out.

"How do you know?" asked the chief engineer.

"Leach told me," said the weapons officer.

Simenon shook his scaly head in disbelief. "The way that woman twisted Picard around her finger . . . it was disgraceful. And now we're all going to pay the price for it."

"You think she led us into a trap?" asked one of the other engineers, a man named Pernell.

Werber chuckled bitterly. "Is there any doubt of it?"

Pug Joseph swallowed and pushed his tray away. Suddenly, he didn't feel like eating anymore.

It seemed to him that Werber was right. Santana *had* led the *Stargazer* into a trap. In fact, she must have begun plotting it long before she set foot on the ship.

But it wasn't just Commander Picard whom she had hoodwinked. She had pulled the wool over Joseph's eyes as well. If he had been his usual alert self, he might have figured the woman out in time and warned Captain Ruhalter not to trust her.

But he had allowed Santana to charm him, to draw him in. He had let his guard down. And as a result, they had lost their captain and their first officer, and come within inches of losing their ship.

Joseph promised himself that as long as he lived, he would never let someone like Santana fool him again.

Idun Asmund made a small course adjustment to avoid some space debris and watched the stars slide to starboard on the viewscreen.

Commander Picard, who was standing behind her, nodded approvingly. The hollows under his eyes gave him the look of a man sacrificing sleep and other creature comforts for the sake of doing what needed to be done.

But then, he was laboring under a great burden. He had already scoured the ship for survivors, gotten repairs underway on key systems, and moved the ship away from the coordinates of their battle in case other enemy vessels were on their way.

Truly, Picard was a warrior.

However, he seemed unequal to his task in one respect and one respect only—though he moved around the bridge like a caged *targ,* he refused to settle into the center seat.

Of course, the captain had perished less than fourteen hours ago. Quite likely, Picard still thought of the seat as Ruhalter's and avoided it out of respect.

On the other hand, a Klingon wouldn't have hesitated to sit down. In fact, Idun reflected with a secret smile, a Klingon might have put a dagger in his superior to secure such an opportunity.

The helm officer frowned, regaining her composure. She was a Starfleet officer, she reminded herself. She had sworn allegiance to the Federation and the ideals it held dear.

But she had been raised as a Klingon, and part of her still thought as Klingons did—which was why she couldn't find solace in a leader who shied from leadership.

No matter the reason.

For the next hour or so, Picard continued to haunt the bridge, checking on this console or that one, stealing glances at the viewscreen every now and then. Then, apparently satisfied that the ship's most critical needs had been met, he tapped his communicator badge.

"This is Commander Picard," he said. "I would like the following personnel to meet me in the main lounge." And he reeled off a list of names, which included all of the surviving senior officers.

A staff meeting, Idun mused. The commander was going to address the men and women working under him, just as Captain Ruhalter had addressed them when he was still alive.

Picard hadn't yet deposited himself in the captain's chair, the helm officer noted. He hadn't yet seized the reins that had been turned over to him by default.

But at least he had made a start.

* * *

Picard surveyed the personnel seated around the lounge's black, oval table, their faces turned to him with varying degrees of expectation.

There were eight of them there—Jomar, Ben Zoma, Simenon, Greyhorse, Cariello, Werber, Paxton, and Picard himself. Eight of them who would attempt to survive in an unknown part of space and salvage what they could from the embers of disaster.

Normally, Captain Ruhalter would have conducted this meeting, wringing the best out of each of them and making them more than the sum of their parts. But Captain Ruhalter, unbelievable as it seemed, was dead—and Commander Leach was in a coma from which he might never emerge. For better or worse, it was Picard's meeting to conduct . . . Picard's ship and crew to command.

The second officer hadn't asked for this. He hadn't imagined himself ensconced in a center seat until years later, when he would have had a good deal more experience under his belt. But the situation was what it was, and he was determined to do what it demanded of him.

"I called you here for two reasons," he began. "One is to announce that, effective immediately, Lieutenant Ben Zoma will assume the post of acting second-in-command. At the same time, Lieutenant Ang will take over Mr. Ben Zoma's duties in the security section."

There were nods around the table, though not from Werber, Simenon, or Jomar. No surprise there, Picard thought. Ben Zoma had never been a favorite of Commander Leach or his friends.

"The second reason for this meeting," the commander said, "is the difficult set of circumstances in which we find ourselves. As you all know, we have taken heavy damage to our primary systems. Still, it remains our duty to survive . . . and to warn the Federation that the Nuyyad are every inch the threat of which we were warned."

No one seemed inclined to argue the point. However, he did receive some wary looks—predictably, from Leach's camp.

"There are two options open to us," Picard went on. "Two choices. We can make a run for the galactic barrier in our diminished condition and hope we don't run into the Nuyyad again. Or, as an alternative, we can try to find Serenity Santana's colony and seek replacement parts there."

"Her *colony?*" Werber echoed, a look of disgust and disbelief crossing his face. "Are you insane, Picard?"

The second officer felt a spurt of anger. He swallowed it back. "You will address me as you would have addressed Captain Ruhalter," he said in a clipped tone, "or I will find a weapons officer who can."

Werber went dark with anger. "You want the respect accorded a commanding officer? Then exercise the *judgment* of a commanding officer. That Santana woman led us into a trap, Commander. She almost destroyed us. I wouldn't trust *anything* she told us."

Picard glared at the weapons officer. "Despite appearances, we do *not* know for certain that Ms. Santana engaged in any treachery."

Werber looked at him wide-eyed. "Are you blind? She led us to the slaughter like a fat, little lamb. She—"

The second officer tapped the Starfleet insignia on his chest. "Security," he said, "this is Commander Picard. I would like an officer posted outside the lounge immediately."

"Right away, sir," came the response.

The weapons chief drew in a breath, then let it out. Clearly, he didn't relish the idea of being led away by a security officer. "What I *meant* to say," he amended with an effort, "is that, under the circumstances, it would be imprudent to believe anything Santana told us."

"I agree," said Jomar, albeit without emotion. "Who knows? There may never have been any *Valiant* survivors in the first place. And even if this colony exists, Santana might not have divulged its true coordinates."

Werber looked at him. "Hang on a second. You mean to say you've never heard of this colony?"

"Never," the Kelvan confirmed.

The weapons chief seemed confused. "But aren't you from this side of the galactic barrier?"

"I am," Jomar told him. "However, space is as enormous here as it is in your galaxy, and I only became familiar with a small portion of it before I emigrated to Nalogen Four."

It was Paxton who dragged the discussion back on track. "Even if Santana's colony exists," he said, "and even if she gave us the right coordinates, her people may not be all that glad to see us."

"True," Jomar remarked without inflection. "Especially if we're right in our assumption that Santana led us into a trap."

"Plus," Simenon hissed, "our technologies may be incompatible—in which case their parts would be useless to us, even assuming they're generous enough to give them away."

"Then you're in favor of trying to reach the barrier instead," said Picard. "Is that correct?"

"It is," the engineer agreed.

"Unfortunately," Ben Zoma said, "heading for the barrier may put us in an even worse bind."

"How so?" asked Cariello.

"For one thing," the acting executive officer noted, "it's just what the Nuyyad would expect us to do—retreat and regroup. For another thing, our shields are in no shape to protect us from the barrier's energies. We would only be creating the kind of supermen that nearly destroyed the *Enterprise* and the *Valiant*."

They were good points, Picard reflected—especially the one about crossing the barrier without shields. Judging from their expressions, his officers agreed with him. Even Werber seemed a trifle less certain of himself than he had been before.

But in the final analysis, it was Picard's decision. He took a moment to mull what he had heard to that point.

"Well?" Jomar asked of him, making no effort to disguise his impatience. "What do you plan to do, Commander?"

The second officer frowned. "Like some of you, I prefer the idea of returning to the galactic barrier."

Werber nodded. "Now you're talking."

"However," Picard added, "I do not wish to create any additional threats to the Federation—nor do I relish the prospect of destroying my vessel in order to negate such threats. And as Commander Ben Zoma points out, retreating through the barrier without sufficient shielding could create some prodigious threats indeed."

Werber paled as he realized where Picard's comments were leading him. "Oh no. You're not—"

"I *am*," Picard insisted, his posture unyielding. "I am going to try to find the colony Ms. Santana described, in the hope that it will equip us to eventually make it through the barrier unscathed."

He eyed each of his companions in turn, gauging their reactions. They didn't all look happy about his decision.

"If we're to come through this crisis intact," Picard said, "and warn the Federation about the Nuyyad, I will need the help and cooperation of everyone aboard this vessel." He glanced at Werber. "Without exception."

The lounge fell silent. It wasn't exactly the vote of confidence he had been hoping for.

"I respectfully request that you reconsider," Werber said, his tone anything but respectful.

"So do I," Simenon rasped.

"You are leading us into disaster," Jomar added bluntly, undeterred by any need to observe Starfleet protocol.

Picard smiled a grim smile. Clearly, his stint as commanding officer would not be an easy one. "My decision stands. You are dismissed." He looked around the room. "All of you."

One by one, his officers and the Kelvan left the room. Ben Zoma was the last to depart. Finally, the second officer was alone.

"Navigation," he said out loud, activating the intercom system. "This is Commander Picard."

"Asmund here," came the response.

Picard licked his lips. "Chart a course for Ms. Santana's colony. I believe you have the coordinates."

"I do, sir," Asmund confirmed. If she was surprised, it wasn't reflected in her voice. "Course set."

"Helm," said the second officer, "best speed. Engage."

"Acknowledged," Idun Asmund replied.

Picard leaned back in his chair in the otherwise empty lounge. The die was cast, he told himself. Now he would see if he had made the right choice . . . or the wrong one.

CHAPTER 9

Hans Werber had traveled each and every corridor of the *Stargazer* at one time or another. But he had never before traveled one so quietly or with such serious intent.

Werber wasn't alone, either. He was followed by three other officers—Chen and Ramirez of his weapons section and Pernell of engineering. And all four of them were armed with phaser pistols that Werber had lifted with the help of his security clearance.

The weapons chief knew they didn't have much time. Pausing at an intersection, he peeked into the perpendicular passageway to make sure it was empty. Then he made a left turn, his fellow conspirators in tow.

Their objective was the third set of doors on the right. As soon as he arrived there, Werber removed a small tool from his tunic and inserted the end of it into an aperture in the bulkhead.

A moment later, the doors slid apart, granting him access to a suite. Leaving Pernell to close the doors again, Werber and the others moved into the darkness within.

Reluctant to warn the suite's occupant, the weapons chief decided not to turn on the lights. Instead, his phaser held in front of him, he advanced to the sleeping quarters at the apartment's far end.

So far, he reflected, everything had gone smoothly. But their job wasn't over yet. Far from it.

The door to the bedroom was open. Taking a deep, slow breath, Werber made his way inside. Then he trained his weapon on the vague outline of the bed and reached for the light padd on the wall.

As he turned up the illumination, he fired his phaser. Its lurid, red beam slammed into the bedcovers with enough force to stun an ox—or in this case, the misguided commanding officer of a starship.

But as Werber's eyes adjusted to the light, he saw that something was wrong. Picard's bed was empty . . . except for a small, bronze object of some kind. He took a closer look—

—and saw that it was a combadge.

Suddenly, the weapons chief realized what he had stumbled into. His throat constricting, his blood pounding in his temples, he whirled and launched himself back through the doorway. But by then, the dimly lit anteroom was rife with ruby-red phaser bolts.

Before Werber could do anything about it, one of the beams caught Chen in the chest and drove him into the wall behind him. Then a second shaft slugged Ramirez in the jaw, spinning him around.

As Ramirez collapsed alongside Chen, Werber fired at one of the several cranberry-colored tunics in the room. What's more, he thought he hit one. But as he tried to squeeze off a second shot, he felt something kick him in the wrist and saw his weapon go flying out of his hand.

Cradling his injured wrist, Werber saw who had disarmed him. It was Picard, a phaser in his hand. And there were three other figures behind him—Pug Joseph and two of his fellow security officers.

"Picard to Ben Zoma," said the second officer, making use of the ship's intercom system since his combadge was elsewhere.

"Ben Zoma here," came the answer. "We've discovered a few rats in my quarters, but they won't bother us again. And you?"

"We've taken care of Werber," Picard replied soberly.

The weapons chief scowled at the byplay. "This wouldn't have been necessary if you'd made the right decision," he spat.

Picard didn't argue the point. Instead, he gestured with his phaser, indicating the corridor outside. "Take these mutineers to the brig," he told the security officers. "If they require medical attention, Dr. Greyhorse can see them there."

"Aye, sir," Joseph replied.

Rather than wait to be manhandled, Werber put his head down and made his way to the turbolift.

Picard wasn't sure how many times the chimes sounded outside his quarters before he woke enough to acknowledge them.

Glancing at the chronometer that sat alongside his bed, he saw that it was almost time for him to get up anyway. And if it had been any other morning, he wouldn't have minded doing so in the least.

However, he had been up the better part of the night laying in wait for Werber and his compatriots. And even after the second officer had sprung his trap, he had had trouble sleeping.

It was understandable, he told himself. Armed mutinies had a way of unsettling one.

Swinging his legs out of bed, Picard got to his feet and pulled a robe on. Just in case his visitor was a tardy mutineer, he picked up the phaser he had acquired and tucked it into the palm of his hand. Then he made his way to the next room.

"Come," he said.

The sliding doors whooshed open, revealing the lizardlike form of Phigus Simenon standing in the corridor outside. The Gnalish's eyes were slitted and even more fiery than usual.

"Are you crazy?" he demanded of Picard, gesticulating as he entered the room. "Have you lost your mind entirely?"

Perhaps it was his weariness. Perhaps it was the undeniable frustration in Simenon's voice. Either way, the second officer wasn't inclined to take umbrage at the way he was being addressed.

"I would have to say 'no' to both questions," he answered drily. "Why do you ask?"

"Why do I ask?" the engineer echoed. "Could it have something to do with the way you've treated Werber and half a dozen other officers—throwing them in the brig just for disagreeing with your decisions?" He waddled up to Picard and glowered at him nose-to-snout. "While you're at it, Commander, why don't you throw *me* in the brig as well?"

The second officer waved away the notion. "You misunderstand," he said. "I didn't have Mr. Werber and his friends incarcerated because they disagreed with me. I had them incarcerated because they invaded my quarters with phasers in their hands and mutiny on their minds."

Simenon looked at him askance. "Mutiny . . . ?" he rasped.

"Indeed," Picard confirmed. "And it would have succeeded had it not been for Lieutenant Vigo in the weapons section, who overheard Werber and two of his fellow officers making plans to neutralize me."

The Gnalish gaped at him, then shook his head. "You're lying."

"I assure you," said the second officer, "I am not. Werber led an attempt at mutiny last night. If you have any doubts, you can ask one of the security officers who helped capture the conspirators."

In all the weeks Picard had spent on the *Stargazer,* he had never seen Phigus Simenon at a loss for words . . . until that very moment. The engineer looked positively deflated.

"You know," Simenon grated after a while, "it's not in my nature to admit that I'm wrong."

"So I gather," said the second officer.

"That fact notwithstanding," the Gnalish continued, "it seems I may have misjudged you."

"Actually," Picard said generously, "I may have misjudged you as well."

Simenon's eyes narrowed. "How so?"

"Frankly," the second officer told him, "I expected to find you among the mutineers. In their forefront, in fact. I would say we're both capable of jumping to conclusions."

The engineer snorted. "Apparently."

Picard considered Simenon. He and the Gnalish hadn't ever spoken at length before, especially about personal matters. But now that they had, the second officer found himself liking the fellow.

"I think I'll slink off now," said Simenon. "I've got some friends in the brig who'll no doubt need cheering up." He hesitated. "That is, if it's all right with my commanding officer."

Picard nodded. "Go ahead. Just one request."

"What's that?" asked the Gnalish.

"Don't slip any of the prisoners a phaser. I don't think the guards I've posted would appreciate it."

Simenon chuckled. "You have my word." Then, dragging his scaly tail behind him, he left Picard's quarters.

The second officer watched his doors slide closed behind the engineer. Then he returned to his bedroom and put down his phaser.

Someone had once told him that something good comes out of even the worst circumstances. If he had established even a small bond of trust with Simenon, perhaps there was an upside to the mutiny attempt after all.

In all the months he had spent on the *Stargazer*, Lieutenant Vigo had never visited the captain's ready room.

He had seen plenty of other officers entering and leaving the place from his vantage point at the bridge's weapons console. Sometimes, he had even gotten a glimpse of what it looked like inside. It was just that he himself had never been summoned there.

Until just a couple of minutes ago.

Standing outside the ready room doors, Vigo waited for the internal sensors to recognize his presence and alert Picard to the fact. A moment later, Vigo knew that the sensors had done their job, because the doors whispered open and gave him access.

He could see the second officer standing near an observation port, to one side of the captain's sleek, black desk. Picard smiled. "Please, Lieutenant. Take a seat."

"Thank you, sir," Vigo replied. He pulled out a chair that stood across the desk from the captain's and tried to make himself comfortable—not an easy thing for a being of his bulk.

Picard regarded him for a moment. Then he said, "I take it you heard about Lieutenant Werber."

The Pandrilite nodded. "That he was caught. Yes, sir."

Vigo had been forced to carry out his regular assignments, pretending that he didn't know anything about the mutiny. Otherwise, Werber and his comrades might have suspected a leak and called it off.

Knowing what was taking place elsewhere on the ship, it was difficult for him to keep his mind on his work. Almost impossible, in fact. But somehow, he had managed.

Then, early that morning, while he and two other crewmen were repairing a phaser turret, Vigo had heard the news. Werber and his mutineers had been caught. Picard and Ben Zoma had prevailed.

It hadn't given him any special pleasure to know that he was the one who had scuttled the mutiny. He had only done his duty, after all. There was nothing personal in it—only a sense of relief.

"Obviously," said Picard, "I can't allow Lieutenant Werber to go free. Not after what he tried to do."

"Yes, sir," Vigo agreed.

"And if he's in the brig," the second officer continued, "he can hardly serve as weapons chief."

The Pandrilite began to see where the conversation was going. Why would Picard discuss this with *him* unless . . .

"Sir," he blurted, "I didn't expose Lieutenant Werber's plans so I could replace him as weapons chief."

Picard smiled understandingly. "I know that, Lieutenant. In point of fact, I have had my eye on you for some time. I can tell you that few crewmen in any section, weapons or otherwise, have demonstrated as much dedication to their work as you have."

The Pandrilite was surprised. As far as he had been able to tell, only Werber had had the chance to see how hard he was working—and for whatever reason, the weapons chief had refused to acknowledge it.

"That's kind of you, sir," said Vigo.

"You needn't be humble," Picard told him. "It's part of my job to identify personnel with the potential for advancement. And, I'm happy to say, you have such potential. Even if Mr. Werber hadn't acted as he did, you would still have been considered for a promotion."

The Pandrilite found himself smiling. "It's gratifying to hear you say that, sir."

"Then you'll accept a promotion to weapons chief?" Picard asked.

Vigo's conscience was clear. Under the circumstances, how could he refuse? "I will," he assured the second officer. "Thank you again, sir."

"No, Mr. Vigo. Thank *you*. And by the way, your promotion is effective immediately. I will inform Commander Ben Zoma."

"Yes, sir," said the Pandrilite.

As he left the lounge, he felt a little dazed. But more than that, he felt vindicated. He had acted honorably . . . and contrary to the expectations of his friends, his actions had been rewarded.

There was some justice in the universe after all.

It was part of Gerda Asmund's job to conduct periodic long-range sensor scans—even when they *weren't* in an unfamiliar and potentially hostile sector of space.

Since the attack by the Nuyyad ship, she had been inclined to conduct her scans three times as often as usual. For the first thirty-two hours, she hadn't turned up anything interesting—including the colony described by Serenity Santana. But then, at that point, the place's coordinates were still outside their sensor range.

In the thirty-third hour, one of Gerda's sweeps picked up a concentration of thermal and electromagnetic radiation on what appeared to be a M-Class planet. She knew the signs. This wasn't a natural phenomenon. It was an installation of some kind—manufactured by a sentient civilization.

Just to be certain, Gerda checked its coordinates. Then she examined its sensor profile a second time. It was then that she noticed a second energy concentration—one so close to the first that it was almost indistinguishable from it at this distance.

But the second concentration wasn't on the planet's surface. The navigator could see that now. Unless she was mistaken, it was marginally closer than the first concentration.

In orbit above it.

Gerda turned to Commander Picard. "Sir?"

Picard approached her. "Yes, Lieutenant?"

"I think you should see this," she told him.

Picard again found himself addressing a lounge full of officers. As before, he had convened them on the heels of a tumultuous event that had resulted in a new face among them.

But it wasn't Werber's mutiny that had spurred this meeting. It was something a good deal more ominous.

The second officer leaned forward in his chair. *The captain's chair,* he remarked inwardly, correcting himself. "I called you here to apprise you of our most recent long-range sensor report. Though I normally steer clear of glib remarks, I cannot help describing it as good news and bad news."

"First," he said, "the good news. It seems the colony described by Serenity Santana exists after all. Furthermore, it is located at the coordinates with which she provided us."

There were expressions of relief all around the table. If the long-range sensors hadn't found Santana's colony, their chances of survival would have been almost nil.

"You are certain of this?" asked Jomar.

"Quite certain," Picard assured him.

The Kelvan's pale blue eyes narrowed. "And how long will it take us to reach this colony?"

"Approximately nine days," said the second officer. "Unless, of course, we can find a way to go faster than warp five."

"Which isn't likely," Simenon interjected flatly.

"What's the bad news?" asked Greyhorse.

Picard frowned. "There is a ship in orbit around Santana's colony. We believe it is a Nuyyad vessel."

He could feel the air in the lounge turning sour as his news sank in. He wasn't surprised in the least. The *Stargazer* was in no shape to endure another battle with the Nuyyad.

And yet, the only way to make themselves battle-ready again was to go through the enemy. They were in a quandary, to say the least.

"Clearly," he said, "we need a plan."

Jomar shook his head scornfully. "What we need, Commander, are weapons. And we have very few of those."

"Then we'll make some," Vigo interjected.

The Kelvan turned to him, his features in repose but his posture one of skepticism. "Out of what, if I may ask?"

"That is the question," Picard agreed. He looked around the table. "Considering the ingenuity and expertise represented in this room, I was hoping to get some answers."

It was a challenge, nothing more. However, there was an unexpected edge in Jomar's normally neutral voice as he answered it.

"We could have had weapons specifically designed with the

Nuyyad in mind," he reminded them. "However, you turned down my offer to make them for you. Now it is too late for that."

"With all due respect," Picard told him, "there were reasons we turned down your offer. And as you say, it's too late to contemplate making those weapons now, so let's discuss something we *can* accomplish."

He addressed the entire group again. "In nine days, we will reach Ms. Santana's colony. If by that time, we cannot come up with a way to neutralize the Nuyyad presence there, we will have failed in our duty to the Federation—and I, for one, will not accept such an outcome."

For a moment, no one said anything. Then Vigo spoke up again, his blue brow furrowed with concentration. "I think I have an idea, sir."

"By all means," Picard told him, "share it with us."

The Pandrilite described what he had in mind. It didn't involve any exotic technology. But before he was finished, everyone in the lounge was a little more hopeful.

Even Jomar.

CHAPTER **10**

Picard stood in front of the captain's chair and gazed at the forward viewscreen, where he could clearly see a Nuyyad vessel in orbit around a blue, green, and white planet.

The enemy ship looked exactly like the first one they had encountered. It was immense, flat, diamond-shaped . . . and more than likely, equipped with the same powerful vidrion cannons that had inflicted so much punishment on the *Stargazer* already.

Picard tried not to contemplate how much more damage they could do without any shields to slow them down.

"There it is," said Ben Zoma, who had come over to stand beside him.

The second officer nodded. "Slow to half impulse, helm."

"Half impulse," Idun confirmed.

Picard turned to Vigo, who was sitting in Werber's spot behind the weapons console. "Are the shuttles ready?" he asked.

"They are, sir," came the Pandrilite's response.

The second officer turned back to the screen. "Release them."

"Aye, sir," said Vigo.

Picard watched the viewscreen. If the Nuyyad vessel had picked up the *Stargazer* on her sensors, she wasn't giving the least indication of it. She was just sitting there in orbit around Santana's planet, looking like a large, deadly blade.

Abruptly, a handful of smaller craft invaded the screen from its bottom edge—seven remote-controlled Starfleet shuttles hurtling through the void at full impulse, rapidly leaving the *Stargazer* behind. The shuttles, which ranged in size up to a Type-7 personnel carrier, looked dwarfed by the Nuyyad ship even though the latter was much more distant.

"Status?" Picard demanded.

Gerda answered him. "Eighty seconds to target."

The commander could feel his heart thud against his ribs. Eighty seconds. Five million kilometers. The difference between victory and defeat, life and death, survival and annihilation.

Ben Zoma cast him a look of confidence, a look that seemed to assure Picard that everything would be all right. Then he retreated to the engineering console and began monitoring ship's systems.

Each of the shuttles carried an antimatter payload big enough to punch a hole in the Nuyyad vessel's shields. But to accomplish that feat, they would have to reach the enemy unscathed—and that, Picard reflected, was easier said than done.

He had barely completed the thought when one of the shuttles became a flare of white light on the viewscreen. Cursing beneath his breath, he whirled on his weapons officer.

"What happened, Mr. Vigo?"

The Pandrilite shook his large blue head, obviously as confused by the premature explosion as Picard was. "I don't know, sir. I didn't trigger it, I can tell you that."

"I can confirm that," Ben Zoma interjected. "The payload seemed to go off on its own."

The second officer could feel his teeth grinding. If the other shuttles went off prematurely, they would be all but toothless. The Nuyyad vessel could pick them off at its leisure.

"Fifty seconds," Gerda announced.

It was time for the *Stargazer* to enter the fray. "Full impulse," Picard told Idun Asmund.

"Aye, sir," said the helm officer.

"Power phasers," the commander added.

"Powering phasers," Vigo replied, activating the batteries that could still generate a charge.

"Forty seconds," declared Gerda, her face caught in the glare of her navigation controls.

He glanced at Ben Zoma. His friend returned it—and even managed a jaunty smile. *I've still got confidence in you,* it seemed to say.

Suddenly, a green globe shot out from the Nuyyad ship and skewered one of the shuttles. Again, Picard saw a flash of brilliance. Then a second shuttle was hit. It too vanished in a splash of glory.

That left four of the smaller craft—a little more than half of what they had started out with. And they still hadn't gotten within two million kilometers of their target.

"Evasive maneuvers," said the second officer.

"Aye, sir," Vigo responded, implementing one of the patterns they had programmed in advance.

On the screen, the shuttles began banking and weaving, making the enemy's job that much more difficult. Unfortunately, it would get easier again as they got closer to the Nuyyad vessel.

"Thirty seconds," said the navigator.

Picard desperately wanted to accelerate the shuttles' progress. But he didn't dare have them drop in and out of warp speed so close to a planet, where gravity added a potentially disastrous layer of difficulty.

In the end, he had no choice. He would have to grit his teeth and hope the shuttles did their job.

The Nuyyad fired another series of green vidrion blasts. However, to Picard's relief, none of them found their marks. The four remaining shuttles went on, intact.

Gerda looked up from her controls, no doubt eager to see the drama with her own eyes. "Twenty seconds."

The enemy vessel unleashed yet another wave of vidrion splendor. For a moment, as the *Stargazer*'s shuttles passed through it, Picard lost sight of them. Then the emerald brilliance of the energy bursts faded and he was able to catch a glimpse of the smaller craft.

There were three left, it seemed. Part of that light display must have been one of them exploding.

One less shuttle meant one less shot at success. That was the inescapable reality of it. But they were getting close now to the enemy. With luck, Vigo's plan would pan out.

Again, Picard shot a look at Ben Zoma. As before, the man didn't seem to have a care in the world.

"Phaser range," the weapons officer announced.

"Fire on my mark," Picard barked.

The Nuyyad bombarded the shuttles again, lighting torches of pale green fire in the void. Picard squinted to see through them, to get an idea of whether any of his craft had made it through.

"Five seconds," said Gerda. "Four. Three . . ."

Then Picard spotted them—not just one of the shuttles, but all three. As his navigator counted down to zero, they smashed headlong into the Nuyyad's deflector shields.

And went off.

If the vidrion bursts had been showy, the shuttle explosions were positively magnificent, magnified by their reflection off the enemy's shields. But Picard didn't take any time to appreciate their glory. His sole interest was how much damage they could do.

"Fire!" he bellowed.

Instantly, the starboard phaser banks lashed out with everything they had, driving their crimson energy through each of the three spots where the shuttles had exploded.

Picard turned to Gerda. "Report!"

"We've penetrated their shields!" she told him. "Sensors show significant damage to their hull!"

He turned back to the viewscreen, smelling the victory they had been hoping for. "Fire again, Mr. Vigo!"

A second time, the *Stargazer*'s phaser beams slashed through the enemy's tattered shields, piercing the vessel's outer skin and setting off a string of small explosions.

But the Nuyyad wasn't ready to call it quits yet. A moment after Picard's ship fired, the enemy unleashed a salvo of its own.

"Brace yourselves!" the second officer called out.

Fortunately, Idun managed to slip past most of the barrage—but not all of it. The force of the vidrion assault drove Picard to the deck, his head missing the base of Ruhalter's chair by inches.

Consoles exploded aft of him, shooting geysers of white-hot sparks at the ceiling. As a cloud of smoke began to gather, he dragged himself up and glared at the viewscreen.

The enemy ship had suffered extensive damage, her hull plates twisted and blackened from stem to stern. Still, she was functioning—and if she was functioning, she was a threat.

Picard meant to put an end to it. "Mr. Vigo," he said, trying not to choke on the smoke filling his bridge, "fire again!"

On the screen, the Nuyyad vessel seemed to writhe under the impact of the *Stargazer*'s phaser beams. She was wracked by one internal explosion after another as the directed energy ripped into key systems. Finally, unable to endure the torment any longer, she flew apart in a splash of gold that blotted out the stars.

Picard wasn't a bloodthirsty man and never had been. However, he found himself nodding in approval as pieces of Nuyyad debris spun through space in an ever-expanding wave.

He glanced over his shoulder at the ruined aft consoles. Ben Zoma and a couple of other officers had gotten hold of fire extinguishers and were spraying foam over the flames, though the control panels themselves would require extensive repairs.

Ben Zoma seemed to sense that his friend was watching him. Returning the look, he smiled a big smile. You see? he seemed to say. I told you you could do it.

The second officer turned to Gerda. "Report."

The navigator consulted her monitor. "Damage to decks three, four, and six," she replied. "Photon torpedo launchers are off-line. Likewise, the starboard sensor array."

Picard grunted. They were shieldless and half-blind, and their once-powerful arsenal was limited to a couple of battered phaser banks. But it could have been worse.

Much worse.

"Casualties?" he asked.

Gerda paused for a moment, then looked up at him. "None, sir. Everyone made it through intact."

It was better than the second officer might have guessed—better even than he might have hoped. "Excellent," he said.

There was only one thing left to do. After all, they had come all this way for a reason. He regarded the forward screen, which now showed him an unobstructed view of the planet.

"Mr. Paxton," he said, "hail the colony."

"Aye, sir," came the response.

Almost a minute passed as Paxton tried one frequency after another. Finally, he seemed to hit on the right one.

"They're returning our hail," he told Picard.

The commander folded his arms across his chest. "On screen."

Abruptly, the image on the viewscreen was replaced by that of a long-faced, middle-aged man with thick eyebrows and dark, wavy hair. He seemed to stare at Picard for a moment, as if he couldn't believe his eyes.

Then he smiled.

"You're from Earth," he concluded. "So Daniels and Santana must have reached you."

"They did indeed," Picard confirmed. He identified himself as the commander of the *Stargazer.*

"My name is Shield Williamson," said the colonist. "I'm in charge here. Speaking for everyone, I have to tell you how grateful we are that you chose to help us."

"Especially after you led us into a trap," Picard expanded, hoping to nail down at least that bit of information.

Williamson's smile faded. But far from denying the charge, he nodded soberly. "Yes. After that."

"I trust the Nuyyad ship we destroyed had something to do with it?" the commander suggested.

The colonist sighed. "It had everything to do with it."

"I would like very much to hear the details," said Picard. "But first, I need to know if you will assist us. We have suffered considerable damage at the hands of the Nuyyad. We were hoping—"

"That we could help with repairs?" Williamson spread his hands out. "Absolutely—however we can. As I said, Commander, we're grateful for what you did for us—especially in light of what happened before."

"Thank you," said Picard.

"It's the least we can do," the colonist told him. "And if I may ask, how are our people—Daniels and Santana?"

The second officer frowned. "Daniels was detained for security reasons by our Starfleet. There were suspicions about him and Santana, as you seem to have anticipated."

"I'm sorry to hear that," said Williamson. "And what of Santana? Is she with you now?"

"She is," Picard told him. "However, she was severely injured in the Nuyyad's ambush."

The colonist looked devastated. "Is she alive?"

"Yes. But she seems to have withdrawn into some sort of coma. Our doctor is at a loss as to—"

"Our physicians will know how to treat her," Williamson assured him. "But we've got to hurry. Her condition sounds precarious."

Picard had no intention of hanging onto Santana if there was any chance her people could help her. She may have led the *Stargazer* into a deadly trap, but it wasn't his place to demand an eye for an eye.

"As you wish," he replied. "I'll notify my ship's surgeon." He tapped his combadge. "Picard to Greyhorse. We're going to beam Santana down to the colony."

"That's fine," came the medical officer's reply. "I'll prepare her for transport immediately. But I want to come along, Commander. The woman is my patient, remember."

Picard regarded Williamson. "Do you have a problem with Dr. Greyhorse beaming down as well?"

The colonist looked at him as if he had grown another head. "Beaming down?" he echoed.

The second officer had forgotten . . . Santana's people were descended from a crew that left Earth nearly three hundred years earlier. At that time, there were no such things as molecular imaging scanners, phase transition coils, and pattern buffers.

As Earth pushed out into the galaxy in the twenty-second century, there had been a need for a quick way to board and disembark from spacegoing vessels—and transporter systems had filled that need. However, the colonists might never have been impelled in that direction.

"It's a sophisticated procedure," he explained, "in which a subject is disassembled at the subatomic level, transmitted to another location and reassembled at the other end."

Williamson looked at him. "Impressive. And are there any . . . casualties when you employ this technology?"

"None when the equipment is working correctly," Picard assured him. "And without question, it would be the fastest way to convey Ms. Santana to your planet's surface."

The colonist hesitated—but only for a moment. "Very well. Where should we expect your medical officer and Santana to arrive?"

"Where would you *like* them to arrive?"

Williamson thought about it. "What about the plaza outside our central medical facility? It's shaped like a hexagon and it sits between two of our tallest towers."

Picard glanced at his communications officer. "Mr. Paxton?"

Paxton responded without looking up. "I'm relaying the information to Lieutenant Vandermeer now, sir."

"Actually," Williamson interjected, "you may want to consider accompanying your medical officer. At some point, Commander, you and I will need to speak in person. It might as well be now."

"Sir," said Paxton, before Picard could give the colonist an answer, "Lieutenant Vandermeer says she's located the hexagonal plaza."

"Acknowledged," the second officer responded.

Ben Zoma, who had returned to the engineering console, whispered, "You're not going down there without a security escort, are you?"

Picard glanced at him. It was the type of sentiment he might have expressed to Captain Ruhalter just a few days earlier. But somehow, it sounded less urgent when one was on the other side of the rail.

He turned back to the colonist. "I would like to take you up on that," he said diplomatically. "However, I am not the only one who would like to speak with you."

"Bring whomever you wish," Williamson responded. "Even a security team, if you feel you need one. But as you'll see, Commander, we no longer have any reason to deceive you."

After their experience with Santana, Picard had no business believing Williamson. But for some reason, he did.

CHAPTER **11**

Evening had already fallen on the colonists' continent when Jean-Luc Picard and his entourage beamed down from the Stargazer.

The second officer could have accompanied Greyhorse and Santana to the medical facility as he originally intended. However, he had instead accepted Shield Williamson's invitation to meet him in his offices.

Picard was instantly pleased that he had made that choice. Looking out from a semicircular balcony, he found himself gazing at the most impressive city he had ever seen.

It was sleek, elegant, magnificent in scale . . . a titanic landscape of hundred-story-high buildings with proud, rounded shoulders and breathtaking, sky-spanning footbridges, cast in soft pinks and yellows by an abundance of tethered, softly glowing globes.

Hovercars of different sizes and shapes sailed effortlessly through the spired landscape, looking like graceful, exotic fish in the depths of an alien ocean. As for foliage . . . dark blue trees and shrubs were everywhere, defining spacious, ground-level plazas and overhanging public balconies, filling the air with a pleasant, slightly tart fragrance.

Picard had never been here before. And yet, it seemed to him that he *had* been here, or at least someplace very much like it.

And he knew why. As a cadet at Starfleet Academy, he had studied many things—archaeology, drama, and astrophysics, to name a few. He had also developed more than a passing interest in architecture.

In the year 2064, a year before the *S.S. Valiant* left Earth orbit, a Frenchman named Goimard had unveiled his vision for rebuilding a world that had been wracked by its third World War. Unfortunately—at least from Picard's point of view—that vision had only blossomed in dribs and drabs, a series of perhaps thirty buildings in nearly as many locations.

Evidently, he reflected, one of the *Valiant*'s survivors had been a Goimard aficionado—because here, on a planet a great many light-years from Earth, the Frenchman's dream had been realized in all its glory. Picard felt compelled to smile at the irony.

"Not bad for a ragtag band of survivors," Ben Zoma quipped.

"They've had almost three hundred years to build," Picard reminded him. "This place could be thirty years older than our colony on Mars."

"Welcome to Magnia," said Williamson.

The second officer turned and saw their host approaching them through a wide, arched set of sliding doors. In person, Williamson was considerably taller than he had appeared on the viewscreen. He was also alone—a clear demonstration of trust.

Picard smiled. "Magnia," he said, letting the word roll off his tongue. "Goimard's name for his perfect city."

The colonist's eyebrows shot up. "You know his work?"

"I do," said the second officer. "And frankly, I'm delighted to see it expressed here so faithfully. No doubt, Goimard himself would have been delighted as well."

"We like to think so," Williamson replied.

"How is Santana?" Picard inquired.

The colonist's expression sobered. "She suffered considerable damage. However, our physicians tell me she'll be all right."

"That's good to hear."

Williamson indicated the arched doorway with a gesture. "Shall we?" he said, and led the way.

His offices were expansive, with rounded, pastel-colored furniture, ornate moldings, and an entire wall full of oval monitors. Each screen showed them a repair effort in a particular part of the city.

Picard looked at their host. "Your defenses, I take it?"

"Yes," said Williamson. "I dispatched teams to our shield generators as soon as I knew that the Nuyyad were gone." He gazed critically at one screen in particular. "Unfortunately, they're not gone for good. The Nuyyad are eventually going to figure out what happened to their ship—and when they do, they'll be merciless."

Picard had no doubt of it. After all, he had experienced the Nuyyad's propensity for violence firsthand.

"I don't suppose you've had a chance to plan for that contingency?" the colonist asked him optimistically.

The second officer shook his head. "I must admit, I have not. However, I am of the mind that Magnia and the *Stargazer* can help each other out of this predicament . . . if they so choose."

"Rest assured," Williamson told him earnestly, "my people will do anything you require of them."

"I am glad to hear you say that. Mainly, we are in need of parts to replace those the Nuyyad destroyed. Though I realize your technologies and ours may have developed along different lines, I am hopeful that you either have the necessary parts on hand or can manufacture them for us."

The colonist shrugged. "I would be glad to have my engineers take a look at the specifications."

"And in return," said Picard, glancing at the oval screens, "we will see what we can do to expedite your repair schedule."

Williamson nodded. "That would be much appreciated."

"Are you familiar with the Kelvans?" Ben Zoma asked.

Unexpectedly, the other man's expression seemed to sour. "I am," he said. "Why do you ask?"

"We have a Kelvan on board," Ben Zoma explained, "an engineer named Jomar who seems to know Nuyyad tactical systems pretty well. You may want to consult with him."

Williamson didn't answer right away.

"Judging by your expression and your silence," Picard asked, "am I to infer that you've had conflicts with the Kelvans?"

The colonist frowned. "They're not the Nuyyad," he said, "I'll grant you that. But those few we've met have been arrogant and untrustworthy in their dealings with us."

Picard smiled. "Jomar *can* be arrogant at times. On the other hand, he's absolutely dedicated to stopping the Nuyyad from invading the Federation. If I were you, I would take advantage of that dedication."

Williamson thought for a moment, then nodded. "All right. In the interest of working together, we'll welcome this Jomar as well."

"Good," said Picard. "But before we work out the details, I would like to know more about the Nuyyad's interest in your world . . . as it may shape some of our tactical decisions."

"Of course."

"From what I have seen so far," the second officer went on, "the Nuyyad did not have any presence here on your planet's surface. They seemed content to remain on their vessel."

"That's true," the colonist responded.

"Then why bother to come here at all?" asked Ben Zoma.

Williamson smiled ruefully. "Actually," he said, "it was your fault. Your Federation's, I mean."

Picard was surprised. "The Federation's?"

"That's right," the colonist told him. "A short time ago, the Nuyyad got wind of your existence—apparently, from a species that routinely crosses the galactic barrier. They're known as the Liharon."

Picard nodded. "Yes . . . I am familiar with the Liharon. They are traders, for the most part."

"They trade, all right," said Williamson. "But not material goods. Their main business is information."

Again, the Earthman was surprised. "The Liharon are spies? No one in Starfleet has ever suspected . . ."

"Of course not," said the colonist. "If everyone knew the Liharon for what they are, they wouldn't be very effective."

"I guess not," Ben Zoma allowed.

Williamson continued. "Once the Nuyyad knew something about the Federation, they couldn't help seeing it as a potential conquest. But before they could launch a military offensive on the other side of the barrier, they needed to know more about your defensive capabilities."

The second officer began to understand. "And even the Liharon couldn't obtain that kind of data. Then someone pointed out the similarities between your people and the human species . . ."

"Exactly," said the colonist. "An intrusion into our database confirmed the connection. We were human, the Nuyyad discovered. Even better, we shared a common history with Federation humans. And if we sent a plea for help to the Federation, it would likely be answered."

Picard grunted thoughtfully. "So it *was* our fault that the Nuyyad were drawn to you."

Williamson smiled again. "As I said. Mind you, none of us wanted to cooperate with them. We had no desire to be part of their plans for conquest. However, we had little choice in the matter."

"Because the Nuyyad had taken your world hostage," Ben Zoma observed.

"Yes," said the colonist. "Once they had us where they wanted us, they went through our records. After a while, they selected two 'volunteers' on the basis of intelligence and resourcefulness."

"Daniels and Santana," said Picard.

"Daniels and Santana," Williamson confirmed. "They were to

visit Federation territory and lure a Starfleet vessel out past the barrier."

"Judas goats," Ben Zoma noted.

"Yes," said the colonist. "Though quite unwillingly. After all, they hated the Nuyyad species and all it stood for. However, the alternative to cooperation was to see their families and friends tortured to death, and that was too bloody a scenario for either of them to contemplate."

Picard couldn't help sympathizing with Santana's plight. Had he been given the same choice by the Nuyyad, he would have had a difficult time deciding which road to take.

"I hope you understand," said Williamson, "how terrible we feel about this. We're a proud people. The notion of being forced to do something against our will is anathema to us."

Picard nodded. "And the fact that you were betraying your own species must have made it even more difficult."

The remark elicited an unexpected change in the colonist's demeanor. He seemed aloof for a moment, almost resentful. However, he continued to look the Starfleet officer in the eye.

"Clearly," he said, "we didn't warm to the prospect of deceiving anyone. But to be perfectly honest, Commander Picard . . . we feel no more kinship with Earth than we do with any other inhabited world."

At first, the second officer thought he might have heard incorrectly. Then he saw the boggled expression on Ben Zoma's face.

"And why is that?" Picard asked the colonist.

Williamson shrugged. "Put yourself in our ancestors' positions. You've risked your life to push out your people's boundaries, to further Earth's knowledge of the galaxy. And yet, when you fail to return, what does your homeworld do for you?

"Does it plan a rescue? Does it dispatch another vessel to go after you, to see if there were any survivors of your flight? Even after Federation technology allows your people to cross the barrier unscathed, does even one Earth ship come out here to determine your fate?"

"The *Valiant*'s captain sent out a message buoy," Picard noted. "It suggested that he was going to destroy his ship."

"And that was enough?" Williamson asked evenly. "Nobody cared enough to pursue the matter further?"

There was little the commander could say to that. "Apparently not," he conceded, feeling a twinge of shame on the Federation's behalf.

The colonist spread his hands out. "Then I ask you . . . is it any wonder we no longer feel any particular kinship with Earth? Is it a surprise that we've come to see ourselves as a separate civilization . . . even a separate species in some respects?"

Picard saw Williamson's point. As far as the Magnians were concerned, Earth and its people were a distant memory . . . and under the circumstances, not an especially sweet one.

Of course, he still didn't approve of what Santana had done. It was still an act of treachery that had cost some of his comrades their lives. However, he understood now why she was willing to contemplate it.

"I would like to return to my ship now," said Picard, "and put together the engineering teams that will help you."

"Excellent," Williamson told him. "And I will put some teams together to help *you.*"

It seemed like an arrangement from which both sides could only benefit. Picard hoped that it would actually work out that way.

Greyhorse peered through the oval window at Serenity Santana and her Magnian physicians. Then he turned to Law, the medical center's director, who stood beside him in a white lab coat.

"This is how you treat *all* your patients?" he asked.

Law, a small man with Asian features, shook his head. "Only those who *can* be treated this way. Direct mental stimulation is a valuable tool, make no mistake. But in many cases, we're still forced to resort to pharmaceuticals or even scalpels."

On the other side of the window, Santana was lying on a narrow bed under a set of low-hanging blue lights. None of the four doctors surrounding her was actually touching the woman. Instead, they seemed to be leaning over her, eyes closed, focusing on an invisible process.

"What's your success rate using this kind of procedure?" Greyhorse wondered aloud, his inquiry sounding more blunt than he had intended.

Law smiled. "Very high, I'm pleased to say. More than ninety-eight percent. And we are constantly trying to improve on that." He watched his colleagues work on Santana. "Of course, in the present case, the problem was a little more complicated, since the patient's injury took place days ago and had already been treated in other ways."

The ship's surgeon looked at the smaller man. "Are you saying I actually set you back?"

The colonist shrugged. "Just a little. The important thing is that Serenity will be fine."

"You sound as if you know her," Greyhorse observed.

"I do," said Law. "She was a playmate of my eldest daughter. But then, most people in Magnia know each other, if only by family or reputation. After all, Doctor, we're a small community. It's only recently that our population has begun to nudge a hundred thousand."

"In the city, you mean?"

The Magnian smiled again. "Very few people live *outside* the city. Despite the complications created by our telepathic abilities, we have come to enjoy the feeling of having others in close proximity."

Greyhorse didn't understand. "It seems to me that proximity would tend to preclude privacy."

"Not here," Law told him.

* * *

Picard saw Simenon's blood-red eyes narrow in disbelief. "You promised them *what?*" he spat.

The second officer, who was sitting on the other side of the lounge's black, oval table, frowned at the engineer's response. "I made available our technical expertise to help them repair their shield generators. It seemed like an eminently reasonable offer, given their willingness to come up with the parts we need."

Simenon harrumphed. "You call it reasonable to put your crew in the hands of the same people who led you into an ambush?"

Picard regarded the Gnalish, one of three individuals whom he had invited to this meeting. The other two were Jomar and Vigo, the acting weapons chief, who sat on either side of Simenon.

"It is true," said the second officer, "that we may be placing the fox in charge of the hen house. Nonetheless, I am inclined to trust the Magnians' intentions in this regard."

"After what they did to us?" the engineer asked.

Picard nodded. "Shield Williamson could have denied his people's role in the ambush, but he chose not to do so. He told me what they had done and why, without pulling any punches."

Simenon's eyes narrowed, but he didn't try to interrupt. The second officer took that as a good sign.

"Furthermore," he said, "Williamson could have refrained from mentioning his mixed feelings about the Federation—but again, he chose the path of honesty." He leaned forward in his seat. "I believe the Magnians will hold up their end of the bargain, Lieutenant. And I also believe that my people will be safe on the planet's surface."

The chief engineer folded his scaly arms across his chest, obviously still somewhat skeptical of the colonists' motives. "You're the one in command," he rasped, recognizing the fact if not quite approving of it.

Next, Picard turned to Vigo. "You have been sending data as to what parts we require to bring our weapons systems back up to snuff?"

The Pandrilite nodded. "I have, sir."

"And the Magnians' response?"

"They don't have anything like them on hand," said Vigo. "However, they're confident they can manufacture what we need in short order."

"Excellent," Picard replied. Last, he looked to the Kelvan. "I have not forgotten your concerns about dealing with the Magnians, Jomar. And as you are not technically a member of this crew, I am not in a position to give you orders. However, you are our expert in vidrion technology, which the colonists need desperately if they are to withstand the Nuyyad's next attack. With that in mind, I hope you will honor the agreement I made."

The Kelvan's stare was as blank as ever. For a moment, he remained silent. Then he said, "I will help."

It didn't quite answer Picard's question. But under the circumstances, he supposed it would have to do.

CHAPTER 12

A spike?" Picard echoed. "In her brain waves?"

On the other side of Greyhorse's desk, the doctor nodded. "It was difficult to miss, believe me. And it began before we were hit with enemy fire, so it couldn't have been a reaction to the battle itself."

"What are you saying?" asked the second officer.

"It's just a theory, of course," Greyhorse noted. "But when I saw the spike, it occurred to me that Santana might have been communicating with the other colonists."

"Even in her comatose state?" Picard wondered.

The doctor nodded. "It's the most viable explanation. I would've mentioned it sooner, but there wasn't a chance to do so. I was too busy rushing my patient down to the planet's surface."

"I understand," said the second officer.

He considered the implications—and didn't like what he found himself thinking. "Doctor Greyhorse . . . you mentioned earlier that Ms. Santana's coma might have been self-induced."

"That's correct," Greyhorse confirmed.

"Is it also possible that she was never in a coma in the first place—and only gave the appearance of it?"

The doctor mulled it over. "According to my instruments, the woman was definitely in a coma. And just a little while ago, in the Magnians' medical center, I saw their doctors working on her—which wouldn't have been necessary if she were just faking it."

"What sort of work were they doing?"

Greyhorse shrugged. "They were using the power of their minds."

"Just standing there?"

"Yes," said the doctor.

"Which, if you were a suspicious person, you might have discounted as window dressing."

Greyhorse looked at Picard. "You're suggesting that their procedure was a sham, Commander? A show for my benefit?"

"I am not suggesting anything," said the second officer. "I am merely bringing up the question."

The doctor's dark eyes narrowed. "I don't understand. I thought you trusted the Magnians."

Picard sighed. "I am so inclined, yes. However, in the position I now occupy, I feel compelled to consider all the angles."

Including the angle that assumed he was wrong about Shield Williamson . . . and that he was placing his people in deadly danger.

Not for the first time, the commander wished he had the benefit of Captain Ruhalter's input. But the captain was in a long, coffinlike capsule in one of their cargo bays, pending their return to the Federation, and in no position to offer advice.

"Thank you for your input," he told Greyhorse.

"It's my job," the physician reminded him.

Yes, thought Picard. Just as it's my job to see to it we're not caught by surprise a second time.

Captain's log, supplemental. Despite the questions that have been raised concerning the Magnians in general

175

and Serenity Santana in particular, I am still willing to trust them. Even as I speak, the colonists are manufacturing critical replacement parts for our propulsion system, phaser banks and shield generators. In exchange, we are applying our own expertise to the rebuilding of the several deflector stations that form a perimeter around Magnia, making those installations even more effective than before. I'm on my way to the planet's surface to see how the work is progressing.

Picard tapped his combadge, automatically ending his log entry, and entered the *Stargazer*'s main transporter room.

Vandermeer was the operator on duty. Nodding to the woman, the second officer crossed the floor to the transporter platform and took his place there. Then he turned back to Vandermeer and said, "Energize."

The next thing he knew, he was standing in a grassy valley full of rocky gray outcroppings, dwarfed by one of the Magnians' shield generators. Rising at least a hundred and fifty meters into the air, the device looked like a child's ice cream cone—minus the ice cream.

The nuclear reactor that powered the device was located several hundred meters underground, where the Starfleet officer couldn't see it. Fortunately, there wasn't a problem with the reactor; the problem was with the mechanism that converted the reactor's energy into a stream of polarized gravitons and projected them out into space.

A group of four was laboring at the squat, squared-off base of the generator, where an access panel had been removed. Three of the four were Magnians; the fourth was Simenon, who was showing the colonists how to alter their equipment to produce vidrion particles.

Teams were working on the city's five other shield generators as well. They hoped to have all six locations producing vidrions as well as gravitons by the time the Nuyyad returned.

As on the *Stargazer,* the retrofit process looked to be a tedious one. However, if it bought the colonists another few minutes in the upcoming confrontation, it would be well worth it.

Picard's hair lifted in the rising wind, a harbinger of the blue-gray storm clouds piling up behind the pastel skyline of Magnia. The birds that had circled the splendid towers in twos and threes earlier in the day were gone, having fled to more secure positions.

They knew a storm was coming, the second officer reflected. They just didn't know how fierce a storm it would be. But then, he had a storm of his own to worry about.

He approached Simenon without the engineer seeming to notice him. "How are we doing?" he asked, his voice echoing.

Simenon turned and stared at him blankly for a moment. Then he held up a scaly hand as if asking for Picard's forbearance, closed his eyes, and concentrated on something.

Never having seen him act that way before, Picard became concerned. Just as he was about to hike up the hill and try to rouse him, the Gnalish opened his eyes again.

The second officer studied him. "Are you all right?" he asked.

Simenon snorted. "I'm fine. I was just trying to show our friends here how to link a couple of EPS circuits."

Picard looked at him. "You were . . . *showing* them . . . ?"

The engineer scowled. "Telepathically, of course."

"Ah," said the second officer, as understanding dawned.

It made perfect sense, now that he thought about it. In a telepathic society, teamwork would bypass the spoken word. He was a little surprised that an alien mind fit in so well with the others, but he was hardly an expert on the subject.

"Come down here and bring me up to speed," said Picard.

Simenon seemed reluctant to abandon his work, but he made his way down the hillside nonetheless. When he reached the second officer, he said, "You don't really want to know how the work is going . . . do you?"

"I do," Picard told him. "But as you seem to have guessed, I also want to know about your coworkers. No doubt, you've gotten some insights into them by virtue of their telepathic contact."

The engineer looked back over his shoulder at the Magnians. "I've gotten some insights, all right. I've learned that they're a private bunch, as Eliopoulos told us. They don't like to expose any more of themselves than they have to. But I've seen enough of them to say they're also among the most courageous people I've ever met."

Picard looked at him. "Courageous . . . ?"

Simenon nodded his lizardlike head. "I know. Just a few hours ago, I was saying you were crazy to get involved with them, and now I'm extolling their virtues. But it's true about their courage. The Nuyyad may be on their way with an armada at this very moment, but these people don't let it faze them. They just go about their business as if they were fixing cooking equipment instead of shield projectors."

A glowing assessment, the second officer reflected. Perhaps *too* glowing. By the engineer's own admission, he was seldom inclined to admit that he had been in error. Yet here he was, admitting it—and with uncharacteristic enthusiasm, no less.

Simenon indicated the open access panel with a gesture. "If there's nothing else, I ought to get back to work."

"By all means," said Picard.

But as he watched the engineer climb the hillside, he had to wonder . . . was his crew really in danger of being influenced by the colonists? Was that something he needed to be concerned about? Or with an entire ship full of people to look after, was he just being a mother hen?

As he weighed the possibilities, his combadge beeped. Tapping it, he said, "Picard here."

"This is Ben Zoma, Commander. Shield Williamson just contacted us. He wants to know if we're ready to beam up his engineers."

The second officer had expected the call. After all, the Magnians couldn't supply the *Stargazer* with parts until they saw firsthand what kind of damage had been done.

He frowned, suddenly reluctant to give the colonists access to his ship. If his suspicions had any basis in reality . . .

But what was the alternative? To refuse the assistance they had risked so much to obtain? To spurn what they so desperately needed if they were to survive and warn the Federation?

"Inform Mr. Williamson that we're ready," Picard told his friend. "But see to it that his people are provided with an escort everywhere they go. And I mean *everywhere.*"

"Acknowledged," said Ben Zoma, in a tone that assured the second officer that his order would be taken seriously.

"And beam me back up as well," Picard added. He gazed at Simenon and his Magnian coworkers, who were still cooperating without the benefit of vocal expression. "I believe I've seen all I needed to see."

Pug Joseph watched the trio of colonists make their way past the brig, escorted by Ensign Montenegro. There were two men and a woman, all very human-looking, all dressed in the same green jumpsuit that Santana had worn.

And all curious enough to glance in the direction of the incarcerated mutineers as they walked by.

"He's making a mistake, you know," Werber announced with unconcealed disdain. "A big mistake."

Joseph glanced at the deposed weapons chief, who had walked up to the inner edge of his cell's translucent electromagnetic barrier. Werber's eyes looked hard with hatred and resentment.

"I beg your pardon?" said the security officer.

"Your friend Picard," the prisoner elaborated. "He's making a mistake. That Santana woman couldn't be trusted—we all know that now. And if her people are anything like her, they can't be trusted either."

Joseph frowned at Werber's remark. Since Santana had played him for a fool, he had come to resent her as much as the prisoner did—maybe more. However, he wasn't going to discuss his feelings with someone he was guarding. That was how he had gotten himself into trouble the last time.

From now on, the security officer promised himself, he was just going to do what was expected of him and leave the conversations to other people. "Whatever you say," he said.

Werber swore under his breath. "You know I'm right. And you know if I were free, I'd do something about it."

"But you're not," Joseph reminded him.

The prisoner paused for a moment. *"You* are," he said at last. "Free, I mean. You could stop these people . . . maybe even stop Picard."

"That would be mutiny," the security officer noted.

Pernell, who occupied the cell next to Werber's, laughed at the comment. Joseph frowned at him.

"Would it?" asked Werber. "Or would it be an act of heroism? You know what they say, Lieutenant . . . history is written by the victors."

Joseph didn't say anything in return. He just listened to the Magnians' footfalls recede in the distance.

"Admit it," said Werber. "Seeing those people gets under your skin the same way it gets under mine. We've been burned, both of us—and no matter what, we don't want to get burned again."

Still, the security officer didn't answer him.

It wasn't that he couldn't find a kernel of truth in what Werber was saying. It was just that Pug Joseph wasn't a mutineer.

At least, he didn't think he was.

Picard looked around the chamber into which he had materialized. It was high—at least two stories tall—with pale orange walls, a vaulted ceiling, a white marble floor, and fluted blue columns.

It was also the location, buried deep in the heart of Magnia, from which the city's half-dozen shield generators were operated.

In the center of the chamber was a steel-blue, hexagonal control device that was twice the second officer's height. Each of its six sides featured an oval screen, a keypad, and a sleek attached chair.

Five of the chairs were occupied by Magnians. The sixth was occupied by an equally human-looking figure, though his loose-fitting black togs and unruly red hair marked him as Jomar.

Some of the colonists glanced at Picard, then went back to their work. However, the Kelvan seemed not to notice him. He was too busy tapping data into his keypad.

Picard approached him. "Jomar?"

At the sound of his voice, the Kelvan turned. His pale eyes acknowledged the second officer without emotion. "Commander."

"I came down to see how you were doing," said Picard. "Mr. Williamson informs me that your work is proceeding more slowly than expected."

Jomar frowned ever so slightly. "It proceeds as it proceeds" was all the answer he seemed inclined to give. Then he returned his attention to his pale-green screen.

"Is there a problem?" asked the second officer. "Something I can help you with, perhaps?"

The Kelvan didn't look away from his work this time. "There is no problem," he stated.

Picard was far from satisfied with the response, but he nodded. "Carry on, then," he told Jomar.

He considered the Kelvan a moment longer as Jomar went about his labors. Something *was* wrong, it seemed to the second officer. Every now and then, a Magnian would frown in the alien's direction.

He decided to speak with Williamson again. With luck, the colonist could shed some light on the matter.

He had raised his hand to tap his combadge when someone said, "Commander?" The voice sounded awfully familiar.

Then he realized it wasn't a voice at all. It was just a word in his head, planted telepathically.

Turning, Picard saw Serenity Santana come through the control chamber's only doorway.

The colonist was as beautiful as when he first saw her. Her lips were full of color again, her eyes deep and searching, her long, black hair loosely cascading over one shoulder.

"Ms. Santana," Picard replied.

She feigned disapproval. "People generally use their first names here. Please . . . call me Serenity."

Remembering what she had done to the *Stargazer,* he kept his response to a single word. "Serenity."

Santana's eyes crinkled at the corners as she looked into his. It seemed to Picard that the woman was skimming the surface of his mind. "You're surprised to see me."

"I am," he admitted freely. "Apparently, your people's medical techniques are even more formidable than I was led to believe."

"To an outsider," she said, "I can see how they would appear that way." She paused. "I owe you an apology, don't I?"

The second officer shook his head from side to side. "Mr. Williamson has made your apologies for you. He spoke of the pressures the Nuyyad placed on you and Daniels."

The woman looked relieved. "Then you see I had no choice? I had to do as the Nuyyad demanded."

"So it would seem," he responded flatly, keeping his thoughts to himself as much as possible.

Santana studied him a little longer. Then she smiled wistfully. "You know," she said, "I thought we had the makings of an intriguing friendship. I hope what happened doesn't make that impossible."

Picard wanted very much to tell her that their friendship could still develop unimpeded. However, he couldn't allow himself the luxury. He held the fate of an entire crew in his hands, and he wasn't about to jeopardize it by giving rein to his emotions.

No matter how strong they might be.

Besides, Picard thought, Santana had caused the deaths of Captain Ruhalter and several other crewmen, and injured a great many more. It wasn't easy to forget that.

"I will try to keep an open mind," he told her, his tone as devoid of emotion as Jomar's.

The woman sighed. "Under the circumstances, I suppose that's the best answer I can hope to get."

Picard didn't know what to say to that. But as it turned out, he didn't have to say anything at all—because at that moment, an argument was breaking out on the other side of the shield control device.

"Are you out of your mind?" someone hollered.

"Insulting me will not mask your ineptitude," came the response.

Picard couldn't identify the first voice right off the bat, but he could certainly identify the second one. Quite clearly, it was Jomar, and his tone was an edgy one.

Circumnavigating the control device, the second officer saw what the dispute was about. The Kelvan was tapping away at one of the colonists' keypads, erasing work that had already been done.

"If you cannot follow directions properly," Jomar added, "do not participate in this activity."

The Magnian in question, a dark-haired man who had been introduced to Picard as Armor Brentano, looked around angrily at his fellow technicians. "Did you see what he did to my screen? He's insane!"

"No," said Jomar, looking up from the keypad. "I am meticulous. Perhaps it is you who are insane."

Brentano took a couple of steps toward the Kelvan. "Am I the one who just wrecked half a day's work?"

"Perhaps it was half a day's work," Jomar remarked coldly, "but it was not half a day's progress."

Picard had heard enough. "Calm down," he told the combatants, moving forward with the intention of getting between them.

Santana reinforced the commander's sentiments with her own. "Cut it out, both of you. We're not going to beat the Nuyyad by squabbling."

But Brentano and the Kelvan didn't seem to hear them—or if they did, they weren't inclined to take the advice to heart. The colonist planted a finger in Jomar's chest.

"You think you know everything," he shouted, "don't you? You slimy, tentacled son of a—"

Brentano never completed his invective.

One moment, he was standing nose-to-nose with the Kelvan, poking his forefinger into Jomar's sternum. The next, the colonist seemed to disappear, completely and utterly.

Picard couldn't believe his eyes—and he wasn't the only one shocked by what he had seen.

"What did you do to him?" demanded Santana.

The Kelvan turned to her with his customary lack of passion. "I did *this*," he replied calmly. And he pointed to a small, coarse-looking object sitting on the ground.

Picard took a closer look at the thing. It had four triangular faces, making it a perfect tetrahedron.

"What the blazes are you talking about?" snapped another of the Magnians. "Where's Brentano?"

"He is here," Jomar told her, unperturbed by the woman's display of emotion. "However, he has assumed a less disagreeable form."

The colonist still didn't understand. But Picard, to his horror, was beginning to. Kneeling, he picked up the tetrahedron and turned it over carefully in his hands.

"What he means," the commander said, "is that *this* is Brentano." He looked up at the Kelvan. "At least, it was."

The colonist screwed up her features in disbelief. "What are you talking about?" she asked Picard.

He didn't blame her for reacting that way. A hundred years earlier, Captain Kirk had to have doubted his own sanity when he discovered that his ship had been littered with tetrahedron-shaped blocks . . . and was told that they were distillations of his crew.

Just as the block in his hands, Picard surmised, was a distillation of Armor Brentano.

He put the tetrahedron back on the ground, then looked up at Jomar. "Change him back," he said.

The Kelvan's eyes narrowed, but he didn't answer.

"Change him *back*."

"He was insolent," Jomar remarked.

"Nonetheless," Picard insisted, his tone unrelenting.

The Kelvan reached for one of the studs on his belt. A moment later, as if by magic, Brentano was standing in front of them again, looking a trifle dazed but otherwise unharmed.

"What happened . . . ?" he asked.

"That's what *I* would like to know," said Santana. She glared at Jomar with unconcealed animosity.

"A misunderstanding," Picard assured her. "Nothing more. Nor is it likely to happen again." He glanced at Jomar. "Isn't that right?"

The Kelvan shrugged. "It will not happen again," he agreed.

"It would be best," the second officer advised, "if we forgot about this and resumed our work."

Taking her cue from him, Santana managed to submerge her anger. "Commander Picard is right," she told the other Magnians. "Let's just get back to what we were doing."

Having done her part to smoothe things over, she helped Brentano back to his seat. A moment later, Jomar and the other colonists returned to their workstations as well.

Nonetheless, the damage had been done. The second officer could see that with crystal clarity. None of the colonists would be comfortable working with Jomar after what they had just seen.

Nor could Picard blame them.

Unfortunately, the Kelvan was still the foremost authority on vidrion generation. Despite everything, he would have to remain in the control chamber for the foreseeable future.

But he wouldn't remain the *Stargazer*'s only representative there. The second officer resolved to dispatch one of his other engineers as well—perhaps Simenon himself, since he and the Kelvan seemed to have a good rapport.

As for Santana . . . she seemed inclined to remain alongside Brentano for the moment, helping him see what it was about his work that had produced the Kelvan's objection. A good idea, Picard reflected.

He had barely completed the thought when Santana glanced at him. *I'm glad you think so,* she replied.

The second officer acknowledged her remark with a nod. Then he tapped his communicator and asked Vandermeer to beam him up.

He would still speak with Williamson, to at least let the man know what had taken place. Despite Picard's concerns about the Magnians, this alliance was still important to the *Stargazer.*

And he didn't want Jomar's penchant for insensitivity to wreck it.

CHAPTER 13

Picard watched Shield Williamson's reaction from across a large and ornate wooden desk.

"With luck," the man said, "what the Kelvan did was an isolated incident and we'll see no repeats of it."

"That is my hope as well," the Starfleet officer told him.

Williamson sat back in his chair. "Actually, Commander, I'm glad you're here. My engineers have pointed something out to me."

"Oh?" said Picard.

"They see an opportunity to not only repair your equipment, but to modify it—much as your people are modifying our shield technology to make use of the Kelvan's vidrion particles."

"Which systems are we talking about?" asked the second officer.

"Sensors and tractors," said Williamson. "However, I should tell you . . . for these modifications to be of any utility, you'll require Magnian operators." He paused. "And from what I gather, you're already uncomfortable with our presence aboard your ship."

Picard was surprised by the remark, but he absorbed it without flinching. "Am I to assume you've been reading our thoughts?"

The colonist smiled. "We haven't had to. It's apparent in the way your people look at us, the way they follow us wherever we go."

"As I instructed them," the second officer admitted.

"Because you don't trust us?"

Picard sighed. "Because I cannot afford to."

"An honest answer," Williamson observed.

"To an honest question," Picard replied.

They both fell silent for a moment.

"Consider this," Williamson said at last. "We're operating on faith as much as you are. Once we help you repair your warp drive and your weapons systems, what's to keep you from taking off for Federation space . . . and leaving us to defend ourselves against the Nuyyad?"

The second officer frowned. "Which could be why you want to place some of your people on the *Stargazer* . . . to keep us from reneging on our bargain when the attack comes."

The Magnian's eyes narrowed. "Touché."

Picard shrugged. "My apologies. It seemed to be the obvious response."

This time, the room seemed to echo with their silence.

"Any agreement," said Williamson, "is only as strong as the intentions of the parties involved in it. If there's some way I can convince you we mean only good . . ."

Unfortunately, Picard couldn't think of one.

"Mind you," he said, "I *want* to trust you. My instincts *tell* me to trust you. I just don't have the *luxury* of trusting you."

And his trust had been watered down by recent events, though he didn't feel compelled to mention that.

Williamson smiled a little sadly. "Does that mean that you're turning down our offer?"

The second officer couldn't deny the appeal of sensor and tractor enhancements, considering they didn't know how many

Nuyyad vessels they might eventually be facing—or how power-ful they might be.

He took a moment to weigh the benefits against the risks—and made his decision. "In the interest of defending Magnia as well as the *Stargazer*," he said, "I'll accept your operators."

Williamson nodded. "You've made the right choice, Com-mander."

I certainly hope so, thought Picard.

Lieutenant Vigo sat with his back against the curvature of a Jefferies tube and watched another piece of conduit casing go sailing past him.

A couple of colonists were waiting to receive the component farther down the line. Even from a distance, the acting weapons chief could see the concentration on their faces—a concentration that had been there since earlier that morning, when the *Stargazer* beamed up a supply of replacement parts from the planet's surface.

"How's it going?" asked Lieutenant Iulus, a curly-haired secu-rity officer, as he made his way toward Vigo from a perpendicu-lar tube.

"Rather well, it seems," said the Pandrilite, watching the Mag-nians snatch the piece of casing out of the air and fit it into the conduit they were building. "These people have hauled more parts in the last hour than you and I could have lugged in a day."

Iulus nodded. "Amazing."

"Very much so," said Vigo. "And yet, separately, none of them can move one of these parts even an inch."

The security officer looked at him. "So how do they do it?"

"By working together," the weapons officer replied. "When they pool their efforts, they raise their effectiveness in leaps and bounds. At least, that's how it was explained to me."

"You know what?" said Iulus. "They can do it anyway they want—as long as they're finished before the Nuyyad get here."

Vigo grunted softly. That was one way of looking at the situation.

Unfortunately, Picard had insisted that every colonist on the *Stargazer* have an escort. Clearly, the *commander* didn't want the Magnians to do their jobs any way they wanted.

It seemed like a shift from Picard's earlier stance, when he had been willing to place more trust in the colonists. But then, Vigo mused, even commanding officers were allowed to change their minds.

"Lieutenant?" called one of the colonists from his place at the end of the tube. "Could I see you for a moment?"

It was the first time any of the Magnians had asked for Vigo's help. He wondered what the man wanted.

"I'll see you later," he told Iulus.

"Sure," said the security officer.

Then the Pandrilite moved his bulk through the tube, wishing fervently that he could have glided through it like one of the casing components instead.

Jean-Luc Picard entered his quarters, sought out his bed and sank into it gratefully. It had been a long day.

All in all, the work had gone well—both on the *Stargazer* and on the planet's surface. Simenon had reported that the warp drive was almost functional again, and the colonists were on the verge of bringing their shield generators back on-line.

And having had a chance to look at Williamson's proposal regarding the *Stargazer*'s sensor and tractor systems, it appealed to him even more. If it meant having a few colonists on board during the impending battle, he could live with it.

After all, he had gotten this far taking chances. With luck, the same approach would get his ship home.

The only fly in the ointment was the incident with Jomar. However, there hadn't been any reprise of it, nor had Picard been forced to deal with any other instances of hostility.

He closed his eyes, knowing the work on his ship would continue unabated throughout the night. By morning, the second officer hoped, there would be even better things to report.

Abruptly, as if fate were intent on being cruel to him, he heard a beeping sound. Envisioning an emergency, he swung his legs out of bed and returned to his anteroom.

"Come," he said.

The doors to his quarters slid apart, revealing Lieutenant Vigo. The Pandrilite entered the room a little tentatively.

"What is it?" Picard asked wearily.

"I have some news for you, sir." Vigo looked apologetic. "News you are not going to like."

Picard ran his fingers through his hair. "Go ahead."

"Remember the shuttle that exploded prematurely? When we were trying to liberate the colony?"

The second officer nodded. "Of course."

"At the time," said the Pandrilite, "it appeared to be an accident. But just a little while ago, one of the Magnian engineers came across some evidence that indicates otherwise."

"You're saying it was sabotage?" Picard asked.

"Judge for yourself, sir," Vigo told him.

Crossing to the second officer's workstation, he brought up a red and blue diagram of a secondary command junction. "This is one of the switching points from my bridge console to the remote control node. During the battle, all my signals to the shuttles passed through it."

"All right," said Picard.

"Take a close look," Vigo advised. "What do you see?"

The second officer did as the Pandrilite suggested. After a moment, he realized what Vigo was talking about. The junction had been modified—purposely, it appeared.

A second data line had been spliced in, allowing the command junction to simultaneously accommodate two completely separate sets of signals. And since the first signal would go through unhindered, the change wouldn't show up on a routine diagnostic.

If someone had wished, they could have taken advantage of this situation to blow up one of the *Stargazer*'s shuttles without warning. In fact, they could have blown up *all* the shuttles.

Picard looked at the acting weapons chief. "It seems we have a saboteur on our hands."

"That was my conclusion too, sir."

"Do you have any idea who it might be?" the second officer asked.

Vigo shook his hairless, blue head. "No, sir. However, I believe there are ways to find out."

"See that you pursue them," Picard told him. "However, you must do so without letting anyone know what you're doing. We need to keep this privileged information for the time being."

"Yes, sir," said the weapons officer, and left the room with a laudable sense of urgency.

Picard watched the doors to his quarters slide closed, leaving him alone again. Dropping into a chair, he heaved a sigh.

Just when he thought the dawn might be in sight, the shadowy figure of a saboteur had appeared on the horizon.

He needed to think this through, he told himself. But he was too fatigued to do so on his own. Looking up at the intercom grid in the ceiling, he called upon the one man he felt he could trust implicitly.

"Mr. Ben Zoma," he said, "this is Commander Picard."

"Ben Zoma here," came the reply.

"Meet me in my quarters," the second officer told him. "I've learned something you may find interesting."

Gilaad Ben Zoma sat back in his chair and considered the problem with which his friend had presented him.

Finally, he spoke. "There were only two unknown quantities on the ship when we came up with the notion of using shuttles as tactical weapons. One of them was Jomar. The other was Serenity Santana."

"Ms. Santana was unconscious," Picard reminded him.

The second officer was seated on the other side of his quarters' anteroom, a cup of hot tea resting on a table beside him. He looked as if he would much rather have gone to bed than begun unraveling a mystery.

"True," Ben Zoma conceded. "But do you remember what you told me about her brain activity? How it remained elevated even when she was unconscious? For all we know, she could have been manipulating someone in order to sabotage that shuttle."

The second officer tilted his head. "You mean . . . one of us?"

"A crewman," Ben Zoma suggested. "You, me . . . anyone, really. They might not even have a recollection of having helped her."

"On the other hand," said Picard, "Santana has already admitted her treachery regarding the ambush. If she had used a pawn to sabotage the shuttle, why wouldn't she have admitted that as well?"

"Good point," Ben Zoma acknowledged. Suddenly, something occurred to him. "Unless she had two different agendas . . ."

"I beg your pardon?"

"What if Santana's role in the ambush was what she claimed it was—a response to the Nuyyad's threats—but her sabotage of the shuttle was for a different purpose entirely?"

Picard mulled it over. "That would explain why her fellow colonist didn't think twice about bringing our attention to the altered junction."

"On the other hand," said Ben Zoma, arguing with his own proposition, "what could she have gained by blowing up the shuttle?"

"The same as Jomar," said the second officer. "Nothing—except possibly the sacrifice of their own lives."

"We're lacking a motive," Ben Zoma noted.

"So it would seem," said his friend.

Ben Zoma looked at him. "You might want to confront one of

them about this. Or maybe mention it to our friend Williamson. One of them is bound to tell you something interesting."

The commander considered it. After a while, he shook his head. "I don't think so, Gilaad. I want to identify the culprit before he or she realizes we have suspicions."

"Then we need to keep tabs on them around the clock. Follow their every move until they slip up."

"If you say so," said Picard.

"I'll volunteer to hound Jomar," Ben Zoma offered.

"And Santana?"

"I'll send Pug down to do that. He knows her as well as any of us. And after the way Santana humiliated him, he'll be that much more determined to catch her redhanded."

The second officer took a deep breath. "We need to unmask this saboteur—and quickly. Otherwise, there is no telling when a key system might betray us, repairs or no repairs."

Ben Zoma sympathized with his friend. Commanding a vessel was a difficult task at the best of times. In a situation where the ground kept shifting underfoot, it was nearly impossible.

"We'll catch your saboteur," he assured Picard.

The second officer grunted. "You sound rather certain."

Ben Zoma smiled. "I've never let you down before," he said, wishing he were even half as confident as he sounded.

It was early the next morning, as Picard was getting dressed, that he got a call from Shield Williamson.

Taking it in his quarters, he saw the Magnian's face appear on his monitor screen. "Is everything all right?" asked the second officer.

"That depends," said Williamson.

"On what?"

"On how you feel about having Serenity Santana board your ship again."

Picard looked at the colonist. "For what reason?"

"One of the technicians we planned to send up isn't feeling

well. Santana is the only other Magnian who's qualified to do the job."

Troubled by the proposition, the second officer shook his head. "You must know how this looks."

"Like I'm trying to pull a fast one," Williamson conceded. "Of course, the decision is entirely yours."

Picard considered his options—and the old saying came to him: Keep your friends close and your enemies closer. And it would certainly be a simpler matter for Pug Joseph to keep an eye on Santana if she was working there on the *Stargazer.*

"Send her up," he told the Magnian.

But even as he extended the invitation, he could feel himself inching further out on the limb he had chosen.

CHAPTER 14

Captain's log, supplemental. At last, we are ready. Magnia's defenses have been fully resurrected—and thanks to Jomar, they should be in a better position to withstand the Nuyyad now that their shields will be laced with vidrion particles. The Stargazer's systems have been restored as well, from our warp drive to our deflector grid. What's more, the colonists have made use of their technical expertise and their inborn talents to provide us with a couple of tools we didn't have before—improved sensor and tractor functions. Unfortunately, we have made no discernible progress in our search for a saboteur, but we remain hopeful. After all, we have some of our best people on the case.

Pug Joseph entered the tiny engineering support room on Deck 26 and spotted Serenity Santana among her colleagues.

The dark-haired woman was shoulder to shoulder with them

on her knees, fitting the forward dorsal tractor control node with devices capable of marrying telekinetic energy to the attractive and repellant forces in a directed graviton stream. Every so often she would glance at one of her fellow colonists and receive a glance in return, then go back to work.

None of the Magnians said a word. However, they all seemed to know what to do with the equipment they had brought with them.

Ensign Montenegro, an engineer, was standing in the corner of the room, his arms folded across his chest. Like Joseph, Montenegro was just a spectator. Their guests were the ones applying all the elbow grease.

The security officer felt uncomfortable being in the same room as Santana. If it had been up to him, he would have left. But he was under orders, so he stayed and kept an eye on the woman.

After a few minutes, she seemed to sense his scrutiny and looked back over her shoulder at him. He didn't look away, but he didn't acknowledge her either. He just stood there and did his job.

Santana worked for another ten minutes or so. Then she got up, stretched her muscles and walked over to Joseph. He felt his jaw clench.

"Long time no see," said the colonist.

The security officer didn't utter a word in response. He just stood there, returning her scrutiny.

"I'm sorry for pulling the wool over your eyes," she said.

Joseph didn't give her the satisfaction of an answer.

"I mean it," Santana added. "I've already told Commander Picard, but I want to tell you as well."

Still, he remained silent.

"You've got to want to say *something* to me," the woman told him.

He did. But he didn't say it.

Santana looked at him a moment longer, her dark eyes full of what appeared to be pain. Then she returned to her work.

Joseph didn't like the idea of hurting her. However, as he had said to himself often enough, he was determined not to give the colonist an opportunity to fool him again.

Carter Greyhorse had been busy over the last few days, to say the least—busy with Santana and Leach and the less severely injured survivors of their encounter with the Nuyyad.

And with the exception of a few helpless moments, he hadn't spent any of that time thinking about Gerda Asmund.

But when the medical officer returned from Magnia, he hadn't had the option of burying himself in patient care any longer—and his preoccupation with the navigator had threatened to paralyze him in a duranium straitjacket of despair.

Despair, because he had no chance with her. He had come to accept that, at least on an intellectual level. They were too different. She was vibrant, vigorous, full of life. And he was . . . *not.*

So, in the absence of an urgent need for his medical skills, Greyhorse had come up with another project in which to immerse himself—a project he had begun even before he saw Gerda in the gym. He had renewed his interest in the creation of synthetic psilosynine.

The doctor had even gone so far as to replicate a batch of the neurotransmitter himself, following the guidelines of the Betazoid scientist who had pioneered the process. And now, having brought the stuff back to sickbay, he was testing its integrity at his office computer.

It was turning out to be a success, too. Not just the psilosynine itself, but its ability to take his mind off Gerda.

Just as Greyhorse acknowledged that, he caught a glimpse of someone walking into sickbay.

Turning away from his screen, he saw that it was Joseph from security. Under normal circumstances, the doctor would have completed his tests, then gone to see what Joseph wanted from him. However, their circumstances were anything but normal these days.

Getting up from his computer terminal, Greyhorse exited his

office and emerged into the central triage area. "Something I can do for you?" he asked the security officer.

"I hope so," said Joseph. He looked around. "And I hope you'll keep this conversation confidential—as a matter of ship's security."

Ship's security? "All right," Greyhorse responded, wondering what the problem might be.

"You treated Serenity Santana while she was comatose?"

"I did," Greyhorse confirmed.

"And you told Commander Picard that you saw her brain waves spike when we were approaching her world?"

"That's correct," said the medical officer. Suddenly, it occurred to him where Joseph might be going with this. "Santana's all right, isn't she?"

The other man looked up at him, jolted from his line of questioning. "She's fine, as far as I can tell."

"Then this isn't about her health?" asked Greyhorse.

"No," Joseph assured him. "It's about an act of sabotage." And he went on to describe the way one of their command junctions had been tampered with.

"But what does this have to do with Ms. Santana?" asked the doctor.

"Obviously, she couldn't have sabotaged the shuttle herself. But Commander Picard and Lieutenant Ben Zoma think she might have manipulated someone else into doing it."

"Someone else?" Greyhorse echoed, considering the possibility for the first time. "You mean . . ."

"You," said Joseph. He looked disturbed by what he was saying. "Or me. Or anyone on the ship."

The doctor sat down on the edge of a biobed and thought about it. It was an eerie proposition at best. Unfortunately, he didn't know enough about Santana's abilities to confirm the theory or deny it.

"It's possible," he said at last. "But I can't say for certain."

The security officer looked disappointed. "Commander Picard thought you might say that."

Greyhorse had an idea. "Have you checked the internal sensor logs? They would tell you who might have approached that command junction."

Joseph smiled a tolerant smile. "That was the first thing we tried. But internal sensors aren't very dependable in the vicinity of the warp engines, which is where the junction was located. And whoever did the tampering was smart enough to take off his or her combadge so we wouldn't be able to track them that way either."

The doctor shrugged. "It was just a thought."

"Thanks anyway," said the security officer.

But he didn't leave. He just stood there, his eyes glazing over, as if he had fallen deep into thought.

"Lieutenant?" said Greyhorse.

Joseph looked at him as if he had woken from a dream. "Hmm?"

"Are you feeling all right?" the physician inquired.

"I'm okay. Just a little . . . preoccupied is all." The security officer hesitated. Then he said, "Can I level with you?"

Greyhorse nodded. "Certainly."

Joseph smiled again—a little sheepishly, this time. "To be honest, I don't have a whole lot of friends on the ship. It's always been that way for me, I don't know why. But when I was guarding Ms. Santana, I . . . well, I sort of came to like her."

"As a friend?" the doctor asked.

"That," said the security officer, "and maybe a little more. I know it sounds ridiculous, but I think I fell for her the first time I saw her—when she was sitting on her cot in the brig."

Even Greyhorse had to chuckle at that. "Quite an image," he conceded.

"I thought she liked me too," Joseph confided. "Maybe not the way I liked *her*, but at least a little. Then I found out that she was playing me for a chump, right from the start."

"Playing *all* of us," the doctor interjected.

"But me most of all," the security officer insisted. "I mean, I trusted her. I let a pretty face make me forget my training." He looked embarassed. "I'll bet that never happened to *you.*"

Greyhorse was about to agree with the man, at least inwardly—when a sequence of images flashed through his mind, coming one after the other with jolting familiarity.

Out of the corner of his eye, he saw someone carrying a wounded Gerda into sickbay. Then he took another look and realized that it was Gerda who was doing the carrying, and that it was Leach who had been hurt.

The doctor's heart began to pound as it had pounded then. Even if he managed to forget everything else about Gerda, he would never forget that sight as long as he lived.

Greyhorse regained his composure. "Never," he agreed, lying through his teeth. "But that doesn't mean you should be beating yourself up over it. We're people, Lieutenant, not machines. We have feelings. And sometimes, like it or not, those feelings get in the way of our jobs."

Joseph considered the advice. "Maybe you're right."

But Greyhorse knew the security officer didn't mean it. He would continue to berate himself, advice or no advice.

Well, he told himself, at least I tried.

"If you think of anything that might shed some light," said Joseph, "let me know, all right?"

"I will," the doctor promised him.

But as the security officer left, Greyhorse wasn't thinking about Joseph's problem. He wasn't thinking about psilosynine either. He was thinking about Gerda Asmund again.

Phigus Simenon looked up at the wedge of blue sky caught between the spires of Magnia's tallest towers.

He couldn't see the *Stargazer.* But then, he hadn't expected to. The ship was too far away even to be spotted at night, when the atmosphere of this world wasn't suffused with its sun's light.

Abruptly, the engineer heard his communicator beep. It was what he had been waiting for. Tapping it, he said, "Simenon here."

"This is Commander Picard. I'm taking us out of orbit."

"Acknowledged," said the engineer.

"Good luck," Picard told him.

"To you, too," Simenon replied.

"Picard out."

The Gnalish stared at the sky a little longer. Then he turned to Armor Brentano, who had been attending him patiently.

"Ready?" asked the colonist.

"Ready," said Simenon.

Then he followed Brentano across the plaza to the elegant pink building that housed the shield control center, where they would bide their time until the enemy arrived.

Less than seventeen hours after Picard removed the *Stargazer* from Magnia's sensor range, he heard Gerda Asmund announce the approach of two vessels she had spotted on her monitor.

The second officer had been leaning over Vigo's weapons panel, supervising some last-minute diagnostics. Moving to a position just in front of the captain's center seat, he gazed at the viewscreen.

"Can you give me a visual?" he asked.

Gerda worked for a moment. Then the screen filled with the sight of not one Nuyyad vessel but two, both of them as big and powerful-looking as the ones Picard had seen earlier. Obviously, the enemy believed that would be more than enough to put down the *Stargazer.*

We will have to show them the error of their ways, thought the second officer. "Red alert," he said. "All hands to battle stations. Raise shields and power up phasers."

"Raising shields," Gerda confirmed.

"Diverting power to phasers," said Vigo.

"Their speed?" asked Picard.

"Full impulse," Idun reported.

This was it, the second officer told himself, glaring at the enemy. This was the test of all their hard work. They would either turn the Nuyyad back or be destroyed in the attempt.

"Any sign that they see us?" he asked his navigator.

"None, sir," said Gerda, her hands darting over her control panel. "They're heading straight for the colony."

As we expected, thought Picard. But he couldn't help thinking of Simenon, whom he had left to help defend Magnia.

He hoped that he and the engineer would both be around to congratulate each other when the battle was over.

"Here they come," said Simenon, tracking the two yellow blips on his black sensor screen.

Brentano, who was seated to the engineer's left, cast a thought: *Shields are at full strength.*

Phasers powered and ready, replied Hilton-Smith, the blond woman to Simenon's right.

"Target phasers," intoned Shield Williamson, who had taken up a position behind the Gnalish.

Targeting, Hilton-Smith responded.

Range in thirty seconds, Brentano informed them.

On Simenon's screen, one of the yellow blips unleashed a series of green energy bursts. A moment later, the other blip followed suit. Apparently, the engineer reflected, the Nuyyad's weapons range was a little greater than that of the colonists.

Direct hits, said Brentano. *But no damage to report. Shields are holding at eighty-six percent.*

Range in fifteen seconds, thought Hilton-Smith.

Simenon watched the blips get closer. Again, they fired their vidrion cannons, and this time he thought he could feel a little tremor in the floor beneath him.

Shields down to seventy-two percent, Brentano told them.

Range in five seconds, Hilton-Smith reported, her eyes reflecting the light from her screen. *Four. Three. Two . . .*

"Fire!" Williamson commanded, his voice ripping through the chamber.

On Simenon's monitor, a half dozen red phaser beams reached out and pummeled the enemy vessels. Inwardly, the Gnalish cheered. After all, he had personally helped increase the force of those beams.

"Their shields are taking a beating," observed Brentano, pure excitement in his voice.

Of course, none of them expected to win this battle from the ground. If the Magnians were going to prevail, their allies in the heavens would have to take the lead.

Just as the engineer thought that, he saw a third blip enter the picture. *The* Stargazer *has arrived,* he announced silently, but not without a certain amount of pride.

Picard eyed the bright, diamond-shaped ships on his viewscreen. "Fire again!" he thundered.

A second time, the *Stargazer*'s phasers stabbed at the enemy vessels, wreaking havoc with their shields. What's more, the Magnians' sensor enhancements allowed each beam to find its precise target.

Finally, the Nuyyad must have realized that something new had been added to the mix. Both ships peeled away, resorting to evasive maneuvers.

But Picard knew he had the enemy off-balance. The last thing he wanted to do was give them time to regroup.

"Stay on them," he told Idun Asmund.

"Aye, sir," said his helm officer, following one of the Nuyyad ships as it sped away.

"Get a lock on their aft shield generators," he told Vigo.

Again, they were able to benefit from the Magnians' participation in their sensor operations. The Pandrilite looked up. "Got them, sir."

"Fire!" barked Picard.

The *Stargazer*'s phasers raked the enemy's hindquarters with a devastating barrage. Unfortunately, they could dog only one vessel at a time—and the second officer was wary of getting caught in a crossfire.

He turned to his navigator. "Where is the other one?"

"Bearing two-five-two-mark-six," Gerda told him. "But it's got its hands full with what the Magnians are throwing at it."

Picard nodded, satisfied with the way the battle was going. It was just the way they had planned it.

Suddenly, Gerda swiveled in her chair, her eyes wide with surprise and anger. "Shields are down!" she snarled.

The second officer didn't understand. "We haven't even been hit," he pointed out.

"Nonetheless," the navigator insisted, "shields are down!"

Picard cursed beneath his breath. "Fall back!" he told Idun, the words leaving a bitter taste in his mouth.

But as if the Nuyyad had sensed the *Stargazer*'s untimely vulnerability, the enemy vessel wheeled and came after her. The second officer looked on helplessly as the Nuyyad's cannons belched vidrion fury.

"Brace yourselves!" he cried out.

A moment later, the deck slid out from under him and sparks shot across the bridge. No, Picard thought. This cannot be happening. We *had* them.

Hadn't the enemy been at a distinct tactical disadvantage? And hadn't they just reconstructed the *Stargazer*'s deflector grid unit by unit? How could it have failed again so quickly?

Abruptly, a chill climbed the rungs of the second officer's spine. *The saboteur,* he thought. It was the only explanation.

A second vidrion barrage pounded them, sending the *Stargazer* reeling to starboard. Flung into the side of the captain's chair, Picard heard the deckplates shriek like banshees.

"Evasive maneuvers," he told Idun. "Pattern Omega!"

As the helm officer sent them spiraling out of harm's way, Picard tried to take stock of his options. Shields or no shields, he told himself, he had to create an opportunity to strike back.

Then Vigo called out the best thing the second officer could have hoped to hear. "I've got the shields back on-line, sir!"

Uncertain as to how long they would *stay* on-line, Picard turned to the viewscreen. The Nuyyad vessel was bearing down on them, following up on the surprising damage done by its volleys. Quite possibly, the enemy commander expected to finish them off.

The fellow was going to be disappointed, the second officer thought. With the *Stargazer*'s shields restored, Picard had all his options in front of him again—and he knew which one he wanted to use.

"Divert power to tractor beam," he snapped. "Target a point on their shields in line with their main emitter."

Normally, a tractor beam was useless against an enemy's shields. However, this wasn't just any tractor beam. It was one that had the minds of more than a dozen Magnians to strengthen and manipulate it.

"Ready phasers and photon torpedoes!" the second officer called out.

But even as he gave the order, he saw the enemy release a volley of bright green vidrion packets. They loomed on the forward viewer, growing gigantic before Picard could do anything about them, finally filling the screen from edge to edge.

Then they tore into the *Stargazer* with all their savage, disruptive force. But Jomar's vidrion-laced deflectors seemed to hold against the Nuyyad assault, keeping its destructive potential at arm's length.

"Engage tractor!" the second officer told his navigator.

Gerda did as she was told—and used the ghostly beam to punch a hole through the enemy's shields. Seeing the aperture, Picard smiled a grim smile and glanced at Vigo.

"Fire!" he said.

Instantly, the weapons chief drove his phaser bolts through the

gap created by the tractor beam, piercing the outer skin of the
Nuyyad ship. Then he followed up with a couple of photon torpedoes.

With neither shields nor hull to stop them or even slow them
down, the torpedoes entered the enemy vessel and vented their
matter-antimatter payload in a massive outpouring of yellow-
white splendor.

Even if he had wanted to watch the resulting debris spin off
into space, the second officer didn't have the time. He had to turn
his attention to his other adversary.

"Give me a visual of the other ship," he told Gerda.

The image on the viewscreen changed, showing him the lone
surviving diamond shape. It was exchanging fire with the planet's
surface, perhaps unaware that its sister vessel had been destroyed.

"Target their deflectors," said Picard, "just as we did before.
Ready phasers and torpedoes."

"Ready, sir," came Vigo's reply.

The Nuyyad vessel began to come about, leaving Magnia
alone for the moment. Obviously, its commander had recognized
a more pressing concern.

"Engage tractor beam!" snapped the second officer. On the
viewscreen, the pale, barely visible shaft of the tractor opened a
window in the enemy's shields. "Fire!" he commanded.

The diamond shape didn't stand a chance. Before it could
launch an offensive of its own, before it could try to get out of
the *Stargazer*'s range, a pair of crimson phaser beams sliced
through the opening in its defenses and penetrated its hull.

As before, Vigo followed the phaser attack with a pair of photon torpedoes. And as before, they exploded inside the enemy
ship, blotting out the stars with a splash of deadly, yellow-white
brilliance.

"Well done," said Picard. He turned to Gerda. "Damage?"

"Shields are down twenty-two percent," the navigator reported.
"Otherwise, all systems are functioning at rated capacity."

The second officer was pleased beyond all expectation. "Well done indeed," he told his officers.

"Sir," said Paxton from his communications console, "Mr. Williamson is hailing us from the surface."

Picard smiled. "Put him on screen, Lieutenant."

A moment later, the Magnian's visage appeared. "Tell me our instruments are accurate, Commander. The Nuyyad . . . ?"

"Have been destroyed," the second officer confirmed.

Williamson looked relieved. "And the *Stargazer?*"

"Has not been," Picard said. "How is Magnia?"

"Unharmed as well," the colonist reported. "Our only casualty was a stand of old trees of which I was rather fond."

"It could have been worse," the second officer told him.

He glanced at Vigo, recalling their momentary shield failure, and contemplated the danger in which it had placed them. If the weapons chief hadn't managed to get the deflectors back on-line . . .

"Much worse," he added.

CHAPTER **15**

Picard sat behind Captain Ruhalter's desk and regarded his acting weapons chief. "What happened out there?" he asked.

Vigo frowned. "Honestly, sir . . . when we lost our shields, I was too surprised to even think for a moment. After all, nothing like that had ever happened to me. Then I thought of the saboteur."

"As did I," the second officer admitted.

"I remembered how he had run a parallel data line through that command junction, and I started thinking of which command junctions were involved in the deflector function. As it turned out, there were only four of them, so I began bypassing them one after the other. After I bypassed the third one, we regained shield control."

"And you brought the deflectors back up," Picard concluded.

The weapons officer nodded. "That's correct, sir."

Picard sat back in his chair. "I hope I don't have to tell you how critical that action was. If not for you, Lieutenant, our encounter with the Nuyyad might have had a very different conclusion."

Vigo looked a little embarassed. "I was glad to be of help, sir."

"You can be of further help," the second officer told him. "I want you to examine this altered shield command junction. See if you can glean anything from it—perhaps in comparison to the first altered junction we discovered. Then report back to me."

"Aye, sir," said Vigo. But he didn't get up from his chair right away.

"What is it?" asked Picard.

The Pandrilite looked apologetic. "Begging your pardon, sir, but are we going to return to the Federation with the saboteur on board?"

The second officer was about to ask why that would be of particular concern to his weapons chief. Then it hit him with the impact of a directed energy beam: *the galactic barrier.*

If their shields dropped just before they went through it, they would be naked to the phenomenon. The crew would be completely and utterly exposed to the barrier's mysterious and volatile energies.

Kirk's ship had had some protection, primitive as it might be by contemporary standards, and Gary Mitchell had still become a being capable of enslaving his entire species. How much more monstrous an entity might be created on a vessel that had no shielding at all?

"I see your point," said Picard.

Clearly, they couldn't go back to the Federation as they had planned. Not yet, anyway. First, they would have to identify and neutralize the saboteur, then scour the ship for lingering signs of his or her handiwork.

"I will find the saboteur," the second officer promised. "I don't yet know how, but I will do it."

"I'm sure you will, sir," said Vigo, his expression an earnest one. "If there's anything I can do . . ."

"I'll let you know," Picard told him. "And Lieutenant . . ."

"Aye, sir?" said the weapons officer.

"As before, not a word of this to anyone."

"You can trust me, sir," Vigo assured him.

No doubt, Picard mused. He wished he could say that about *everyone* aboard the *Stargazer.*

Carter Greyhorse walked into the *Stargazer's* lounge, where Commander Picard was already seated at the black oval table.

"Doctor," said the second officer, by way of acknowledgment.

"You wanted to speak with me?" asked Greyhorse, pulling out a chair opposite Picard's and sitting down.

"I did," said the commander. "But I'd prefer to wait until the others arrive before I begin our discussion."

Others? Greyhorse wondered.

He had barely completed the thought when Ben Zoma, Simenon, Paxton, and Cariello walked into the room, one right after the other. Nodding to the doctor, they took their seats.

Greyhorse hadn't realized that this was to be a staff meeting. But then, he could easily have missed that part of Picard's summons.

Ever since his visit from Pug Joseph, the medical officer had been unable to keep from thinking about Gerda Asmund again. He was so preoccupied, so distracted, he hadn't even felt an urge to complete his tests on the psilosynine he had synthesized.

And with renewed longing had come a renewed sense of despair. Gerda was so forceful, so graceful, so vibrant . . . so unlike Greyhorse. What chance could he possibly have with her?

"Doctor Greyhorse?"

Greyhorse turned to Picard. "Yes?"

"I would like to get underway now," said the second officer.

The doctor looked around and saw that Vigo and Jomar had joined them without his realizing it. They were sitting at the table along with the others. My god, he told himself, it's worse than I thought.

"The reason I called this meeting," said Picard, "is to discuss what course of action we should adopt next."

Simenon looked at him. "I'm a little confused. Aren't we supposed to be going home?"

"Yes," said Cariello, "to warn the Federation about the Nuyyad?"

"Indeed," Picard replied, "that is the agenda I had intended to follow. However, it occurs to me there is something more we can accomplish here before we return."

"Explain," said the Kelvan.

"As you will recall," said Picard, "we were told about a supply depot that the enemy had set up on this side of the galactic barrier—one that seemed to be a critical part of their invasion plans."

Greyhorse thought he could see where the second officer was headed. "You want to scout out this depot?"

Picard shook his head from side to side. "No," he told his assembled officers and allies. "I want to destroy it."

The doctor looked at him, struck dumb by the audacity of his declaration. So, apparently, was everyone else sitting around the table.

"Are you sure that's wise, sir?" asked Paxton.

"I believe it is," said the second officer. "For one thing, you saw how easily we handled those two Nuyyad ships."

"But not without the help of the Magnians' phaser batteries," Ben Zoma reminded him.

"No question," Picard responded, "the colonists on the ground played a critical part in our victory. However, I believe we would have defeated the Nuyyad even without their assistance. Our enhanced sensor and tractor functions provided us with a much greater tactical advantage than I would ever have imagined possible."

"Let me understand this," said Simenon, his slitted eyes narrowing in his scaly face. "You want to attack an enemy installation—where we're liable to face a force considerably larger than two ships? And you want us to do it entirely on our own?"

The second officer leaned forward. "I want to take the Nuyyad by surprise—and they won't be expecting a countermaneuver so

212

soon after their assault on Magnia. On the other hand, if we opt
to alert the Federation and watch them put together a task force,
the Nuyyad will have had time to increase the strength of their
defenses."

"Are we even certain there *is* a depot?" asked Greyhorse.
"Wasn't that just the bait in the Nuyyad's trap?"

"It exists," the second officer insisted. "Shield Williamson has
given me the coordinates."

"Can we believe him this time?" asked Cariello.

"A fair question," Picard told her. "But since our arrival here,
the colonists have made good on all their promises. I no longer
feel compelled to question their sincerity."

"Nor do I," Simenon conceded.

"The elimination of the depot is a worthwhile goal," Vigo observed. "One worth taking a risk to achieve."

"Exactly right," said Picard. "We can vastly improve Starfleet's tactical position, giving Command the time it needs to
prepare for an invasion . . . or perhaps even head it off."

"If we're successful," Simenon argued.

"Of course," the Pandrilite conceded. "However, we can
send out a subspace message either way, so the Federation will
be warned about the Nuyyad even if the *Stargazer* is destroyed."

"Well?" asked the second officer. "Do we go after the depot or
not?"

Glances were exchanged as everyone present considered the
question. It was Jomar who finally broke the silence.

"I am in favor of attacking the depot," he said.

Vigo turned to Picard. "So am I."

Ben Zoma shrugged. "I'm convinced."

"Same here," said Paxton, though without as much enthusiasm.

Simenon shook his head stubbornly. "I'll grant you, the Magnians give us an edge in a fight—and so do Jomar's vidrion-laced
shields. But it's not *that* big an edge."

"I'm with Simenon," said Cariello. "I was on the receiving end of a Nuyyad advantage once. I don't look forward to being there again."

That left Greyhorse.

As the others looked to him, he frowned at the scrutiny. "I'm no tactician, you understand. However, I too have to agree with Mr. Simenon. Enhanced shields, sensors, and tractor beams don't inspire much confidence when stacked against an indeterminate number of enemy ships."

Picard nodded. "Thank you for your input." He swept the table with a glance. "All of you."

"You're welcome," said the engineer, his ruby eyes gleaming. "But what are you going to do?"

The second officer looked at him. "I have not been swayed from my original inclination," he noted. "We will break orbit and head for the depot as soon as I can coordinate the details with Mr. Williamson."

Simenon snorted. "Captain Ruhalter was the same way."

Picard turned to him, his eyes flashing with restrained emotion. "And what does that mean?"

The engineer returned his glare. "He had an opinion when he walked into a meeting, and he had an opinion when he walked out—and as I recall, they were always the same."

The second officer seemed to take the remark in stride. "I had a great deal of respect for Captain Ruhalter, as you are no doubt aware. However, he and I are by no means the same. When I come into a meeting, Mr. Simenon, it is with an open mind."

The Gnalish wasn't the type to let a matter go if he felt strongly about it. But to Greyhorse's surprise, he let *this* one go. "I guess I'll have to take your word for it," he said.

Picard nodded, clearly satisfied with Simenon's response. Then he turned to the others. "You are all dismissed," he told them.

As the doctor pushed his chair back and got up, he couldn't

help wishing that the second officer had some secret weapon he hadn't informed them of. He was still wishing that as he left the room and returned to sickbay.

As the doors to his quarters whispered closed behind him, Picard made his way to his workstation, sat down and established contact with a terminal elsewhere on the ship.

A moment later, Ben Zoma's face appeared on the screen. "We've got to stop meeting like this," he quipped.

"Well?" asked Picard, ignoring his friend's remark. "What did you think of my performance?"

Ben Zoma shrugged. "I thought they bought it."

"You don't think any of them were suspicious?"

"Not at all. I think they believe that you're determined to attack the supply depot." Ben Zoma smiled. "For a moment, even I believed it, and I was in on the game from the start."

The second officer nodded. "So far, so good. Now let's hope the saboteur takes the bait."

In truth, he had no intention of attacking the supply depot. The only reason he had announced his desire to do so was to encourage the saboteur to rig another command junction.

That was what he or she had done the last two times a confrontation with the Nuyyad was imminent. With luck, the saboteur would be moved to give a repeat performance.

Except this time, Picard would have Vigo monitoring every command junction in the ship, looking for anyone who might want to crawl into a Jefferies tube when no one was looking. And when they found that person, they would have their saboteur.

Or so the theory went.

"The question," said Ben Zoma, "is how far are we willing to go with this charade? Halfway to the depot? Three quarters of the way?"

The second officer posed a question of his own. "And what will we do if no one has been tripped up by then?"

"You're the acting captain," his friend reminded him.

"So I am," Picard acknowledged, his demeanor as grave as the situation demanded. "And *as* the acting captain, I think I'll worry about it when the time comes."

Greyhorse sat at his desk and tried to focus on the results of his psilosynine research. But try as he might, he couldn't keep his mind on them. He was thinking about Gerda Asmund again.

The doctor wondered what she thought about the idea of their going into battle. Was the Klingon in her looking forward to the challenge? Or was she as concerned about the prospect of facing all those ships as Greyhorse himself was?

He wished he could come up with something to make it a more even battle—and not just for the positive affect it might have on the outcome of their mission. A contribution like that would make Gerda notice him. It might even earn him her respect.

The medical officer dismissed the notion with a deep-throated sound of disgust. Who am I kidding? he asked himself. He wasn't an engineer, as so many others had been in his family. He didn't have the expertise to add anything to the *Stargazer*'s arsenal.

He was just a doctor. He could treat the wounded as they were brought into sickbay, but he couldn't do anything about the odds of their getting hurt in the first place.

The only battle he had ever won was on a chessboard, back in medical school. His first-year roommate, a gregarious and energetic man named Slattery, had taught him how to play the game—not the modern three-dimensional version, but the original.

At first, Slattery had beaten him every time. Then, little by little, Greyhorse had given him more of a run for his money. Finally, just before spring break, he managed to checkmate Slattery's king.

He remembered the man's reaction with crystal clarity. "Damn," Slattery had said with undisguised wonder and admiration, "when did you turn into a mindreader?"

The doctor's eyes were drawn to the series of chemical reactions represented on his computer screen, each of which played a part in the creation of psilosynine. If he had been born with such a neurotransmitter in his brain, he might have been a *real* mindreader.

Of course, back at the Academy, Greyhorse had never met a real mindreader. Now he could actually say he had treated one in his sickbay. What would Slattery have to say about . . .

He stopped himself, his brain suddenly ranging ahead of his recollection. He was making connections that he hadn't made before, connections that seemed so obvious now that he felt mortified.

A real mind reader, he repeated inwardly.

The medical officer studied the screen again, staring at the complex chains of molecules that had figured in his re-creation of psilosynine. *If he had been born with such a neurotransmitter . . .*

Greyhorse's heart was pounding. He had to speak with Commander Picard, he told himself, and he had to do it quickly.

Picard gazed across the captain's desk at the hulking, stony-featured form of Carter Greyhorse. "You made it sound as if this were a matter of some urgency," he told the doctor.

Greyhorse leaned forward in his chair. "It is. Or rather, it might be. All I need is a chance to find out."

The second officer wasn't in the mood for riddles. "Perhaps we should start at the beginning," he suggested.

"Of course," said the doctor. He drew a deep breath and let it out slowly. "Ever since we left Earth, I've been attempting to duplicate the work of a Betazoid scientist named Relanios."

Picard nodded. "I've heard of him."

Greyhorse looked at him, surprised. "You have?"

The commander smiled. "I have other interests beside beating the tar out of hostile aliens, Doctor. As I recall, Turan Relanios was synthesizing the neurotransmitter that give Betazoids their—"

He stopped himself in midsentence, grasping the import of what Greyhorse must have done. "You've synthesized psilosynine?"

"Yes," said the doctor, his dark eyes bright beneath his jutting brow. "Then you see the possibilities? You see how important this substance might be to us?"

Picard nodded. "Indeed."

In a human being, the neurotransmitter might create a fleeting capacity for telepathic communication. But in a mind already developed along such lines . . . a mind like a Magnian's . . .

Then something occurred to him.

"There's a danger here," said the second officer.

"That the psilosynine might trigger a reaction in the colonists' brains," Greyhorse acknowledged, dismissing the idea in the same breath. "That they might develop even greater powers . . . along with the personality aberrations experienced by Gary Mitchell."

Picard regarded him. "You don't seem especially concerned."

"I *am* concerned," said the doctor. *"Deeply* concerned. However, I made a study of Serenity Santana's neurological profile before I came to see you. And on a preliminary basis, at least, I would have to say there isn't anything to worry about."

"But you cannot be certain?"

Greyhorse shook his massive head. "Not until I have had a chance to conduct clinical tests."

"Which would have to be conducted under the most closely monitored conditions," Picard maintained.

After all, he already had a faceless saboteur to contend with. He didn't need a burgeoning superman prowling his ship in the bargain.

"You mean guards," said the doctor. "In my sickbay."

"Yes," the second officer insisted, refusing to yield on this point. "Several of them. And all armed."

Greyhorse obviously didn't like the idea. But given what was at stake, he seemed willing to acquiesce. "All right," he told the second officer. "But we need to begin as quickly as possible."

"As quickly as we can find a Magnian who will agree to be your guinea pig," said Picard.

The doctor looked unperturbed. "Leave that to me."

The second officer knew that they were about to tread new ground in the field of biomedical research. They were about to go where no human scientist had gone before.

He just hoped they wouldn't end up regretting it.

CHAPTER **16**

Captain's log, supplemental. I have discussed Dr. Grey-horse's idea with Mr. Ben Zoma, the only other officer on this ship who knows every facet of my mind in these complicated times. Unfortunately, he is less sanguine about the doctor's scheme than I am. Ben Zoma had come to think of our attack on the Nuyyad supply depot strictly as a ruse to bring our saboteur to the surface, in keeping with our original intention. Now that I am suggesting we actually go through with the assault—providing the doctor's clinical studies pan out—Ben Zoma is like a man who thought he was playing Russian roulette with a toy phaser and has discovered his weapon is real. One thing is clear to me—if we are going to attack the depot, we need to put our saboteur problem behind us. I am not oblivious to the irony in this sort of thinking. Before, we pursued the depot strategy as a way of eliminating our saboteur. Now, in ef-

fect, we have to eliminate our saboteur in order to pursue our depot strategy.

As Picard walked down the corridor, he reflected on the charge Simenon had leveled against him: *Captain Ruhalter was the same way.*

As the second officer noted at the meeting, he had respected and admired Ruhalter. However, he realized now that he wasn't completely comfortable with the man's approach to command.

Ruhalter had indeed relied on his instincts, often to the exclusion of other potentially valuable information and opinions. For a long time, of course, that method had worked for him—but in the end it had produced a bloody disaster.

Picard wasn't spurning the value of instinct—quite the contrary. He had gone with his gut more than once since his captain's demise. But he preferred to poll his officers, to obtain their feedback and draw on their expertise before he made a decision on a major point of strategy.

And not *just* his officers. He was willing to solicit advice even from the most unlikely sources.

Like the one he was about to visit at that very moment.

Up ahead, the second officer saw the open entrance to the brig and caught a glimpse of Lieutenant Pierzynski, who was leaning against a bulkhead inside. The rangy, fair-haired Pierzynski was the security officer who had taken Pug Joseph's place on guard duty.

As Picard got closer, Pierzynski must have caught sight of him, because he straightened up suddenly. If his behavior wasn't enough of a clue, the ruddy color in his face gave away his embarrassment.

"Anything I can do for you, sir?" asked Pierzynski.

"There is indeed," said the second officer. As he entered the brig area, he spotted Werber sitting on his cot behind the electromagnetic barrier. "You can repair to the hallway for a moment, Lieutenant. I would like to speak with the chief in private."

The security officer hesitated, no doubt weighing the wisdom of leaving Picard alone with seven mutineers. In the end, however, Pierzynski must have thought it was all right, because he said, "Aye, sir. I'll be right outside if you need me."

"Thank you," the second officer replied.

As Pierzynski left the room, Picard pressed some studs on a nearby bulkhead panel and altered the polarity of six of the seven barriers—Werber's being the exception. The effect was to make those barriers impervious to sound as well as light. Then he pressed another stud and saw the doors to the corridor slide shut.

Finally, he turned to Werber and nodded. "Chief."

The weapons officer shot him a dirty look. "Nice of you to visit," he declared, his voice dripping with sarcasm. "I'd offer you a chair, but I don't seem to have any lying around."

The second officer didn't take the bait. "This isn't a social call," he replied. "I've come on ship's business."

The prisoner laughed bitterly. "What do I care about your ship, Picard? If you're in the center seat, she'll be debris soon anyway."

"That's certainly a possibility," the commander said.

Clearly, it wasn't the comeback Werber had expected. "And what's that supposed to mean?"

"Since I thwarted your mutiny attempt, the *Stargazer* has been the victim of sabotage," Picard explained. "Not once, but twice now. The third time, it might prove our undoing."

That seemed to get the prisoner's attention. However, he resisted the temptation to inquire about it.

"I thought a veteran weapons officer might have some interest in identifying the saboteur," Picard went on. "Especially when he's someone who took his oath as seriously as you did."

Werber scowled. "To hell with my oath. Look where it got me."

Ah, the commander mused. Progress.

"I'll be honest with you," he told the prisoner. "I need your help. I need to pick your brain the way Captain Ruhalter did."

Werber looked at him askance. "Is it my imagination, or are you telling me you want to cut a deal?"

Picard shook his head. "No deals."

The weapons chief lifted his chin, which had grown a golden brown stubble during the time of his incarceration. "Then why should I even think about helping you?"

"Perhaps you shouldn't," the commander answered. "Think about helping *me,* that is. But you might want to help this ship, or the crewmen who served so ably under you. Or you might want to get involved purely for the sake of your own preservation."

Werber stared at him for what seemed like a very long time. Then he said, "All right. Tell me what you've got."

Picard told him, holding nothing back.

He informed the prisoner of Vigo's findings concerning the shuttle explosion. He described the way the ship's shields had dropped without notice during the second battle for Magnia. And he spoke of Vigo's second discovery, which only served to corroborate the first.

The prisoner considered the information, his eyes narrowing as he turned it over and over in his mind, inspecting it from different angles. But after a while, he shook his hairless head.

"I need more to go on," he said.

The commander was disappointed, but he didn't show it. "Right now, I'm afraid I haven't got anything more. But if additional information turns up, you will have it as soon as I do."

Werber grunted. "I can't wait."

"I will speak with you soon, I hope," said Picard. "Until then, I hope you will keep what I've told you confidential—so as not to diminish our chances of catching the saboteur." And he reached for the control panel that would open the doors to the corridor again.

But before he could press the padd, he heard the mutineer call his name. Turning again, he said, "Yes?"

Werber was on his feet, approaching the barrier. "I'm not surprised that the ship was sabotaged," he remarked, "considering how trusting you are of people like Santana."

The second officer allowed himself an ironic smile. "Interesting that you should say that, Chief. Mr. Ben Zoma is of the opinion that I'm placing too much trust in *you.*"

And with that, Picard opened the doors and emerged from the brig, allowing Pierzynski to resume his lonely vigil.

Gerda Asmund entered the turbolift ahead of her sister and punched in her destination on the control panel. Then, as Idun joined her in the compartment, Gerda watched the doors begin to slide closed.

"The end of another shift," her sister commented.

"And an uneventful one," said Gerda, as the turbolift began to move.

Idun glanced at her, her lip curled in amusement. "Another three such shifts and we'll have reached the Nuyyad supply depot. That promises to be *far* from uneventful."

Gerda nodded. "True."

"And," her sister added, "we haven't exactly been idle for the last week and a half. We were hoping for just *one* battle, remember? And so far, we've gotten three of them."

"I know," said Gerda. "Still . . ."

"What?" asked Idun.

"I don't know," the navigator told her. "It still feels to me as if something is missing."

"Something?" her sister echoed.

Gerda shrugged. "I can't put my finger on it. It's just not as satisfying as I thought it would be . . . as I *wanted* it to be."

Idun rolled her eyes. "Some saber bears aren't happy until they've eaten the entire *targ.*"

Gerda looked at her. "You think I'm a glutton?"

"Honestly?" her sister asked. "Yes."

Gerda knew Idun was seldom wrong about her. "Maybe you're right," she said. "Maybe I ought to be grateful for what I've got."

And yet, she couldn't help feeling there should be *more.*

* * *

Pug Joseph stood at the entrance to sickbay's triage area and watched Greyhorse press a hypospray containing psilosynine against Serenity Santana's naked arm.

As far as the security officer was concerned, it was insanity. If Santana was the saboteur and wanted to see the *Stargazer* destroyed, why give her yet another tool to accomplish that?

But then, he told himself, if they didn't subject Santana to the same tests as the other Magnians on board, she might catch on to their suspicions about her. And Commander Picard didn't want that.

Besides, there were precautions in place. For one thing, Greyhorse was introducing his synthetic neurotransmitter gradually, bit by tiny bit. For another, Joseph and a half dozen of his fellow security officers were on hand in case anything went awry.

Santana stole a glance at him. She knew he was here, of course. And she knew also that he still didn't trust her, no matter what she had done in the most recent battle.

It made him the perfect choice to keep an eye on her. After all, Joseph's feelings of mistrust had begun with the ambush the woman had led them to, not the discoveries of sabotage. So even if she got close enough to reach into his mind, he wouldn't be giving anything away.

Eventually, he reflected, she would slip up. She would try to rig another command junction when she thought no one was looking. And when she did, he would be there to catch her.

That is, if anyone still could.

As Gilaad Ben Zoma entered the *Stargazer*'s spare and economical engineering section, he saw the unmistakable figure of Jomar standing in front of a sleek, black diagnostic console.

The Kelvan had spent much of the last two days at the console, checking and rechecking for flaws in his vidrion injectors. Ben Zoma knew that because he had monitored Jomar's computer activities from security.

The Kelvan hadn't given even a hint that he meant to damage anything or obstruct any aspect of the ship's operations. He had simply run the same program, over and over, as if he were searching for something.

Ben Zoma wanted to know what it was. And since he couldn't ask that question of his computer screen, he had come down to engineering to get an answer from the horse's mouth.

Taking up a position at the console to Jomar's right, the human went through the motions of initiating a diagnostic of his own. Then he turned to the Kelvan, as if he were just trying to be friendly.

"It must be hard," he said.

Jomar glanced back at him. "I beg your pardon?"

Ben Zoma smiled. "You know . . . having made your contribution already. All you can do is mark time until we reach the depot."

The Kelvan returned his attention to his screen. "Inactivity is not as distasteful to my species as it is to yours—so even if I *were* marking time, it would not be a problem. However, I am not merely keeping myself busy. I am seeking the source of the shield lapse we suffered during our most recent encounter with the Nuyyad."

"That's right," said Ben Zoma. "There *was* a lapse, wasn't there?"

Jomar turned to him again and scrutinized him with his unblinking, pale-blue eyes. "Let us be honest with each other, shall we?"

"What do you mean?"

"Despite your casual reference to the recent shield failure," the Kelvan continued, "I believe it was of grave concern to you and Commander Picard. The fact that you have not asked my advice in the matter, nor made any public efforts to keep it from happening again, tells me that you may suspect me of having caused it."

Ben Zoma laughed. "You've got quite an imagination."

"Do I?" asked Jomar. "Because I also imagine that the only reason you came to engineering is to see if I will say something incriminating. If that is the case, let me put your mind to rest—I did not tamper with your shields. Your time would be better spent spying on Serenity Santana and her fellow colonists. If there was indeed an incident of tampering, it is they you should hold accountable."

"Do you have any proof that they did anything?" asked Ben Zoma.

"Gathering proof is not my job," said Jomar. "It is yours." Then he went back to his diagnostic program.

The officer looked at the Kelvan a moment longer. Then he turned back to his own console, where he continued to run a diagnostic of his own.

Well, he thought, that could have gone better.

Carter Greyhorse sat back in his chair and tapped his combadge. "Commander Picard," he said, "this is Dr. Greyhorse."

"I've been meaning to speak with you," said Picard, his voice filling the physician's office. "Have you got something to report?"

"I do," Greyhorse told him. "I've completed my clinical work and I've come to a conclusion."

"Which is?" asked the second officer.

"That, as far as I'm concerned, there's no reason not to give the Magnians full doses of the synthetic psilosynine."

"They've shown no personality aberrations?"

"None that I have noticed. No erratic increases or reductions in their telekinetic or telepathic abilities either. In fact, nothing at all that we need to be concerned about."

"But their abilities can be amplified?" asked Picard.

"Significantly," said the doctor. "By fifty to seventy percent, depending on the individual. Enough, I imagine, to make a difference in the effectiveness of our enhanced tractor beam."

"To say the least," the second officer agreed. "Tell me . . . if you began administering full doses to the Magnians now, how long would it be before they took affect?"

"Two to three hours—again, depending on the individual."

"We will arrive at our target in approximately thirty-six hours," said Picard. "Plan accordingly."

"I will," Greyhorse assured him.

"Picard out."

His conversation with the second officer completed, the doctor got up from his desk to check on his last remaining patient. Bypassing the triage area, which was occupied wall to wall by Magnians, he proceeded to his sickbay's small critical care facility.

There, he saw Commander Leach.

The first officer was laid out on a biobed, a metallic blanket covering him from the neck down, a stasis field preventing his condition from deteriorating. But even with all that, Leach looked deathly pale, an unavoidable consequence of his coma.

Greyhorse used the control padd on the side of the first officer's bed to check his vital signs. They were stable, which was about all the doctor could hope for at the moment.

If and when they reached a Federation starbase, there were things that could be done for Leach—procedures that would give the man an opportunity for a full recovery. But on the *Stargazer,* with its limited equipment, Greyhorse had done all he possibly could.

More satisfying was his work with the colonists. His efforts there would give Picard and his tactical people an advantage— the edge they needed to achieve a victory, perhaps.

I should be pleased, the doctor thought.

Unfortunately, his accomplishment hadn't obtained the thing he wanted most—Gerda Asmund's attention. He had seen her on two occasions over the last couple of days, once in a corridor and once in the lounge, and she hadn't even acknowledged his presence.

She must have known about his work. It had to be the talk of everyone on the ship. But it hadn't fazed her.

In that respect, at least, Greyhorse's victory seemed a hollow one.

* * *

Lieutenant Vigo was sitting at the computer terminal in his quarters, running yet another time-consuming scan of the ship's myriad command junctions, when he heard his name called over the intercom system.

The voice was Commander Picard's. Having heard it every few hours for the last couple of days, the Pandrilite would quite likely have recognized it in his sleep.

"Aye, sir?" said Vigo.

"Anything?" asked Picard.

"Nothing at all," the weapons officer told him. "I haven't seen even a hint of impropriety."

The commander sighed audibly. "I wish I could say that no news is good news, Lieutenant. But in this instance, that is not the case."

"I'll keep at it, sir," Vigo promised. What else could he say?

"I have no doubt of it," said Picard. "And, of course, if anything *does* come up—"

"I'll contact you immediately," the Pandrilite told him.

There was a pause. "Someday," the commander said, "you and I will have more pleasant matters to talk about. But if it's all right with you, Lieutenant, we won't talk quite as often."

Vigo smiled. "I'll be sure to remind you, sir."

For the second time in seventy-two hours, Jean-Luc Picard found himself approaching the ship's brig.

This time, it was Lieutenant Garner who was standing inside the open doorway, keeping an eye on the mutineers. And she wasn't the least bit surprised by the second officer's appearance, because it was she who had communicated with him at Hans Werber's request.

As before, the weapons chief was sitting on his cot. When he saw that Picard had arrived, he stood up. His expression was more thoughtful than belligerent for a change.

"Leave us, please," said the second officer.

Garner did as she was instructed. Then Picard touched the

bulkhead controls and saw to it that he and Werber had some privacy.

"Here I am," said the commander. "Have you thought of something?"

Werber nodded. "I think so."

Picard expected him to say Santana was the guilty party, and attempt to lay out some proof of it. But he didn't. In fact, the weapons officer was no longer quite so sure that the colonist was involved.

"Then who's the saboteur?" asked the commander.

"I don't know," said the prisoner. "But I know how to find him." And he went on to elaborate.

Picard considered the information. "I appreciate your help," he said at last. "If it leads us to the saboteur—"

The mutineer preempted him with a gesture. "Don't make me any promises, Commander. Just get the sonuvabitch."

Picard nodded. "I will certainly try."

CHAPTER **17**

Greyhorse pressed the hypospray against Armor Brentano's arm and released a full dose of psilosynine into the man's system.

The Magnian looked at him. "That's it?"

"That's it," the medical officer confirmed.

"When will I start feeling different?" Brentano asked.

"In the next two to three hours," said Greyhorse. "And you will continue to feel that way for anywhere from four to five hours."

"So we're not far from the depot?" the colonist concluded.

"So I've been told."

Reaching into the pocket of his lab coat, Greyhorse removed a metal disk about the size of his fingernail. Positioning it between thumb and forefinger, he placed it against Brentano's temple—where it remained.

"What's this?" his patient wanted to know.

"A monitoring device," he said. "If your brain waves start to change, I want to know about it."

"So you can shut me down?" asked Brentano.

"Exactly right," said the medical officer. "For the sake of everyone on this ship—you included."

"What if I snap and rip it off?" he asked, smiling.

Greyhorse didn't feel compelled to smile back. "Then I'll know it and the result will be the same."

"I'll remember that," Brentano promised him.

I assure you, the doctor added silently, at least one of us will.

Gerda Asmund had hoped that her mood would improve. However, it had gotten worse with each passing day.

Finally, as the *Stargazer* came within sensor range of her target, the navigator found herself looking forward to the battle ahead. However, the prospect wasn't the blood-roiling elixir it should have been.

What's more, her sister knew it. Idun had been watching her like a mother *s'tarahk* ever since their talk in the turbolift, trying her best to gain some insight into Gerda's feelings.

But how could Idun understand her lack of enthusiasm when Gerda herself didn't understand it?

Abruptly, she was drawn out of her reverie by a beeping sound—a sensor alarm she had set earlier. Looking down at her monitor, she saw that visual information was available on the depot.

Her sister, who had heard the alarm as well, turned to her. Idun, at least, was eager to engage the enemy, and had been for some time. Gerda could see it in her eyes.

The navigator glanced back over her shoulder at Commander Picard, who was discussing something with Lieutenant Ben Zoma in front of the captain's chair. "We're in visual range of the depot," she announced.

Picard regarded her. "On screen," he said.

Working at her controls, Gerda complied.

Pug Joseph was standing just inside the entrance to the engineering support room on Deck 26, watching Serenity Santana and her fellow colonists gather in an approximate semicircle and exert their influence on the *Stargazer*'s dorsal tractor node.

Not that the security officer could actually see the Magnians *doing* anything. After all, they were working solely with the power of their minds, their collective energy amplified by the neurotransmitter Dr. Greyhorse had concocted for them.

The only visible evidence of the colonists' efforts was the flock of triangular, palm-sized devices they had attached to the tractor node days earlier. The things were humming softly to themselves and throbbing with a bright yellow light.

They had hummed and throbbed the same way during the second battle for Magnia. At least, that was how Joseph remembered it. It frustrated him that the Magnians' activities were so foreign to him, so alien, and therefore so difficult to monitor.

How was he supposed to keep an eye on Santana if he couldn't tell what she was really doing? How did he know she was gearing up for the battle ahead and not plotting with her friends to cripple the ship?

The answer, of course, was he *didn't.*

Suddenly, Santana turned away from the tractor node and looked back over her shoulder at him. The expression on her face—one of anxiety—made the security officer wonder what the woman was up to.

Pug, he heard in his head, *something's wrong. We can sense someone tampering with a command junction.*

Joseph looked at her, wary of a trick. "Who's doing it?" he asked.

Santana didn't answer right away. Then she made a single word materialize in his brain: *Jomar.*

The security officer walked over to the nearest console and tapped into the *Stargazer*'s internal sensor net. However, there was no indication of any tampering. There wasn't anyone in the Jefferies tubes at all. And Jomar, apparently, was in his quarters.

He turned back to Santana, wondering what she was trying to pull *this* time. "No one is anywhere near a command junction."

She left the semicircle and came over to him. Gazing at the monitor, she saw what he had seen—in other words, nothing.

"He's there," Santana insisted. She looked up at Joseph. "Dammit, I can *feel* him."

Reacting to the woman's display of emotion, he put his hand on the phaser pistol dangling at his hip. "I'll have someone check Jomar's quarters. In the meantime, you can—"

"No!" she snapped, her dark eyes filled with dread—or so it seemed. "By then, it'll be too late!"

The security officer drew his phaser, leery of what Santana could do with the doctor's neurotransmitter flowing in her veins. "Move back," he told her. "Do it."

She looked at his weapon, then at him again. "You don't understand," she told him.

"Don't I?" he asked.

Then something happened—Joseph wasn't sure what. He seemed to lose control of his limbs, his body becoming a heavy and unresponsive mass of flesh. The phaser fell from his limp, paralyzed hand and hit the deck.

And a moment later, the security officer joined it, his mind spiraling down into darkness.

As Picard watched, Gerda Asmund manipulated her controls. A moment later, the viewscreen filled with the image he had been waiting for.

And what an image it was.

In the second officer's imagination, the depot had been an impressive thing—a large, sprawling facility surrounded by powerful-looking, diamond-shaped warships. It had been equipped with a multitude of cargo hatches and docking ports, everything it needed to facilitate the transfer of food and material goods.

Its reality was even more impressive—and a good deal more

daunting. The depot looked more like a fortress than a supply facility, and more like the crown of an ancient king than either, with its circular configuration of diamond-shaped towers and its circlet of weapons ports and its flawless, almost luminescent surfaces.

As prodigious as the enemy's fighting ships were, the depot was bigger and better-armed by a factor of at least ten. It was perhaps the truest symbol of Nuyyad pride they had seen yet.

"Looks like this is the place," breathed Ben Zoma.

"You know what they say," Picard told him. "The bigger they are, the harder they fall."

"An interesting observation," the other man noted. "But given a choice, I'll take big anyday."

Picard shot him a disparaging glance.

"Except this one, of course," Ben Zoma added cheerfully.

"Of course," the second officer responded. He scanned for the number of Nuyyad vessels. "I'm reading four ships. Can you confirm that, Lieutenant Asmund?"

"I show four as well, sir."

"It could have been worse," Picard allowed.

Suddenly, an alert light on the captain's armrest began blinking red. Noticing it, Picard touched the padd beside it.

"Mr. Vigo?" he asked, feeling an adrenaline rush as he anticipated the weapons chief's response.

"Aye, sir. I've got a problem in the phaser line. Command junction twenty-eight, accessible from Deck Ten."

"Acknowledged," said the second officer. He straightened and glanced at his friend. "Let's go."

"I'm right behind you," Ben Zoma assured him.

Together, they entered the turbolift and punched in a destination. Then they removed the phasers they had hidden in their tunics.

When the turbolift stopped at Deck Ten, they got out and pelted down the corridor. Before long, they came to a ladder and a round door that would give them access to the network of Jefferies tubes that permeated the ship.

Picard went up the ladder first, pulled open the door and crawled into the tube. As Ben Zoma had promised, he wasn't far behind.

It wasn't easy making progress through the tube's cylindrical, circuit-studded confines, which forced the Starfleet officers to hunch over as they ran. However, they reached the first intersection more quickly than Picard would have believed possible.

It was then that they heard the clatter of a violent confrontation. Looking in every direction, Ben Zoma finally spotted it.

"There," he said, pointing.

Following his friend's gesture, the second officer saw two combatants. One appeared to be Santana. The other was a dark, many-tentacled thing that could only have been Jomar in his natural state.

The colonist was trying to hold the Kelvan off with her arms—the way any human might try to hold off something big and monstrous—and not having much luck. But to Picard's surprise and dismay, she was also launching a series of tiny, pink lightning bolts at her adversary.

The Kelvan recoiled wherever the tiny lightnings struck, but the rest of him remained unaffected. Flinging one slimy limb after another at his target, he tried to envelop her, to crush her in his powerful embrace. And no doubt, he would have, had it not been for the energy bolts Santana was able to marshal against him.

As Picard and Ben Zoma moved closer, neither Santana nor Jomar seemed able to gain an advantage. In short, their struggle was a standoff—an impassioned and violent one, certainly, but a standoff all the same.

Ben Zoma swore beneath his breath. "For heaven sakes, Jean-Luc, we've got to do something."

Picard nodded. "But to whom?"

Clearly, one of the combatants was the saboteur they had been looking for. But the other was an innocent bystander at worst, and at best a hero who had risked life and limb.

"We'll stun them both," Picard decided.

"Done," said his companion.

As Picard took aim at Santana, he saw her glance in his direction. Her eyes seemed to reach out to him, pleading for understanding.

It was all the distraction that Jomar needed. Lashing out at Santana, he snapped her head back. The colonist went limp. But before she could slump to the bottom of the tube, the Kelvan caught her up in his tentacles.

Picard still didn't know which of the two was the saboteur. However, he didn't want to see Santana hurt any worse than she was already.

"Let her go!" he barked at Jomar, his voice echoing raucously along the length of the Jefferies tube.

The Kelvan turned to him and underwent a transformation. He seemed to reshape himself before Picard's eyes, his tentacles shrinking and consolidating and giving way to arms and legs. In a matter of seconds, Jomar had assumed his human form again.

With an unconscious Santana in his arms, he approached the Starfleet officer. "I have apprehended the saboteur," he said, his blue eyes steady and unblinking, his voice as flat as ever.

Picard didn't lower his weapon. After all, there was still a lot that had to be cleared up. "That's far enough," he told the Kelvan.

Jomar stopped in his tracks. "Is something wrong?"

Picard declined to answer the question. "Put Santana down and back away," he said.

The Kelvan hesitated for just a moment. Then he knelt, placed the colonist on the curved surface and retreated from the spot.

Picard pointed to Santana with his phaser. "Gilaad," he said, "make sure she's still alive."

Ben Zoma tucked his weapon away and moved to the woman's side. Then he felt her neck for a pulse and looked back at his friend.

"She's still with us, all right. I—"

Before he could get another word out, the tube filled with a hideous, high-pitched scream and Jomar began to change again. Faster than Picard would have thought possible, his human attributes melted away and a swarm of long, dark tentacles took their place.

Picard raised his phaser and aimed it at the center of the monstrosity. But before he could press the trigger, he felt something clammy close around his hand. With a twisting motion that nearly broke his wrist, it wrenched the weapon out of his grasp.

By then, Ben Zoma had drawn his phaser—but he wasn't quick enough either. As Picard watched helplessly, Jomar snatched the man's phaser away with one tentacle and lashed him across the face with another.

Ben Zoma crumpled, stunned or worse. Picard started forward to help his friend, but a moist, black tentacle grabbed hold of his ankle and a half-dozen others knocked him off his feet.

Looking up, he saw a pair of tiny, gray orbs glaring at him above an obscenely pink maw. He tried to crawl away, but he was still held fast by the ankle. Unable to escape, he watched helplessly as a swarm of tentacles slithered toward his throat.

Picard fought some of them away, but he couldn't fight all of them. He felt a tentacle snare one of his wrists, then the other. And finally, as he growled out loud with the effort to free himself, he felt a third tentacle begin to close around his throat.

The Kelvan's grip tightened and Picard's breath was cut off. He tried to claw at the muscular piece of flesh around his windpipe, but his wrists were too well constrained. Deprived of oxygen while his exertions made his need for it even more urgent, he saw darkness closing in on him.

Ben Zoma, the second officer thought. His friend was his only chance now—if he was still alive.

Suddenly, there was a flash of red light. *Phaser light*—Picard was certain of it. But Jomar's tentacle didn't let go.

Then he saw the flash again, even brighter than before—and

this time, it had some effect. The Kelvan seemed to stagger under the impact and lose his grip on his victim's wrists and ankle.

A third flash, and Jomar lost his stranglehold as well. Picard slumped to the floor and drew in a deep, rasping breath.

His instincts told him to run—to get out of range of the Kelvan's deadly tentacles. But he resisted the impulse and did something else entirely. He sought out his captor's face—if it could indeed be called a face—and drove his fist into it as hard as he could.

The yellow eyes blinked and the pink maw let out a blood-chilling scream—not out of pain, Picard thought, as much as surprise. Apparently, the last thing Jomar had expected was a punch in the nose.

It threw the Kelvan off-balance and made him that much more vulnerable to what followed—an intense, red stream of directed energy that got through the mess of dark tentacles and hammered Jomar's grotesque torso.

The Kelvan collapsed, his long, snakelike limbs flying in every direction. He looked disoriented, his maw opening and closing, his gray orbs half-lidded with dark flesh—but not yet out for the count.

Then yet another blast battered his slimy black head . . . and it lolled to the bottom of the tube, senseless.

Picard kicked away a tentacle that lay across his foot and turned to his rescuer. He was eager to thank his friend Ben Zoma for his dramatic and timely phaser assault.

Then he saw that it wasn't his friend at all. It was Pug Joseph, staring wide-eyed at Jomar with his weapon still in his hand.

CHAPTER 18

Mr. Joseph?" said Picard.

The security officer looked as much in need of an explanation as the second officer. "Sir?" he responded.

Before Picard could clear up any of the confusion, he had the Kelvan's other victims to think about. Locating Ben Zoma, he saw that his friend was trying to sit up—a good portent indeed.

Santana, on the other hand, was still stretched out on the bottom of the tube, a sweep of raven hair obscuring part of her face. Kneeling beside her, the second officer took her pulse.

Joseph knelt too, his brow knit at the sight of the stricken woman, his expression giving away his very genuine concern. "Is she . . . ?"

"Her pulse is strong," Picard assured the security officer. "I believe she will be all right."

But she wouldn't be participating in any battles anytime soon, he decided. And not just because of the beating she had taken.

Santana had never demonstrated the ability to create pink

lightning bolts before—but Gary Mitchell had. Kirk reported that he had seen the man do it more than once. If the Magnian's new-found ability was a side effect of the doctor's psilosynine, the second officer was going to shut the experiment down as soon as possible.

Glancing at Jomar, he saw that the Kelvan was still unconscious. However, Picard was uncertain how long he would remain that way.

He tapped his combadge. "Picard to Lieutenant Ang. I need all the security officers you can spare, on the double."

"Aye, sir," said Ang. "Where shall I send them?"

"I'm in a Jefferies tube accessible from Deck Ten. Hurry, Lieutenant. I have injured to get to sickbay."

"On our way," Ang assured him.

"What happened?" asked Ben Zoma, holding the side of his mottled, swollen face as he staggered to his feet.

"We found our saboteur," said Picard.

Gilaad Ben Zoma sat on a biobed in sickbay and allowed Greyhorse to inject him with a hypospray full of painkiller.

Eventually, he would need oral surgery as a result of the blow Jomar had dealt him. But for now, he couldn't afford not to be up and about.

"How do you feel now?" asked the doctor.

"Much better," said Ben Zoma.

"Then you agree?" asked Picard, who was standing beside Greyhorse.

Greyhorse nodded. "Absolutely. We can't let the Magnians direct our tractor beam if even one of them is exhibiting unexpected side effects."

Ben Zoma looked across the triage area at Santana, who was lying on the same biobed she had occupied during her coma. The woman was awake, but dazed—the result of a severe concussion.

Pug Joseph was standing beside her, theoretically to guard

against her doing anything rash. But in truth, the security officer looked more concerned than watchful.

As Ben Zoma understood it, Santana had knocked Joseph out in an effort to reach Jomar before he could carry out his latest act of sabotage. When she found herself unequal to the task, she roused the security officer telepathically—something she couldn't have done without the psilosynine amplifying her abilities—and summoned him to tip the balance.

Ben Zoma was glad she had. And he wasn't the only one.

"For the time being," said the doctor, "I'm going to get the other colonists down here and administer sedatives to them. But I can't make any promises as to the drugs' effectiveness—"

"So you'll need security personnel," Picard deduced. "I understand. Believe me, Doctor, I wouldn't have had it any other way."

The second officer had barely completed his statement when a handful of security officers, led by Lieutenant Ang, escorted Jomar into sickbay. The Kelvan had assumed human form again, Ben Zoma noticed, and didn't appear to be offering the officers any resistance.

"Bring him over here," Greyhorse instructed them, tilting his head to indicate an empty biobed.

Ang looked to Ben Zoma first.

"Do as the doctor says," Ben Zoma told him.

"I am not in need of medical attention," Jomar protested.

"I will be the judge of that," said Greyhorse.

As the Kelvan was brought to the bed, Picard put his hand on his friend's shoulder. "You *are* all right, aren't you?" he asked.

Ben Zoma shrugged. "I've been better. Fortunately, my body doesn't know that right now. How about you?"

"I'll live," the second officer told him. He glanced at Jomar. "If only long enough to find out our guest's motivation for sabotage."

"I'd be interested in that story myself," said Ben Zoma. "And now that we're not headed for the depot any longer, we'll have plenty of time to hear him tell it."

Picard looked at him questioningly. "Not headed for the depot . . . ?"

"Our secret weapon is kaput, remember? Without the Magnians manning our tractor beam, we don't stand a chance. And with our saboteur out in the open, there's no reason to even pretend we're going."

His friend frowned. "Perhaps you're r—"

"Commander Picard?" came a voice over the intercom, interrupting the second officer's remark.

Ben Zoma recognized the voice as Gerda Asmund's.

"Yes, Lieutenant?" Picard responded.

"Sir," said the navigator, "two of the Nuyyad ships have left the depot and are coming after us."

In the wake of the announcement, the security officers exchanged glances. Greyhorse looked disturbed as well.

The muscles rippled in the second officer's jaw. "Then again," he said, "perhaps we'll be having that battle after all."

Ben Zoma acknowledged the grim truth of Picard's statement. The depot was significantly closer to the galactic barrier than the *Stargazer* was. If they wanted to return to warn the Federation about the Nuyyad, they would at some point have to engage the enemy.

"We can't resort to the Magnians," Ben Zoma sighed. "But without them, we'll be outgunned."

His friend shook his head. "Two against one, Gilaad. It doesn't sound very promising, does it?"

"We can still beat them," someone said.

Tracing the comment to its source, Ben Zoma saw Jomar looking at them from his heavily guarded biobed. The Kelvan's pale-blue eyes glistened in the light from the overheads.

"I beg your pardon?" Picard replied.

"I said we can beat them," Jomar repeated without inflection. "That is, if you allow me to complete my work."

"And what work is that?" asked Ben Zoma.

The Kelvan continued to stare at them. "The work I did in an attempt to minimize the effects of your plasma flow regulator and distribution manifold on your phaser system."

Ang looked at him. "What . . . ?"

But Ben Zoma understood. "I get it now. That secondary command line you were laying in . . . you were trying to streamline our plasma delivery system and beef up phaser power."

"That is correct," Jomar confirmed. "The incidents you no doubt attributed to sabotage were inadvertent and . . . unfortunate."

Picard regarded the Kelvan with narrowed eyes. "You were expressly forbidden to tamper with the phaser system."

Jomar looked unimpressed. "The Nuyyad must be stopped, Commander. And I had every confidence that the *Stargazer*'s plasma conduits could tolerate the modifications."

The second officer turned ruddy with anger. "It wasn't your choice to make, Jomar. It was Captain Ruhalter's—and now it's mine. But at no time was it ever *yours.*"

"I stand corrected," Jomar replied evenly, though it was clear he didn't mean it in the least. "However, you now have an option that you would not have had otherwise."

He was right, of course, Ben Zoma reflected. And with a couple of Nuyyad warships on a collision course with the *Stargazer,* they needed all the options they could get.

Picard must have been thinking the same thing. No doubt, he was leery about working alongside someone who had been trying to choke him a short while earlier—and the Kelvan's scheme was still a dangerous one.

But the alternative was to take a chance on making Gary Mitchell-style monsters out of Santana's contingent. And that, in the long run, might be infinitely *more* dangerous.

The second officer looked at Ben Zoma. What do *you* think? Picard seemed to be asking.

"Let's do it," his friend said.

The commander thought about it a moment longer. Then he

turned to Jomar again. "Very well. How much time do you need?"

"Not much," the Kelvan told him. "Twenty minutes, perhaps."

Picard nodded. "You've got it."

Once again, Ben Zoma thought, they were putting their trust in someone who had previously proven unworthy of it. In Santana's case, they had been fortunate enough to make the right choice.

Now they were shooting for double or nothing.

Captain's log, supplemental. Rather than wait for the enemy vessels to come to us, I have decided to go on the offensive and meet them head-on. I hope Jomar's phaser enhancement is everything he claims, or we will find ourselves with a great many regrets.

In the dusky scarlet illumination of a red alert, Picard eyed the pair of Nuyyad vessels on his viewscreen.

"Range?" he asked.

"Twenty-two billion kilometers," said Gerda, "and closing."

At warp seven, the *Stargazer* would cover fifty percent of that distance in the next minute and meet the enemy halfway. It didn't leave them much time to gird themselves for battle.

The second officer turned to Vigo. "Power up phasers and photon torpedoes," he said.

"Aye, sir," Vigo responded.

Picard looked to Gerda again. "Raise shields."

"Raising shields," she confirmed.

The commander took a deep breath and watched the Nuyyad ships loom larger on the screen. For the time being, they were content to fly parallel courses, though that would no doubt change in the next few seconds.

As if on cue, the enemy vessels peeled off in different directions, aiming to catch the Federation ship in a crossfire. Picard thought for a moment and turned to his helm officer.

"Go after the one to starboard," he commanded.

"Aye, sir," said Idun.

Abruptly, the *Stargazer* veered to the right, keeping one of the Nuyyad ships in sight while momentarily ignoring the other. It was the maneuver that had been recommended by all Picard's tactics instructors at the Academy—but not as a long-term solution.

It would buy him a few seconds, at best. But if luck was on his side, that would be all the time he needed.

"Lock on target," he told Vigo.

"Targeting," came the reply.

"Phaser range," said Gerda.

"Fire!" snapped Picard.

Twin phaser beams lanced through space and skewered the enemy ship. At normal strength, the commander would have expected them to weaken the diamond-shape's shields, perhaps even shake up the Nuyyad inside.

The crimson beams didn't do that. They did a lot *more*.

Instead of softening the enemy's defenses, they seared right through them and penetrated the Nuyyad's hull. Before Picard could give Vigo the order to fire again, his adversary suffered a vicious, blinding explosion amidships. With the second officer looking on in morbid fascination, the Nuyyad succumbed to a second explosion and then a third, and finally came apart in a white-hot burst of debris.

"Enemy vessel to port," Gerda reported.

"Bring us about," Picard told Idun.

As they swung hard to port, the viewscreen found their other antagonist. But at the same time, a string of vidrion bundles came slicing from the vessel's cannons, filling the screen with their fury.

The second officer braced himself, but the impact wasn't as bad as he had expected. Their vidrion-reinforced shields were holding up well—he could tell even without asking Gerda for the details.

"Target and fire!" he told Vigo.

A moment later, their phaser banks erupted again—gutting the enemy ship as they had gutted the other one, and with much the same results. The Nuyyad was ripped to shreds in a chain of spectacular explosions, one right after the other. The last of them left nothing in its wake but a languidly expanding wave of space junk.

Suddenly, the *Stargazer* was alone in the void, registering nothing on her forward viewscreen but the light of distant stars. Picard expelled a breath he hadn't known he was holding.

Ben Zoma appeared beside him. "Apparently," he said, "Jomar knew what he was talking about."

"Apparently so," the second officer replied.

But there was still the question they had brought up when Captain Ruhalter was still alive—as to whether the plasma conduits could tolerate the kind of stress Jomar's enhancement would place on them. With that in mind, Picard asked Vigo to run a diagnostic.

After a moment, the weapons officer made his report. "The stress appears to have been considerable, sir. But the conduits held. There's no sign of damage to them."

The commander nodded. "Thank you, Lieutenant."

Ben Zoma looked at him. "Now what?"

Picard frowned. There was really only one option, as far as he was concerned. "Now we go after the depot."

His colleague smiled a halfhearted smile. "I was afraid you were going to say that."

"If you were in my place," asked the second officer, "would you be turning back now?"

"If I were in your place," said Ben Zoma, "I wouldn't have come this far in the first place."

Picard shot him a disparaging look.

"You asked," his friend reminded him.

By the commander's estimate, they were still two hundred and fifty billion kilometers from their target—more than twenty minutes' travel at warp seven. With their pursuers out of the way, there was still plenty of time to change course and head for the barrier instead.

But Picard had undertaken a mission, and he was determined to see it through. "Resume course," he told Idun.

The helm officer seemed to approve of the decision. "Aye, sir," she said, and made a small adjustment in their heading.

Soon, the commander reflected, their struggles would be over—one way or the other.

Pug Joseph looked down at Serenity Santana, whose dark eyes were closed in recuperative repose.

She might have died in her fight with Jomar, he told himself. The Kelvan might have miscalculated and killed her. And then Joseph would never have had the chance to speak with Santana again . . .

And to tell her he was sorry.

Not for being vigilant, because it was a security officer's job to be vigilant. But for not accepting her apology when she tendered it to him in the engineering support room on Deck 26.

On the other side of the triage area, Dr. Greyhorse was puttering around with his instruments. He seemed distracted—as distracted as Joseph had been when he last visited sickbay. Or maybe, knowing how the security officer felt about Santana, the doctor was simply giving him some privacy.

Joseph gazed at the colonist again and resisted an impulse to straighten a lock of her hair. He had been so determined not to get fooled again, he had almost prevented her from going after Jomar.

If he had been successful, the Kelvan would have faced Picard and Ben Zoma alone, without any help from Santana. There was no telling what would have happened to the officers then.

Picard trusted her, Joseph thought. Maybe I should have trusted her too. He resolved to tell her that when she woke.

There's no need, said a voice in his head. *You've told me already.*

And Santana opened her eyes.

He felt his face flush with embarrassment. "You were reading my mind," he said accusingly.

"Are you upset with me?" she asked, her voice thin and reedy from the medication Greyhorse had administered.

The security officer started to say yes, started to protest that she had violated his privacy. Then he stopped himself. "Not anymore," he told her. "Not after what you risked to stop Jomar."

Santana smiled wearily. "I was afraid he would transform me into a tetrahedron," she murmured, "the way he transformed Brentano. That made me fight a little harder."

"So he wouldn't get the chance," Joseph deduced.

"Uh huh." The colonist drew a breath, then let it out. "I'm glad you're not angry at me."

So was he. He said so.

"I'm so tired," Santana told him, stumbling over the words. "Would you do me a favor, Lieutenant?"

"Anything," the security officer answered.

"Would you stand guard over me? Just for old times' sake?"

He nodded. "I'd be glad to."

A moment later, Santana was asleep.

Picard regarded the Nuyyad supply installation on his screen and counted the number of warships circling it.

"Is it my imagination," he asked Ben Zoma, "or are there four vessels defending the depot again?"

"There are four, all right," said his friend. "Apparently, the Nuyyad had other ships in the area."

"And maybe more on the way," the second officer noted. "All the more reason to act quickly."

Ben Zoma didn't respond to the statement, but his expression wasn't one of complete confidence. Then again, he hadn't been eager to go after the depot from the beginning.

Picard took another look at the depot and its fleet of defenders.

Was his friend right? Were they out of their league? Or would their secret weapon be enough to pull off a victory?

There was only one way to find out.

"All hands to battle stations," he said.

All over the ship, he knew, crewmen were rushing to their predetermined posts. He remembered what it was like to respond to such an order, to know that a battle was imminent.

On the bridge, it was a different experience entirely. It was at once headier and more daunting. After all, he wasn't just responsible for one isolated job. He was responsible for *all* of them.

"Strafing run?" Ben Zoma suggested.

The second officer shook his head. He had already considered the idea and rejected it. "I would rather be in their midst, where they will have to worry about hitting each other with their vidrion bursts."

Just as the second officer expressed that sentiment, he saw two more of the enemy ships move out to meet him. Apparently, the choice of approach had been taken out of their hands.

"Phaser range?" he asked Vigo.

"In a few seconds, sir," the weapons officer told him.

"Target the foremost vessel," said Picard.

"Targeting," Vigo responded.

"Range," Gerda announced.

The commander eyed the viewscreen. "Fire!"

The Nuyyad tried to twist out of the way. But the *Stargazer*'s phaser beams punched through the vessel's shields, shearing off its nacelles on one side and cutting a deep furrow on the other.

A moment later, the enemy ship met its demise in a ball of yellow-white flame—a blast so prodigious that it licked at the extremities of the victim's sister vessels.

"Evasive maneuvers!" Picard called out. "Pattern Gamma!"

Accelerating, the *Stargazer* split the difference between the Nuyyad ships and blew right through the remnants of the vessel she had destroyed. The enemy must have been surprised, because it didn't even get off a volley.

"Pattern Alpha!" the second officer demanded. "I want them both in our sights again!"

Idun muscled the ship hard to port until the Nuyyad appeared on the viewscreen. Then she bore down on them.

"Target the starboard vessel and fire!" said Picard.

At close range, their enhanced phasers were even more effective. The beams rammed through one side of the Nuyyad ship and came out the other. And in the process, they started a series of savage explosions that gradually tore the vessel to pieces.

The third vessel raked them with a vidrion barrage, causing the *Stargazer* to jerk to port. But again, their shields kept them from serious harm. Then it was the Federation ship's turn again.

"Target and fire!" Picard told his weapons officer.

Once more, Vigo's aim was impeccable. Their phasers speared the Nuyyad vessel through its heart, causing it to tremble and writhe with plasma eruptions until it was claimed by a massive conflagration.

For the second time that day, the second officer found himself the winning combatant. But he wasn't done yet—not while the supply depot still lay ahead of them.

"Resume course?" asked Idun.

Picard nodded. "And give me a visual of the installation."

Instantly, an image of the depot leaped to the viewscreen. Up close, the thing was even more gigantic, even more daunting than before. It dwarfed its lone remaining defender.

The second officer focused himself on the task ahead. He hadn't forgotten that he chose this course over the objections of others. If it failed, he would have only himself to blame.

That is, if he was still in a position to blame anyone at all.

Abruptly, the last of the Nuyyad ships came after them. No doubt, its commanding officer knew the other vessels had failed miserably, and his was likely to do the same. But it didn't stop him.

"Phaser range," said Vigo.

Picard regarded the enemy. "Target and fire!"

This time, the enemy veered at just the right moment and eluded the *Stargazer*'s first volley. But her second assault nailed the Nuyyad ship. Pierced to its core, it shivered violently and succumbed to a frenzy of yellow-white brilliance.

That left only one target. The second officer considered its mighty sprawl of diamond-shaped plates on the viewscreen.

It hadn't fired a single shot. Maybe I was wrong about its firepower, Picard thought. Maybe it's a sitting duck after all.

"Aim for its center," he decided. "Fire when ready, Lieutenant."

"Aye, sir," said Vigo, his long, blue fingers skittering over the lower portion of his control panel.

But the supply depot struck first.

It sent out a stream of vidrion bundles that far surpassed anything the Nuyyad's ships had thrown at them. Seizing the captain's chair for support, the commander rode out one bone-jarring impact after the other.

"Status?" he called out, as Idun did her best to make them a more difficult target.

"Shields down twenty-six percent," Gerda responded crisply. "No hull breaches, no casualties."

"Sir!" said Vigo, his voice taut with urgency.

Picard turned to him. "Lieutenant?"

The Pandrilite looked stricken. "Sir, phasers are off-line!"

The second officer felt the blood rush from his face. Without the amplified phaser power Jomar had given them, they were all but toothless.

And the depot still hung defiantly in space, ready to serve as the key to a Nuyyad invasion of the Federation . . .

CHAPTER 19

Another pale-green flight of vidrion packets blossomed on Picard's viewscreen, seeking to bludgeon his ship out of space.

Idun gave it the slip with a twisting pattern that tested the limits of the inertial dampers. However, she couldn't keep it up indefinitely. The installation's gunners were too accurate, their weapons too powerful.

And there was no telling how many more enemy vessels were on their way, eager to finish what the depot's vidrion cannons had started.

To this point, Picard had relied on the talents of the Magnians and a Kelvan to get him past the rough spots. Now he was on his own. If he was going to prevail, he was going to have to rely on *himself.*

But what could he do? The depot was significantly better armed than they were, better equipped . . .

Then he remembered something one of his professors had

taught him back at the Academy, when he and his class-mates were studying shield theory. *The larger and more complicated an object's shape, the more difficult it is to protect effectively.*

The depot was very large, very complicated. Its armor had to have some chinks in it. All the second officer had to do was find them.

"Mr. Vigo," he said, approaching the weapons console, "analyze the installation's shield structure. See if you can find a weak point."

He peered over the Pandrilite's shoulder as he called up a sensor-driven picture of the enemy's shields. Together, they pored over it, knowing that they might absorb a vidrion barrage at any moment.

"Here," said Vigo, pointing to a spot between two of the massive diamond shapes that encircled the depot. "There's a lower graviton concentration at each of these junctures. If we can get close enough, we might be able to penetrate one with a few well-placed photon torpedoes."

Picard agreed. "We will get close enough," he assured the weapons officer. Then he turned to Idun. "Aim for a juncture between two of the diamond shapes. We need to hit it with a torpedo barrage."

His helm officer did as she was instructed. Like a hawk stooping to take a field mouse, the *Stargazer* darted for the depot's weak spot.

The Nuyyad gunners must have seen them coming. But unlike a ship, the installation wasn't mobile. It couldn't evade their attack. All it could do was punish its enemy with all the firepower at its disposal.

Picard felt the bridge shiver as the first volley rammed into them. The viewscreen went dead for a second, then flickered back to life.

"Shields down forty-two percent," Gerda called out.

The second volley hit them even harder, rattling the second officer's teeth. An unmanned console went up in sparks and filled the air with the acrid smell of smoke.

"Shields down sixty-four percent," the navigator barked.

The third volley forced Picard to grab Vigo's chairback or be knocked off his feet. As he recovered, he saw that a plasma conduit had sprung a leak.

"Shields down ninety percent," Gerda reported dutifully.

They couldn't take another blast like the last one, the second officer told himself. But then, maybe they wouldn't have to.

"Now, Mr. Vigo!" he shouted over the hiss of seething plasma.

A string of golden photon torpedoes went hurtling toward the depot. Before the enemy could fire again, the torpedoes hit their target—and were rewarded with a titanic display of pyrotechnics.

But did they pierce the Nuyyad's shields? As Idun Asmund pulled them off their collision course, Picard peered at the weapons console and checked the depot's status.

For a moment, he couldn't believe his eyes. Then Vigo said it out loud, giving his discovery the weight of reality.

"We must have hit one of their primary shield generators, sir. They're defenseless from one end to the other."

As defenseless as the *Stargazer* had been after its initial encounter with the Nuyyad. As defenseless as the Magnians had been when the second officer found them.

Picard eyed the viewscreen, which was still tracking the enemy depot as Idun brought them about. The installation didn't look any different to the human eye, but to their sensors it was naked and unprotected.

He had a feeling the Nuyyad would remember this day. Certainly, he knew *he* would. "Target and fire," he told his weapons officer.

Vigo unleashed one torpedo assault after the other, pounding the installation in a half-dozen places. And everywhere the matter-antimatter packets landed, they blew something up.

Finally, the last remaining section erupted in a fit of expanding energy, painting the void with its glory. Then it faded, leaving an empty space where a Nuyyad presence had been.

"Serves them right," said Ben Zoma.

Picard looked at his friend and wished he could disagree.

Captain's log, supplemental. We have returned to Magnia to drop off the colonists who aided us with our tactical enhancements. Fortunately, none of them have shown any lasting effects from their exposure to psilosynine. Though I had reason to distrust these people when I first met them, I now see that they are as trustworthy as anyone I know. They are also what the name of their ancestors' ship proclaimed: valiant. In accordance with Shield Williamson's request, I recommend that Guard Daniels be returned to the colony and that its existence henceforth be kept a Federation secret—for our good as well as that of the colonists. After all, there are those who might try to tap into the Magnians' potential for their own ends. As for Jomar . . . I am grateful for his assistance in destroying the Nuyyad depot, which proved critical to our efforts. However, his arrogance, penchant for violence and insistence on implementing his plans over our objections mark him as someone the Federation should avoid in the future. And while it pains me to paint all Kelvans with the same brush, I find I must do exactly that—or fail in my service to the Federation. My recommendation is that we encourage the Kelvans to remain an insular society . . . indefinitely.

Picard gazed at Serenity Santana, the sun of her world sinking through tall trees into a deep, red-orange miasma behind her.

"Will you miss me?" she asked with a smile, the mountain wind lifting her raven hair.

Torn between emotions, the second officer shrugged. "What can I say? I wish we had met under different circumstances."

"Then . . . you *won't* miss me?"

He couldn't help chuckling a little at her cleverness. "I didn't say that," he told her.

Abruptly, his combadge beeped. He tapped it in response. "Picard here."

"We're ready to leave, sir," said Ben Zoma. "If you're ready to beam up . . . ?"

The second officer glanced at Santana again. "Give me a minute, Gilaad. Picard out."

"You know," she said, "we Magnians like our privacy. But if you ever get the urge to visit us . . ."

Picard nodded. "I'll know where to find you."

"I hope so," Santana told him, her eyes telling him she meant it with all her heart.

Then she and the mountain and the sunset were gone, and he found himself standing on a transporter pad . . . feeling empty and terribly alone.

Carter Greyhorse was on his way to the mess hall to secure some lunch when he saw Gerda Asmund turn into the corridor up ahead of him.

He would never have planned to confront Gerda with his feelings about her in a million years. But something about the moment seemed to reek of opportunity.

"Miss Asmund?" the doctor said, his heart pounding as he hastened to catch up with her.

It was only after he had gotten within a couple of meters of her that the navigator cast a glance back over her shoulder. Her expression wasn't an especially inviting one.

"What do you want?" she asked, as blunt as any Klingon.

"I . . ." Greyhorse stumbled over the words. "I'd like to talk with you sometime. Perhaps over a cup of coffee . . . ?"

"I don't drink coffee," Gerda told him in a peremptory tone. "Leave me alone." And she kept on going.

"Wait," he said, grabbing her arm to hold her back. "Please. I really need to speak with—"

Before he could finish what he was saying, Gerda lashed out at him with the heel of her boot. It was one of the moves he had seen her make in the gymnasium, one of the exercises he had watched in awe.

Without thinking, the doctor reacted—and before the navigator's foot could reach the side of his head, he caught it in his hand.

Suddenly, Gerda's attitude changed. She looked surprised at his quickness—but not *just* surprised. If he were compelled to describe her expression, he would have called it one of . . .

Admiration.

Unfortunately, it didn't last long. As she twisted, out of his grip, the woman's lips pulled back and she lashed out again—this time, with her fist. It hit him hard in his solar plexus, driving the wind out of his lungs.

As Greyhorse doubled over, she struck him in the chin with the heel of her hand. The blow drove his head up and back, sending him staggering into the bulkhead behind him.

For a moment, he thought she would come at him again. But she didn't. She just stood there in her martial stance, feet spread apart, hands raised in front of her, ready to dole out additional punishment if that was what she chose to do.

"I didn't mean to antagonize you," he told her, the taste of blood thick in his mouth.

"I told you to leave me alone," Gerda snarled.

The doctor took a step forward, knowing full well the risk he ran. But he didn't care. He had had her on his mind too long. Once and for all, he had to tell her how he felt.

"Just let me ex—"

As before, she attacked him before he could speak, landing an openhanded pile driver to his mouth. But he kept his balance somehow. And when she followed with another openhanded assault, he didn't just block it with his forearm. He slugged her back.

Either she hadn't expected Greyhorse to retaliate or he just got lucky, because the blow caught her sharply in the side of the head. In fact, it sent her reeling, clutching at the bulkhead for support.

He didn't anticipate that she would remain that way for long, so he spoke up while he had the chance. "You're all I can think of," the doctor told her. "All I *want* to think of. I can't go on like this. If I haven't got a chance, I need to hear you say it."

Gerda's eyes narrowed, giving her a vaguely wolflike expression. But she didn't say anything.

"Well?" he prodded miserably.

"You fight like a child," she told him, the disgust in her voice cutting him even more than the words.

Greyhorse drew a deep breath. That was it, then. Gerda couldn't make it any plainer than that.

He turned and retreated down the corridor, starting to feel bruises where the woman had struck him. But before the doctor could get very far, Gerda spoke again.

"Greyhorse."

He turned to look at her. There was something in the navigator's eyes, he thought, and it wasn't disdain or revulsion. It looked more like the admiration he had seen earlier.

"Meet me in the gym tomorrow morning at eight," she said. "Perhaps I can teach you to fight like a warrior."

The doctor had never been an emotional man. But he felt such joy then, such a rush of heady optimism, that he could barely find the voice to get out a response.

"I'll be there," he promised her.

Picard regarded the six officers whom he had summoned to the *Stargazer*'s observation lounge. Paxton, Cariello, Ben Zoma, Simenon, Greyhorse, and Vigo looked back at him from their places around the oval table.

"I called you here," he said, "because you have all had questions regarding the events of the last several days, during which time I have been forced to sometimes operate on a clandestine basis. I thought I would answer these questions all at once."

Then he proceeded to do just that. When he was done, not everyone was happy—Simenon least of all. But even the Gnalish understood the second officer's need for secrecy at various times.

Greyhorse, who had apparently bruised his chin during an accident in sickbay, didn't fully grasp Werber's contribution.

"Chief Werber," Picard explained, "was the one who predicted that the phaser junctions were likely to be tampered with next."

"But he didn't know *which* junction?" the doctor asked.

"That is correct," said the second officer. "We only found that out when Vigo detected a problem in the line. And it wasn't until we spoke to Jomar in sickbay that we understood his objective."

Greyhorse nodded. "I see."

Picard looked around the room. "If there are no further questions, I thank you for persevering in such trying circumstances . . . and commend you to your respective assignments."

He watched his command staff file out of the lounge, one by one. However, one of his officers declined to leave.

"You have something on your mind," Ben Zoma told him. "And it has nothing to do with flow regulators and distribution manifolds."

Picard nodded. "You're right, Gilaad. You see, my mother taught me that one can learn from every experience. I am trying to puzzle out what I can learn from this one."

The other man shrugged. "Not to listen to your fellow officers all the time—especially if they're as wrong as I was about attacking the depot?"

The commander smiled. "Perhaps. Or rather," he said, thinking out loud, "to draw on every resource available to you . . ."

"Even if it means taking the advice of a sworn enemy as seriously as that of a friend."

Picard mulled it over. "That was certainly the way it worked out."

"You know," said Ben Zoma, "I think your mother would have been proud of you right now."

"I hope so," the second officer replied earnestly.

"Captain Ruhalter would have been proud of you too."

Picard looked at him askance. "You think so?"

His friend smiled. "Don't you?"

The second officer wanted to believe that Ruhalter would have approved of his performance. However, he wasn't so sure that that would have been the case.

And he was even less certain of what they would have to say about it at Starfleet headquarters.

As the *Stargazer* hung motionless in space, her computer running yet another shield diagnostic, Gerda Asmund gazed at the immense, rose-colored expanse of the galactic barrier.

Of course, she didn't blame Commander Picard for wanting to be thorough. The navigator wasn't eager to go through the phenomenon with a soft spot in their shields either.

Beside her, her sister waited with the patience of a hunter for the order to engage engines and send them soaring through the barrier. Until recently, Idun had known everything about her.

But she didn't know about Carter Greyhorse.

Life is funny, Gerda mused. Just when she discovered that battle was no longer enough for her, just when a hole had opened in her life, she found what she needed to fill it.

"Everything checks out," said Vigo, interrupting her reverie.

Gerda liked the Pandrilite. He had been raw and unproven at the time of Werber's mutiny, but no one could have done a better job at the weapons console than he had. In fact, he seemed to gain confidence with each passing day.

Picard turned to Vigo. "Thank you, Lieutenant." Looking to the viewscreen, he said, "Helm . . . warp six." Then, with a gesture that suggested forward motion, he added, "Engage."

And they sailed into the scarlet abyss of the barrier.

CHAPTER **20**

Picard considered the pinched, dark-haired man in the admiral's uniform seated across the desk from him.

Admiral Mehdi was still studying the logs posted by the second officer in the wake of the Nuyyad's ambush. He looked grim as he read from his monitor screen, his wrinkled brow creased down the middle.

Finally, Mehdi looked up. "You had quite a struggle, I see."

Picard nodded. "Yes, sir."

"And a number of difficult choices to make."

Picard sighed. "Admiral," he said, "I am not certain I provided you with a full explanation of—"

Mehdi held a thin, almost spindly hand up for silence. "I can imagine what you're about to say, Commander. However, I believe I already possess all the information I require."

The second officer bit his lip and sat back in his chair. "Of course, sir," he replied.

The admiral's eyes seemed to reach into him. "To summarize,

you pursued several rather unorthodox options. First, you advised Captain Ruhalter that Serenity Santana could be trusted . . . over the official protestations of First Officer Leach."

Picard swallowed. "Yes, sir."

"Second," said Mehdi, "you chose to take your vessel to the Magnians' colony instead of the galactic barrier, even though—as some of your officers were quick to point out—there was no proof the place even existed, much less that it could give you the assistance you needed."

Picard didn't like the way this was going. "That is correct, sir."

"And in so doing," the admiral continued, "you jeopardized not only the lives of your crew, but your ability to warn the Federation about the Nuyyad. Is this also correct?"

"It is."

"Then," said Mehdi, "knowing that the Magnians had already led you into an ambush, you beamed a number of them up to the *Stargazer* and gave them access to strategic systems. In addition, you allowed their mental powers to be amplified through the use of a synthetic neurotransmitter, thereby inviting the possibility of an enclave of Gary Mitchells running amok aboard your vessel."

"I did," Picard had to admit.

"And, finally, you removed the safeguards from your phaser technology in order to take out a single enemy installation—once again, wagering your ship and crew on a long shot. Is this true?"

Picard had only one answer. "It is, sir."

The admiral considered the younger man a moment longer. "In your estimate, Commander, are these the actions of a Starfleet second officer?"

Picard sighed. "I'm not in a position to say, sir."

"Then let me tell you," Mehdi remarked, "they're not. They're the actions of a Starfleet captain—and a damned remarkable one at that."

Picard wasn't certain he had heard the older man correctly. "I beg your pardon?" he said.

"What you did," Mehdi told him, "what you accomplished against staggering odds ... shows me that you're more than ready to command. And since you've already won the admiration of the *Stargazer*'s crew, it stands to reason that you should remain with that vessel—as her captain."

Picard didn't know what to say. "Sir—"

Again, the admiral held up his hand. "You're grateful. I know. But between the two of us, I can't tolerate maudlin displays."

"Actually," said Picard, "I was going to ask about Commander Leach."

Mehdi frowned. "Fortunately, Commander Leach will make a full recovery from his injuries. But I don't believe he was ever qualified to serve as first officer on a starship. Command will find a posting for him that's more in line with his abilities."

"I see," said Picard.

It was almost exactly what Ruhalter had said about Leach. In that respect, at least, Ruhalter and Mehdi thought much alike.

"You're a brilliant fellow," the admiral informed him, "and a thoughtful commanding officer, who is obviously not afraid to take the unorthodox and even the unpopular path. I wish you, and those who serve under you, long and illustrious careers."

This time, Picard *did* want to thank the man. But to his chagrin, he didn't get the chance.

"Now get out of my office," said Mehdi, "and start showing me I made the right choice."

Captain Jean-Luc Picard smiled. "Yes, sir," he replied, and took his leave of the admiral.

Hans Werber had to admit that the accommodations in the Starfleet brig were a little better than in the *Stargazer*'s. But that didn't make him feel a whole lot better.

Hearing the sound of footsteps in the corridor outside his cell, he looked up—and saw a familiar if unexpected face through the barrier.

"Picard?" he said.

"In the flesh," said his visitor.

"I didn't think I'd ever see *you* again," Werber confessed.

Picard regarded him. "You mean because you tried to stun me in my sleep and take over a vessel under my command?"

"Well," said the weapons officer, "yeah."

The other man smiled a taut smile. "I don't believe I will forget that incident anytime soon. But neither will I forget that you helped me uncover Jomar's clandestine activities—or that, in the end, you put your resentment aside and did what your duty demanded."

Werber shrugged. "You didn't have to come here to tell me that."

"I also didn't have to put in a word on your behalf with the judge advocate general," said Picard. "Nonetheless, I did. Perhaps he'll take it into account when he tries your case."

The weapons officer couldn't believe it. "You did that for me? You've got to be kidding."

"I am not," his visitor assured him. "I wanted the court to have all the facts in front of it."

Werber didn't say anything. He couldn't.

"We'll see each other again," Picard told him. Then he turned and started down the corridor.

"Hey, Picard!" the prisoner called, getting to his feet and approaching the energy barrier.

The other man stopped and looked back. "Yes?"

"You know what?" said Werber. "I was wrong. You're going to make a hell of a captain someday."

Picard nodded. "I hope you're right."

Book Three

Valiant

CHAPTER 1

Dennis Gardenhire checked his instruments. "Hold on," he said. "It could be a rough ride."

Activating the reverse thrusters, the navigator felt them slow the escape pod's descent. Then he made adjustments in the shape of their shields to minimize the stress of entry.

Gardenhire had piloted a pod prototype a dozen times before the *Valiant* left Earth orbit, and gone through escape simulations a hundred times more. But penetrating the atmosphere of an alien world with shield generators that hadn't been dependable for weeks and an inertial damper that hadn't worked correctly from the beginning . . .

That was a different story entirely.

Still, Gardenhire asked himself, what choice did they have? Their pod was low on fuel and even lower on nutritional packets and potable water, and this was the only habitable world they had come across.

Through the pod's observation portal, he could see the ragged white of dense clouds ripping past them. But they were high clouds—sixty-five thousand kilometers high. The pod still had a long way to go before it reached the planet's surface.

Gardenhire looked around at the other faces in the escape vehicle. They looked back at him with trust if not complete confidence, knowing he would do his best to land them safely despite the pod's limitations.

There was Coquillette, the little medic who had seen them through everything from seasickness to bedsores. And O'Shaugnessy, the craggy-faced assistant engineer who had nursed their engines as deftly as Coquillette had nursed the crew.

There was Santana, the stoic and uncomplaining security officer, and Daniels, the astrophysicist with the wicked sense of humor. And finally, Williamson, the balding supply officer who had bullied them into surviving one day after another, regardless of whether they wanted to or not.

By getting this far, they had already set themselves apart as the lucky ones, the ones on whom Fortune had smiled. Only twelve of the *Valiant*'s fourteen escape pods had cleared the explosion that destroyed the ship, and one of those twelve had fallen victim to a plasma breach days later.

The units that remained intact were packed with six or seven people each, with so little living space that only one person could move around at a time. But then, the pods hadn't been designed with an eye to creature comfort. They were survival tools, and survival was a grim business at best.

Gardenhire had always prided himself on his ability to stay cool, to perform calmly under pressure. But after just a month of such close confinement, his nerves had frayed to the breaking point. He was tense, irritable, ready to lash out at anyone who looked at him sideways.

Then came the change.

It was subtle at first, so subtle that the navigator had to wonder if he was losing his mind. But as it turned out, he wasn't losing anything. He was gaining something remarkable. He could hear the thoughts of his fellow crewmen.

Not all of them, of course—just a stray reflection or two. But it distracted Gardenhire from his misery. It gave him something to think about as he lay prone in his padded shock bunk and waited for his appointed exercise period.

The navigator wasn't oblivious to the fact that telepathy had been one of Agnarsson's talents too. In the back of his mind, he knew he might become what the engineer had become.

But somehow, he felt confident that it wouldn't happen. After all, it had been weeks since the crew was exposed to the Big Red phenomenon. If Gardenhire was going to be altered to the same extent as Agnarsson, if he was going to mutate into a gray-haired, silver-eyed superman, it seemed likely that it would have happened already.

Besides, it was different when the individual undergoing the transformation was oneself. For obvious reasons, it made the prospect seem a lot less chilling.

Then, one day when the navigator was skimming Coquillette's thoughts, he felt an awareness there—a facility capable of not only recognizing his intrusion, but responding to it.

He was afraid that the medic would balk at his invasion of her privacy—for clearly, that was what it was. And in a tinderbox like the escape pod, that was the last thing they needed.

But as it happened, Coquillette didn't mind his trespass at all. In fact, she seemed to welcome it.

It made her feel less lonely, she told him—communicating not in spoken words, but in precise and evocative thoughts. It let her know she wasn't the only one who was experiencing some kind of transformation.

It made Gardenhire wonder . . . if he and Coquillette had changed, was it possible that some of the others were changing as well? And like the medic, were they too uneasy with the situation to speak of it?

Both of them wanted to discuss the matter with the group. However, they were concerned . . . if they were the only ones who had been affected, how would their companions look at them? Would they see Gardenhire and Coquillette as threats to the welfare of their miniature society—threats that had to be dealt with in a harsh and immediate manner?

Then, while they were wondering what to do, O'Shaugnessy responded to their telepathic intrusions as well. And a day later, Williamson did the same. It was Williamson who insisted that they let the others in on what was happening to them.

As Gardenhire had expected, the revelation didn't go very well. Santana didn't say much, but his thoughts were decidedly frightened ones. And though Daniels made a joke about it, it didn't take a telepath to see he was every bit as scared as Santana.

The atmosphere in the pod became taut and uneasy. No one said anything more about the transformations, but they were a subtext in every conversation, a stubborn and nettlesome ghost haunting them every hour of the artificially induced day and night.

Until Santana and Daniels found themselves with telepathic powers of their own, their discoveries coming less than a day apart. At that point, the air of suspicion went away. They were all equals again, working together toward a common goal.

But there were other surprises in store for them. One day, when Williamson was delving in a locker for a hard-to-reach nutritional packet, he saw the thing move obediently into his outstretched hand.

Apparently, he had developed a knack for telekinesis. Announcing his discovery to his podmates (as if he could have kept it secret from a bunch of telepaths), the supply officer challenged them to test their own talents in that regard.

At that juncture, only O'Shaugnessy and Santana exhibited rudimentary telekinetic abilities. But in the days that followed, the rest of them followed suit. Only Coquillette seemed to lag behind, never becoming anywhere near as adept as the rest of them.

They never figured out why. But then, they never figured out anything else about their powers either. Their newfound facilities were a mystery to them through and through.

Eventually, there was only one more step they had to take.

Since the destruction of the *Valiant,* the pods had maintained periodic radio contact—in the beginning, communicating as often as several times a day. Then, as tedium set in and there was less and less to say, their conversations had become correspondingly less frequent.

But in none of these give-and-takes had Gardenhire and his companions ever mentioned their transformations. The main reason for this restraint was simple—it seemed imprudent to give the crews of the other pods a reason to fear them.

Of course, Santana and Daniels could have sent a message to the other pods when they found out about their comrades' powers. At that juncture, they still appeared to be unaltered human beings, and they might have seen it as their duty to send out a warning.

Why had they hesitated? Not just out of fear that they might get caught, as they quite willingly revealed later. It was because they were explorers by nature, and they wanted to see where their podmates' transformations ultimately led them.

Such considerations notwithstanding, they all knew they would have to spill the beans someday. And that day arrived when the pods came within scanner range of a solar system.

By unanimous agreement, Gardenhire radioed McMillan and the other ranking officers and revealed everything that had happened. But far from exhibiting concern, the other pods appeared to be relieved.

Because they had been experiencing the same things.

It wasn't a possibility the navigator hadn't weighed in the back of his mind. The individuals in his group had been exposed to the same stimuli as the men and women in the other vehicles. It stood to reason that they might be changing too.

But it felt good to know for sure.

Especially when their scanners showed them a habitable planet in the solar system they had discovered. A planet with plenty of water and plant life. A planet where they might have a future.

The same planet toward which Gardenhire's pod was now dropping like a very large stone.

"We're falling too quickly," said Daniels, his brow uncharacteristically creased with concern.

"*Much* too quickly," agreed Coquillette.

Through the observation portal, the navigator could see a faint reddish hue—the play of friction about the shields. And as he had noted earlier, the shield generators had seen better days.

"Something's wrong with the thrusters," O'Shaugnessy said.

"Can you see that?" Gardenhire asked. "Or are you just guessing?"

"I can see it," the engineer assured him, his eyes glazing over as he focused his mind. "One of the release apertures is jammed shut."

The navigator knew that that was no small matter. There were only four apertures and they needed all of them to brake their descent.

"Can you *un*jam it?" asked Coquillette.

O'Shaugnessy shook his head. "This isn't a nutritional packet we're talking about. It's a machine part."

"What if we were to work *together?*" asked Williamson.

Daniels seemed to like the idea. "It's worth a shot—and we don't have too many other options."

Outside the pod, the heat was increasing. What had been a faint red glow was now a deep crimson. They were starting to vibrate as well, starting to experience the roughness Gardenhire had warned them about.

"How's this going to work?" asked Santana.

Gardenhire turned to O'Shaugnessy. "If you can picture the lever that opens the aperture, we can try to access it through you."

"Then we all put pressure on it at once," Daniels added.

"Exactly," said the navigator.

O'Shaugnessy nodded. "Let's do it."

Gardenhire concentrated on linking his thoughts to the engineer's, picturing what O'Shaugnessy was picturing. It turned out to be easier than he had imagined. He could see the lever in question, even feel the place where the thing was stuck.

If the navigator could have reached into the mechanism with his hand, he might have been able to free the offending lever. As it was, he focused on moving it with the power of his mind.

He sensed the others, vague presences all around him. They were pushing with their minds as well.

Come on, came a thought—O'Shaugnessy's. *We can do it.*

And the lever moved.

In fact, Gardenhire was surprised at how little resistance it offered them. It was like moving a feather.

But were they in time? The navigator looked out the observation portal and saw that the aura had become an actual flame. Their shields were rapidly losing their battle with the planet's atmosphere.

Turning to his instrument panel, he checked the pod's rate of descent. It was less than it had been, certainly, but still a good deal more than what safety demanded.

"What's the verdict?" asked Daniels.

"Not good," Gardenhire told him.

"We're still falling too fast," said Coquillette, "aren't we?"

The navigator nodded.

"Wait a minute," said Santana. "O'Shaugnessy couldn't move that lever at all—but when we worked together, it moved easily. Maybe we could slow the pod down the same way."

At first blush, it seemed like a crazy idea. But the more Gardenhire thought about it, the less crazy it sounded.

"Let's try it," said Williamson.

Outside, the flames of their descent had completely obscured their view of the alien sky. Soon, they would feel the temperature begin to rise inside the pod. And after that . . .

"O'Shaugnessy will be our point again," said the navigator, "since he did such a good job last time."

Without a moment's hesitation, the engineer closed his eyes. "All right . . . I'm picturing the underside of the pod. We need to push against it, to slow it down . . ."

Linking his mind to O'Shaugnessy's, Gardenhire could see the flat titanium surface. Surrounded by the four thruster apertures, he pushed up against it. He wasn't alone, either. He felt the others with him, around him and inside him, adding their strength to his own.

At first, he didn't perceive any difference. Then their efforts began to pay off. The pod began to slow down.

Breaking contact with O'Shaugnessy for a moment, the navigator darted a glance at his instruments. They confirmed it—the escape vehicle was falling at a slower rate than before.

Keep it up, Gardenhire told the others.

They did as he asked, continuing to toil against the pull of gravity with all the telekinetic power at their disposal. And little by little, the pod continued to decelerate.

He glanced at the observation portal. The shields were all but gone, but so were the flames that had blocked his view. He could see clouds again. And through them, patches of blue.

If he and the others had had enough time, they might have teamed up with the thrusters to stop their descent altogether. Unfortunately, they didn't have that much time. Gardenhire could see that all too clearly on his monitor, the harsh truth expressed in cold mathematical certainties.

The planet's surface was rushing up eagerly to meet them. And when it did, it would crack them open like an egg.

The injustice of it pierced the navigator's heart like a dagger. To have come this far, to have tried this hard, only to be crushed on a hard and unfeeling alien landscape . . .

Then he saw a way out.

"We need to do more than slow down," Gardenhire said. "We

need to push ourselves *that* way." And he pointed to the bulkhead behind Daniels.

"What for?" asked Williamson.

"So we can splash down," the navigator explained. "Or would you prefer to crack up?"

"Let's *push,*" said Daniels.

What Gardenhire was asking of them was a lot more complicated than what they had done before. They couldn't push in two directions at once; they had to find just the right vector.

Somehow, they managed it.

Then the six of them pushed for all they were worth. The mingling of their talents created an unexpected level of force, one that seemed to be more than the sum of their individual abilities.

The navigator moved closer to the window and looked down. He could see land through breaks in the cloud cover. He could make out a large, blue bowl of a bay, embraced by a hilly, green coastline.

It would be a good place for a settlement, he thought, a good place to make a future for themselves. That is, if they survived long enough to think about such things.

Push, he insisted.

They poured every last ounce of their energy into the effort, nudging the pod away from the land and out to sea. Gardenhire followed their progress on his instruments, cheering inwardly with each minute alteration in their angle of descent.

We're going to do it, he told the others.

It encouraged them to keep it up, to shove the pod as far out over the bay as they could. With a couple of kilometers to go, the navigator was certain of it—they had earned a water landing.

Brace yourselves, he thought.

They looked at each other as they slid into their shock bunks, needing no words—silent or otherwise—to communicate their feelings. Whether they survived or not, whether their temperamental dampers held or failed, they had fought the good fight.

They had discovered a strength in themselves that few members of their species ever came to know.

Neither Gardenhire nor any of the others had a single regret.

Then they punched through the surface of the bay. The impact sent rattlings of pain through the navigator's skeleton, despite the gelatinous padding that lined his bunk. For a moment, he wondered if they might have hit something more than water—some submerged spine of land, perhaps.

Then he craned his neck to look out the observation portal and saw silver bubbles clustering around them like living seacreatures, enveloping them in an intricately woven cocoon of oxygen-rich atmosphere.

Slowly, feeling for injuries all the while, Gardenhire emerged from his bunk. One by one, the others did the same.

"Everyone all right?" asked Williamson, who looked a little dazed.

Santana felt his jaw. "Could have been worse."

Daniels kneaded his neck muscles. "You can say that again."

"How far down are we?" asked Coquillette.

The navigator checked his control panel, but his screen was blank. "I wish I could say. We must have lost external sensors when we hit."

O'Shaugnessy looked out the portal. "Who needs external sensors? I'd say we have five meters of water above us, tops."

"And we're rising," Williamson added, his eyes closed in concentration as he made the judgment.

Gardenhire concentrated as well and came to the same conclusion. Their mantle of bubbles was dissolving, abandoning them, and the waves above were getting closer. Finally, with an effervescent bounce, the pod broke the surface of the bay.

"Look!" said Santana, pointing to the portal.

The navigator looked through the transparent plate, which was dappled with prismatic droplets. In the distance, past a stretch of undulating blue water, he could see the rocky coastline they had managed to avoid. From here, it looked friendly, even inviting.

"I want to get out," Coquillette said suddenly.

Daniels grinned. "Me too."

Gardenhire considered it. There might be jagged rocks just under the surface, or a school of carnivorous sea monsters. But he knew how much the others wanted to leave the pod, because he wanted to leave it also.

"Let's get a little closer to shore first," he advised, running contrary to the current of enthusiasm.

Despite their urge to leave their artificial womb behind, the others agreed to do as the navigator asked. By then, working in concert had become almost second nature. They got the pod skidding through the waves rather easily and came within twenty meters of shore.

At that point, even Gardenhire couldn't stop them. They pried open the hatch cover and spilled out into the water—first Coquillette, then Daniels, then Williamson and Santana. Gardenhire was about to come out too when O'Shaugnessy gave him an unexpected shove.

As the navigator was immersed, he found that the water was warmer than it looked—so warm, in fact, that they were all inclined to linger in it. Gardenhire felt like a kid again, splashing and getting splashed, feeling the sun and the waves wash away weeks of tension and fear.

He wished Tarasco had lived to see this. He wished, at the very least, that the captain could have seen the fruits of his sacrifice.

Finally, the navigator and his comrades got too tired to splash anymore. They struck out for shore with long, easy strokes, tugging the pod along in their wake. That is, five of them did.

O'Shaugnessy chose to try to glide above the waves. But then, as Gardenhire had learned from weeks of sharing a pod with the man, O'Shaugnessy could be something of a showoff.